ZANE

NO
MORE
TIME-OUTS

BI

ebor Books
. Box 6505
o, MD 20792
//www.streborbooks.com

book is a work of fiction. Names, characters, places and incidents
roducts of the author's imagination or are used fictitiously. Any
blance to actual events or locales or persons, living or dead, is
ly coincidental.

1 by Thomas Slater

78-1-59309-348-8
78-1-4516-0820-5 (ebook)
011928054

bor Books trade paperback edition November 2011

ign: www.mariondesigns.com
otograph: © Keith Saunders/Marion Designs
: © Shutterstock Images

5 4 3 2 1

red in the United States of America

tion regarding special discounts for bulk purchases,
ct Simon & Schuster Special Sales at 1-866-506-1949
simonandschuster.com

& Schuster Speakers Bureau can bring authors to your
r more information or to book an event, contact the
uster Speakers Bureau at 1-866-248-3049 or visit our
w.simonspeakers.com.

Dear Reader:

No More Time-Outs by Thomas Slater blew my mind...literally. The characters, their storylines, the suspense, and their candid and brutally honest dialogue all create a mix for wonderful reading. What happens when a family is destroyed by one tragic event and one disheartened patriarch? Complete chaos.

Slater weaves a tale of a highly regarded minister who is a complete nightmare to the clergy. He sleeps with his congregation, openly disrespects his wife, and has no morals whatsoever. Therefore, it is no surprise when his behavior trickles down to his offspring and throws all of their lives into turmoil as well. From the oversexed daughter who is attracted to thugs outside of her marriage to a drug-addicted son who snatches purses from senior citizens to feed his habit, their family is on the brink of destruction. But one son is determined to try to pull their household back together when the mother suddenly takes ill. However, he must battle his own demons of the past and make one of the toughest decisions ever...when there are no more time-outs.

As always, thank you for reading the authors that I present under my imprint, Strebor Books. We strive to bring you the best and most prolific authors around. Please check out Slater's first novel, *Show Stoppah*, as well. I am sure that you will enjoy *No More Time-Outs* as much as I did.

Blessings,

Zane

Zane
Publisher
Strebor Books International
www.simonandschuster.com

ALSO BY THOMAS SLATER
Take One for the Team
Show Stoppah

WRITING AS TECORI SHELDON
When Truth is Gangsta

ZANE PRESEN

NO
MOR
TIME-O

THOMAS S

STREBOR
NEW YORK LONDON

PRA

IN LOVING MEMORY OF MY NEPHEW: JERMAINE SLATER, JR.

As a writer, my nephew, Jermaine Slater, Jr., was my biggest supporter. In those dark days when the doors that held access to the literary world were welded shut, Jermaine was there as a constant source of inspiration when I was ready to pull the plug. Cheering me on intensely, he would often say: "Unc, you're crazy to give up your dreams when you're so close—you feel me?" Of course, I couldn't do anything but laugh. He was right. I had come too far. The doors and windows had been opened wide enough for me to live how I dreamed.

Unfortunately, I could not physically share this wondrous testimony of faith with Jermaine Slater, Jr.

My nephew tragically departed this life April 15, 2011, leaving nothing behind but the devastation of heartache and emotional pain. After his untimely death I didn't care much about anything, least of all, my dreams for literary greatness. Unfamiliar with the new air I was breathing, my nephew was my familiar oxygen; one that I could count on for a positive word whenever I emerged from a creative solitude. I could remember taking deep breaths, but couldn't feel my lungs expanding.

Slipping into a sullen, somber sadness, weeks passed as I felt myself ascend into the darkness of depression and pitching a tent in the name of "permanent residency." But before I could get comfortable, God reminded me that my nephew wasn't dead—and neither was my dream. The Lord let me know that anything He loved never died. And, Lil Maine, as long as I have oxygen in my lungs and blood coursing through my veins, I will honor your memory. Not by simply existing inside of the dream, but living it in the form of high-octane fiction that will become my staple for years to come.

Jermaine, with every word I write and every meditation I type, you will live.

So, from here on out, my writing career is dedicated to you, my loving nephew. Between you and me, one book at a time, we're gonna stake our literary claim inside the minds of readers—all with God leading the way, of course.

The boy with the charming, mega-watt smile, slick swagger, accompanied by crazy, cool charisma will always occupy a special place in my heart! I love you, Lil Maine!

—Your uncle

ACKNOWLEDGMENTS

God is my light! In Him I shall find my way home!

To my brother, Jermain Slater Sr., no father should have to follow his son's walk from the cradle to the grave. May God comfort you in the absence of Jermaine Slater Jr.

I'm acknowledging my niece, Marcia Marks! A week after the release of my first title, *Show Stoppah*, Marcia was at the library searching for another title when she stumbled across mine. And of course, she tossed the other title to the side and only left with *Show Stoppah*—well, that's how I imagined it probably went down. I would've wanted it to go something like that—Marcia, please tell me that it went something like that...

I'm sorry—where was I?—oh yeah, acknowledgments. Zane, I can't thank you enough for the opportunity!

Last but certainly not least: Mama, this is my sophomore project. Please sprinkle some guardian angel dust over this one so that I'm one step closer to accomplishing my first goal. I can't tell you guys about that goal. It's between me and my mama, Mary Slater. I love you!

To all the readers, I would just like to say: Thank you all for putting up with the insane, message-driven entertainment that I like to call "high octane fiction." I love you guys!

YAZOO

The thoughts going on inside the young boy's mind after he slipped off a gigantic boulder he and his two brothers were fishing from and into the frigid lake was beyond comprehension. Terror filled the air as the two brothers desperately struggled to pull the younger boy from the water and back onto the boulder. Tears filled their eyes as they watched their younger brother slip from their grasp. All hell broke loose as the current swept the young boy further and further away from shore.

One of the two older boys became alarmed. He thought about jumping in, but not knowing how to swim fueled the desire to get help. One more glance revealed that his brother was struggling to stay afloat. Seeing the whole scene put his steps into motion as he ran up a dirt trail cutting through dense vegetation, yelling, screaming and waving his arms like he was trying to direct an airplane onto the runway. But this was no airport. His brother was in the water.

It wasn't long before the commotion drew the attention of two older men who were standing and fishing from the bank. Once they understood what was going on, there was no time to waste with details. The boy was quickly shoved off the path as the larger of the two men started up the dirt trail, knocking away tree branches as he rushed through, kicking up a cloud of dust. Fear urged him on as he could finally hear the commotion ahead. The shorter man was on the heels of the larger one—followed by the boy. The larger man mumbled something incoherent.

Coming upon the clearance, he could see his older son frantically motioning out to the middle of the lake. Not seeing his baby boy only confirmed his fears. In one fluid motion, without thinking, the larger man leapt from the boulder, kicking his legs as though he were a record-breaking broad jumper.

Splash!

He hit the water. It was a miracle. His baby was still afloat. The young boy had been swept into the middle of the lake, but he was still alive. Chopping, splashing and kicking, the father made his way to the boy. With one mighty push, he shoved the confused little boy all the way to shore and into the awaiting arms of the shorter man.

Seeing his son to safety had been a small victory over the Reaper, but reality presented another deadly circumstance. The father couldn't swim. He'd saved his son, but he was now faced with the critical task of saving himself. And since no one on the banks of that river could swim, the father fought and wrestled with the water like it was a dark foe who'd come to take his life. With the baby boy safely on shore, the group was made to watch in sheer horror as the father desperately splashed around, screaming, "Throw me a pole!"

The shorter man followed direction. He wrapped the end of the durable fishing line around his left hand and cast the pole out toward the drowning man. The pole failed to reach the father as he went under once, twice, the final time.

✪ ✪ ✪

"Shit!" Yazoo flung his arms around violently, falling out of the bed, landing dead on his backside. Sweat profusely poured down his face, making his brown skin resemble the glaze on a doughnut. He sat up dazed, as he stared around his bedroom. The spooky face of old man darkness stared back. Yazoo had been having this recurring nightmare ever since that sad, gloomy day in August when he and his half-brothers watched his father drown. Yazoo's beloved father had died saving the life of his youngest stepson—a son who had turned out to be a junkie. In Yazoo's mind, there was no fair trade. His father was gone. Now his life was a void of darkness and despair. And where was God while all this was going on—on lunch break? His mother had tried hard to explain life to him, but Yazoo's mind had been made up. He wasn't going to believe in God. From that moment on, God was no longer in his vocabulary. He would dog out anyone who attempted to get him to go to church.

He would be a rebel.

Yeah, that's it; a rebel against God.

After all, God had been to blame for taking the life of his father, and cursing him with years of nightmarish slumber. What a serious injustice: his father's life for his brother's, Jordan. What a pillar of humanity he turned out to be—an alcoholic by day and a junkie by night.

Yazoo hated his life. But it was his stupid name that he hated the most: Yazoo Washington. What kind of self-respecting mother would name her eldest child after a small fly speck of a county in Mississippi?

As he stared off into the dead of night, he chuckled. His chuckling turned into deep, booming laughter with a super-sized dose of insanity. Then, all at once, the laughter turned into painful sobbing. The kind of sobbing that happens after the loss of a loved one. His chest heaved; tears flushed his cheeks. He held his head in the palms of his hands and thought to himself, God would pay for wrecking his life.

As quickly as it started, the sobbing shut off like a faucet. He was a gangster again. And gangsters didn't show weakness.

He picked himself up off the floor and went into the bathroom to wipe his face, then returned to the bedroom, making a phone call.

"Yeah, man. It's on and popping," Yazoo spoke into the receiver with tons of bass. He made another phone call and got dressed. He thought about his dad. He thought about death. He thought about power. He made a pact with himself: he would pick when and where to meet death. No one or nothing would take his life until he was ready to lay it down…not even God Himself.

Yazoo walked out into early morning darkness. He jumped into his hooptie, and with one tail light glowing, sped off into the night.

WISDOM

"Schmuck"—was the only word that came to mind in describing the bone-headed situation who was now calling me her baby-daddy.

"I don't know why I mess around with yo' broke ass, Boo-Boo. You know I need money for new paternity clothes—"

"That's maternity clothes," I corrected. "And every time that you squeeze money from me you end up over at Wanita's Bumper and Curl salon."

"Whatever. You know what I mean, Boo-Boo. We gonna see how smarter-than-a-fifth-grader you are when them Friends of the Court pit bulls get off in yo' shit."

"Yes, Malisa," I spoke softly into my cell. My frustration grew with every dissecting moment. I hated when my ghetto girlfriend called me while I was on my job delivering packages. It wasn't enough that these packages were heavy, and my supervisor was always checking up on me at every stop, but my girlfriend was always carrying on about money and randomly shaking me down for it.

I'd messed up, royally. I could admit that, I, Wisdom

Jones, being of sound mind and schmuck, had truly screwed the pooch. One defective condom had cost me the heaviest hurt of three lifetimes. What had started out as an inebriated booty call was now a coerced relationship held together by a pregnancy and promising threats of diming me out to the Friends of the Court.

Bluntly put: I hated that broad with all my heart's heart.

"Malisa, hold on." Another call came in. I didn't recognize the number. Against my better judgment, I answered it. I usually didn't answer unknown phone calls. "Yeah," I said, trying to disguise my voice.

"Don't put me on…"

I clicked on to the other line.

"Wisdom," my father's voice spoke with urgency, "your momma has had a crisis. We're down at the hospital."

"All right. I'm on my way."

Worried, I threw my Metro PCS on the passenger seat, forgetting about Malisa. Two minutes later, my cell violently vibrated. My home number appeared on the caller ID. It was my own little devil in pumps. Malisa was an angry person. Mean to the bone. It had gotten so bad, I could distinguish the disgruntled vibrations of her calls over others. Malisa was short, and light-skinned. I was enchanted by her hourglass figure. And the fact that she had the biggest booty and the smallest waistline of any girl I'd ever seen. But she was downright nasty. I didn't want to answer the phone, but I had to.

"I'm sorry, Malisa." I tried to sound as apologetic as I could, hoping that it would soothe the little savage beast.

"What the hell did you hang up on me for?" Malisa ranted. She didn't give me a chance to get a word in. "I know you don't want me to put those child support dogs on you, do you?"

By this time, I had the pedal to the metal, rushing to the hospital. I was hoping like hell that I wouldn't be pulled over for speeding. God knows my license couldn't stand any more points. I was already hanging on to my mail delivery job by a wing and a prayer. The insurance company that my job carried was ready to burn my license over a campfire.

"No, Malisa." I stopped at a red light, fearing my mother would die before I got there.

"You know I got a doctor's appointment," she huffed into the phone. "You will be there!"

"My momma—"

"Your momma ain't got nothing to do with this conversation."

I sat there in a daze, not realizing that the light had changed color. A loud blurring horn by an irate motorist from behind brought me back to my senses. I took off like a shot.

"My momma's in the hospital," I said, observing my rearview mirror.

"You *will* come to pick me up—like I said!" She hung up the phone. I couldn't think straight. All my thoughts were of my mother. Malisa didn't matter. But as I drove through the streets to the hospital, I recognized that there would be hell to pay if I missed her appointment.

Fearing the worst, I parked my mail delivery van in the visitor's parking lot. I'd been in the middle of my route when I received the phone call. Somehow, my boss was going to trip because I had put my route on hold. Bosses never understood when someone had a family crisis.

Making my way through the parking lot, the high humidity made it almost impossible to breathe. People were everywhere. As usual, all eyes were on my robust, six-foot-five frame. I figured height to be a curse. The unwanted attention made me remember the dream that I'd never accomplished. I had made the Dean's List three years straight at Michigan State University. I'd won a NCAA championship, and MVP honors in my junior year. There were many in my ear telling me that I could make millions in the NBA. So I packed it up after my third year and entered the NBA draft.

On the eve of the draft, to relax, I went out to the park to run some ball. I got involved in a heated pick-up game, which turned out to be the worst mistake of my entire life. I blew out my ACL (anterior cruciate ligament). I was crushed. After the surgery, I rehabbed like a lunatic, but didn't come back 100 percent. I was toxic in the NBA. None of the teams wanted to gamble on me. And if it weren't for my mother, I probably wouldn't be here today. I never could get my life back on track after that. And because I'd thought with the pockets of an athlete and not my brain, I was now reduced to driving this damn mail van!

I hated hospitals. They always smelled like ammonia and bland food. I checked in at the front desk. And as expected, they gave me hassle. Told me that I could only go up if somebody came down. That let me know that the whole family was up there. I pinched the bridge of my nose in dying frustration. If my family members were up there, trouble, arguing and resentment were visiting as well. My poor mother. My siblings were way out of control. So much hatred existed in our family. One word described us: dysfunctional.

Before the middle-aged, fat black woman could hang up the telephone, I'd made my way to a huge bank of elevators. I wasn't gonna wait. Because of my enormous size, I banked on no one coming after me. Sometimes being huge had its advantages. This was definitely one of those times.

I entered the elevator and stood with my back resting against the wall. I watched the numbers fly by, wondering what fate awaited me in room B-213 on the thirteenth floor. Didn't believe in bad luck. But I wished they could've placed Momma on another floor.

As I rounded the corner, my worst fears were confirmed: chaos. Total chaos. My older brother, Yazoo, had his finger all up in my only sister, Tempest's face. My sister wasn't backing down, though. Spit was flying everywhere. His mouth was moving so fast I couldn't figure out what he was saying until I got up on them.

"If you kept your ass out of that married man's house,"

he yelled loud enough to warrant the attention of the nurses sitting at the nurse station, "you would've known what the hell was going on!"

"No you didn't, punk!" Tempest popped her neck, and snapped her fingers. "Judging by that same tired, funky outfit you've been wearing for the past few weeks, it would be safe to say that your hustle game is lame. You need to stop gym shoe-crack rolling and get yourself a real job, you bum," my sister shot back.

"Did somebody say crack?" my cracked-out younger brother, Jordan, chimed in.

"Somebody sit his crackhead behind down!" Tempest yelled.

All this was going on and I hadn't made my way into my momma's room. They were carrying on as though I was invisible. I had to assert my dominance.

"Shut the hell up!" I roared, causing a nurse to fumble with her tray of utensils and almost sending Jordan into cardiac arrest. My booming voice had shut Tempest completely up, leaving my hard-head-butt older brother. At six feet even, Yazoo thought of himself as a hardcore hoodlum. A real gangster. He wasn't crazy. He wore an Ice Cube snarl on his grill for a minute but when I increased mine, he took a walk.

"Is that you, Wizzy?" a very sickly voice called out from inside the room. I snarled at Tempest one more time before I entered. She dropped her head as though she knew what I was thinking.

"Jordan, sit your ass down somewhere." I hated to see my baby brother in his chemically dependent state. Frank, Yazoo's biological father's, death had had quite an affect on Jordan. Yazoo had a different father from the rest of us. My mother didn't marry Frank because of his playa's mentality. She married my father instead. Frank never held it against my mother. Wherever he took Yazoo, he took me and Jordan as well. And that's what we were doing at the lake on that fatal day. Frank was a nature man. Hunting and fishing were the two main loves of his life. I was with him when I'd shot my first deer, killed my first rabbit. Unfortunately, I was there the day of his death. We were at a lake in Pontiac. Jordan had fallen in. Yazoo ran and got Frank. Frank jumped in to save Jordan and drowned in the process. I had a strong feeling Yazoo hated us for it. He became cold, hard, disgruntled. Although he was the eldest, everybody gave me that respect. Even Yazoo looked up to me.

That's why the chump was standing in the doorway staring at me out the corner of his eyes. I would hate to have to snatch those cornrows out of his head.

"Wizzy," my mother called out. "I'm glad to see that you made it." She coughed weakly. That's when I noticed the older gentleman sitting right next to her bed. It pained me heavy whenever I saw his sneaky mug.

"Hi, son," my father greeted me. I gave him a serious look of disgust as I glanced down at the black leather-covered Bible he was clutching, like he actually believed. I let a feisty look do my talking as I walked past him over to kiss Momma.

"How you doing, Ma?" I asked. She looked tired. Before her illness, Momma used to have a vibrant figure. That was all behind her now. Years of worrying about her wayward husband had taken its toll on her vivacity. CRF or Chronic Renal Failure was the doctor's fancy way of saying that Momma's kidneys were about as worthless as one-half of a missing, torn hundred-dollar bill. Hypertension had been the culprit. Momma had been carrying around high blood pressure for years and didn't know it. Her extreme hatred for bad news had kept her from regularly scheduled doctor's examinations. Even when she'd started losing weight, Momma still wouldn't go. It wasn't until she'd started experiencing bloody stools, severe bouts of nausea and intense vomiting that she made a doctor's appointment. Momma's health had been slowly declining ever since.

"The doctors said that I have to go on Hemodialysis and be put on the organ donor list."

"God said that everything is going to be just fine." My father saw a chance to get into the conversation. He stood up, smelling like extremely expensive cologne. Raising the Bible over his head, Pop went to work quoting scriptures involving faith.

"Isaiah 40:31—*they that wait upon the Lord shall renew their strength. They shall mount up with wings as eagles,*" my father preached rather loudly, bringing my sister and brothers into the room. The room was a private room. No bigger than a shoebox. It was barely able to accommodate three people. "Romans—"

"Shut up, you jackleg preacher!" Yazoo screamed.

That ignited Tempest.

"You bum, listening to some of that might do your heathen behind some good!" Tempest shouted, her tongue scolding hot buckshot.

Yazoo had taken just about enough verbal abuse. Without further delay, he rushed her, his hands out front as if he was charging to choke her. Being the peacemaker that I was, I jumped between the two combatants, subduing Yazoo.

"Please, y'all," Momma said, sitting up in the bed almost out of breath. "Do anybody recognize"—she caught her breath—"that this is a hospital and there're sick people all around us, even in this room?" Momma's long salt-and-pepper-colored hair hung around the first bow tie of her hospital gown.

Pops stood there holding his Bible up like he was trying to ward off evil spirits. I struggled with Yazoo as he yelled back at my sister.

"What's in that book," Yazoo shouted in Pops' direction as he struggled around inside of my bear hug, "about her harlot, married ass sleeping with other men?"

"This is getting on my nerves. I'm going for a drink," Jordan said, immediately leaving the room.

"Honor thy father and thy mother," Pops quoted, holding the Bible in the direction of Yazoo.

"You ain't my old man," Yazoo blazed. "You an ol' jack-leg preacher. Holding that Bible, you don't even believe in it yourself. Taking your congregation for all their money, using it for your tramps—"

"Yazoo, what did I say?" Momma said a little bit stronger this time, standing to her feet.

"Excuse me," a soft voice said from the doorway. When we looked up, there was an itty-bitty nurse standing in front of three rough-looking, beefy security guards. Two black, one white. "Some of you are going to have to leave."

Yazoo stopped struggling. I sized up the three men behind the nurse. The two brothers were my height and wore identical builds. I went to say something but one look from Momma silenced me. She was the only one who could do something with me once I got going.

"Nurse," Momma said, "I'm sorry about this blatant disrespect shown by my 'supposed to be' behaved children." She gave all of us that cold, motherly glare. "They're leaving right now!"

Yazoo caught the white security guard staring at him as though there were something personal in his eyes.

"You got a problem, honky?" Yazoo hollered in his direction. The guard looked as though he wanted to take some steps toward Yazoo. But the Mike Tyson-like look on my face was enough to stall the schmuck's efforts. The tension inside the small room was becoming hostile. Then, it was as if God Himself had spoken to the nurse.

She turned, but not before mean-mugging us, and walked off with security in tow.

Momma lay back on the bed and covered herself. "I want everybody, except Wizzy, to leave the room."

There was some grumbling but everybody started toward the door.

Tempest kissed Momma on the jaw and told her she would be in touch. Yazoo didn't even offer a backward glance when he left. And Pops said he had some mission work to do. I shook my head in disgust. His only mission was grinding on top of some other man's wife. He asked did she need anything and looked at me as if to offer some sort of kind gesture, but he looked at the bulldog scowl on my grill and decided against it.

It wasn't that I didn't like my father; I hated how he used his ministry for his own personal gain. He was the most crooked pastor I'd ever seen. Most of all, I didn't like the way he was doing my mother.

"Momma, I'm sorry for all that drama they put you through." I sat in the chair that Pops had occupied earlier.

Momma looked up at me and smiled. "Wizzy, you don't have to apologize for them. We all know that they mean well, but they're ignorant when it comes to respect."

"Momma, are you scared?"

"Son," she said, taking her time, "of course I get scared. But I've learned to keep my hand in God's hand. We are all going to have to go through something in this life. We have to be prepared."

Amidst all the confusion that had gone on in the room,

I hadn't paid attention to all the machines Momma was hooked up to. And because she had risen, one of her leads had come off. Like clockwork, the little chimpanzee-looking nurse had returned. She faked a smile and popped the wire back into place. I watched the chimp walk out of the room. Momma smiled foolishly. She knew I had jokes.

"Wizzy, I want you to be prepared for what God's plan is for me. I've fought through a whole lot of bad things in my life: my unfaithful husband, my failing health, my bad kids—except for you—and my husband's other family down in Mississippi." Momma's bright smile faded behind the cloud of Pops' infidelities. "I want you to promise me one thing, Wizzy."

"Momma, you know I'd do anything for you." I took her hand and looked deeply into her eyes. Momma bore an uncanny resemblance to Gladys Knight. She just had longer hair. "I love you. And I know you're going to make it."

Momma pursed her lips together. She gave me a warm, motherly look. "I know, son. I want you to look after your sister and brothers. They're not living their lives right. But I was hoping some of what you have would rub off on them. Find a way to reach them. Yazoo is in reaching distance. He don't believe in God anymore, but that's all because of his father drowning. Promise me that you'll bring them together."

"You're not giving up? Why are you talking to me like you're about to die?"

Momma looked out the window as though she was waiting on God to answer for her. "Son, I don't doubt God, but there are a whole bunch of folks waiting on donors. It would take some kind of a miracle to receive a kidney in time."

I almost broke down. The mere thought of my mother not being here made me want to go to the organ donor office and pull a Denzel-style John Q. My vibrating cell took me by surprise. I almost jumped out of my skin. I looked at the caller ID. It was my nightmare in leather pumps. Malisa was ringing my phone like she had a problem with the world. Out of respect for my momma, I didn't answer it. Didn't feel like getting into an argument. Didn't feel like hearing her scream at the top of her voice. Momma already knew what was up. She knew her son. She could tell what mood I was in by every facial expression.

"You and Malisa fighting again?" Momma had that 'I told you so' look on her face. Momma didn't like Malisa from the very first day she had laid eyes on her.

"No, Ma'am," I lied. "We're fine." I looked at my watch. It was time for me to finish my route. I hated to leave. Didn't want to leave. But if I wanted to keep a roof over my head and continue to eat, I had to get back to work. It was as if Momma was reading my mind.

"It's time for you to get back to work. You don't have any room to get fired."

I wanted to say more but I let my kiss on her jaw do my talking. We both said our good-byes, and then I walked back into my *Twilight Zone* of a life.

TEMPEST

Two hours ago, I was studying my Bible, reading from the gospel of Matthew. What stuck in my mind was committing adultery. My thing was: why make men look so damn attractive? Why is it so hard to follow God's rules? Why make all this stuff appealing to the flesh, and then say, we are not allowed to even think about touching? The more I read the Bible, the more I became confused. This law tried to tell me that I risked a permanent vacation in Hell if I committed this sin, or my soul was going to burn for eternity if I didn't repent. How could I stop my mind from wondering about the appetites of the flesh?

It was a good thing God wasn't in the back of my Escalade because Robert was doing all those little things to me the Bible warned were sinful. My father always said evil lurked around using the cover of darkness, covering up the naughtiness of mankind. We were far away from the city, and even farther from my husband. My truck sat in one of the metro parks. I was too drunk to know which one I'd driven to. At this point, while

Robert was sinking his love deeper and deeper into me, it really didn't matter. Nothing mattered. Yes, I was married, but Robert was my boy-toy. My maintenance man of choice. I hated sounding like a cliché, but I was pushed into this affair. My husband and I owned a huge beauty shop, two apartment buildings and a cluster of single homes. He was a good man, always good to me. But he couldn't satisfy me in the bedroom. He'd come into my life at a time when my self-esteem had been damaged by this bastard of an ex-boyfriend. My husband was cute. Had money. I was lonely. And that's all it took for me to walk down the aisle. I tried for the first year to be a good wife, but when I met Robert, that was it. He had power, passion.

"Tempest Jones, Tempest Jones, damn Mrs. Jones," Robert sang poorly, but passionately let me know that he was appreciating every inch of my womanhood. "Me and Mrs.—Mrs. Jones…Mrs. Jones, Mrs. Jones."

Robert was an attorney from a very prestigious law firm. The man was a sexual beast, too. He understood my body better than me. Plus, the very long thang swinging between his legs had sealed the deal.

We were going at it pretty hot and heavy now. The windows were fogged up and I was trying hard to keep from screaming while he was pleasuring me like no man had ever done. My ass was facing him while I straddled his lap. I tried desperately to keep my wits about me so that we wouldn't find ourselves crept up on by the park rangers. Robert had the task of watching the back and side windows. No matter how hard we tried to keep watch, our lust blinded us as we slipped deeper into erotic bliss. At the height of my climax, I totally let my guard down. No longer was I watching for the law. Hell, we had a good spot anyway. The truck sat in a deserted parking lot a mile off the main road, surrounded by big evergreen trees.

The one thing I did like about having affairs with other men was that they didn't want to cuddle afterward. There was no time to. Really no time for words. Sometimes we did *it*, and said nothing to each other afterward. Just a kiss and a smile and we'd go our own separate ways. And that's what Robert and I did. I drove him back to his truck, kissed him and he went his way, leaving me to go mine.

The night was still young. It was around eleven and I was still very much hungry for flesh. I wondered about my husband, but I knew Darrius was probably slaving away over paperwork as usual, not giving a damn about me. I wanted to go home but my appetite wouldn't let me. I had dined on a corporate power lunch. And for dinner—a young tasty thug.

Within one hour, I'd managed to go from Cristal to Old English, from a thousand-dollar suit to a saggy pants, Timberland boot-wearing, gun-toting, rough house-walking, rap music-blasting, cold-blooded gangster.

I blamed two people for my open legs condition: my

mother and Reverend Poppa Jones. In her day, my mother had one helluva figure. She had all the sexual equipment to leave a man licking his lips and wanting to pay for a sample. Moms had average-sized plump breasts—with absolutely no assistance from a good bra—the girls always stood at attention. Her delectable swell blended in nicely with her narrow waistline. And just when roaming eyes thought it was over, her flawless waistline tapered downward and ballooned into a beautiful, well-proportioned backside. Her legs held muscular definition. My ol' girl used to be strapped. And that's the body I was tramping around town in now. I'd inherited my mom's whole package.

Unlike my mother, though, I was out of control with my hourglass figure. I felt God had given me a hot sports car without the owner's manual. I was an ebony dime piece in search of a ninety cent thug so we could share a whole dollar's worth of good times. Men often told me that my body was a cross between Jennifer Lopez's and Beyoncé's.

I'd been a preacher's kid growing up. That meant we didn't get to experiment with the world like other kids. We were in church more than we were at home. I hated every minute of it, too. Back when my father was the pastor at a small storefront church, times were terrible. The inside of the church was raggedy, and even when he wasn't working at Global Engines and Axles manu-facturing plant, the good Reverend spent the rest of his time making repairs to that dump. In my mind's eyes, kids shouldn't be deprived of life's experiences. They will only end up like me.

It took me forty minutes to get from the suburbs to the hood. I should have been pretty scared driving around the ghetto in my expensive pearl white Lexus LX570 at that time of night. The street looked like a cemetery: old, abandoned houses stood like century-old mausoleums; crackheads emerged from them like zombies preparing to prowl the night in search of slow-death, offered by rock cocaine. Darkness shared the street with gloom. Every other streetlight was out—probably shot out by the lower-level dealers while testing the power and accuracy of the many black market weapons purchased on the streets. The area was also a wasteland of expensive vehicles that crowded vacant lots, alleys and streets stripped to the frame and left sitting on cinderblocks.

After I passed the first block, the street burst with life. The hustlers were hustling, the crackheads were stealing, and people walked the streets searching for whatever people searched for at that time of night. My little twenty-year-old thug was another reason for why I had no concern with being in this part of town by myself. This was his kingdom and according to him, niggas knew what belonged to Geechie. Death came by way of disrespect and nobody lurking inside of a healthy mind knew better than to cross him.

Geechie might've been a shrimp of a man, but it was

his sinister heart that catapulted him into the shoes of a ghetto legend. He was a dark-skinned brother with pearly white teeth, deep dimples and brushed-wavy hair. It wasn't his small frame which was ripped right by mountain ranges of muscle that had earned Geechie the ferocious reputation, but the two pistols he was known for carry-ing on his person—I think I heard one of his boys refer to them as .40-caliber Glocks. Geechie was violent, a major player inside his world who lived as close to the edge as one could get without falling over. He didn't give a damn about the law, and his mouth was foul…but I loved his thuggish drawers.

After I found the house, I pulled up around back. Geechie's company parked in the alley. As I drove up, my headlights flooded the alley, sending big furry rats scattering for cover. As soon as I opened the truck door, the sound of windowpanes were violently vibrating to the point of explosion under the heavy bassline behind Busta Rhymes as he ripped the track to pieces on the Chris Brown song "Look at Me Now."

Stepping from of the truck in this neck of the woods was my least favorite thing to do. It didn't matter the season, the alley behind Geechie's crash-crib aways smelled like pure-dee piss, cheap wine, and garbage. I looked around. Nothing but darkness stared back after the timer on my truck headlights disengaged. I expected somebody to jump from the shadows and drag me into God knows what. That thought caused me to pull and tug at my short dress.

Walking through flickering backyard lights reminded me that I was still wearing my four-carat diamond ring. The dog barking in the distance caused me to walk a little faster. Inside the backyard, I could smell something that I was praying not to step in. The security that I received from the private fences surrounding the whole backyard made me feel a little comfortable. Not to mention the pair of roguish eyes peering out from one of the top bedroom windows. He yelled something as I stepped my high-end pumps onto the back porch. The outside of the house was kept up immaculately. They even had the nerve to have a flower garden in the front yard. It looked like Suzy Homemaker lived here. But that was a facade. The real intentions of the place were much more evil.

I was fidgeting with my alarm keypad when the heavy steel door swung open, which was immediately followed by smoke and a strong marijuana smell that the kids called kush.

"Tell Geechie that his piece is here," the corn-rolled punk with half-opened eyes announced to the others as he intensely stared at my body like I had no clothes on. He was drinking a forty-ounce of something with no shirt on and ran a free hand over the protruding navel of his hanging belly like it was going to be the smoothest thing to see on this ghetto tour of "pimps, hoes, and gangstas." *No, he didn't lick his big pink lips,* I thought as the worm stepped aside to let me pass. The grip I had on my clutch bag would probably rival one exhibited by a wino holding the last bottle of cheap wine here on earth.

I went in through the kitchen, stepping right into a sea of sagging pants gangsters. Just about everybody and their mommas were sporting afros and cornrows like they were staging a *Bring Back the Seventies* rally. There were a few young women on the scene. But none of the little skanks had anything on me, though.

Once I entered, all eyes were wallpapered to me. My mouthwatering cleavage reminded me that, at age thirty-five, I was still the hottest bitch at the party. A strapless, form-fitting, but very gorgeous, bone-colored Dolce and Gabbana dress hugged every curve of my body, yielding about mid-thigh. Manalo Blahnik shoes, Hublot watch—three carats, of course—and a Gucci clutch that cost more than all the outfits and nappy hair weave that these little hoodrats were sporting combined, completed my ensemble. They stared in hot envy—even though they probably weren't up on half the designers I had on.

The rap music was unbearably loud. Unlike the outside of the house, the inside looked like a trash bin. While exposed wiring, cracked ceilings, and peeling paint gave the place a hollowed-out, condemned look, beer bottles, cigarette butts, pizza boxes and the burger wrappers that littered the floor made sure the after-party rodent clean-up crew was fed to ensure a healthy population. The two-legged rats weren't the only hot-ass creatures running around this dump. I remembered one time in the bathroom where I'd broken the heel on a very expensive pair of Jimmy Choos while trying to escape a rat that had the temperament and body of a rodent raging on roids.

I put a real sensual twist in my hips to give those tramps something to really look at. I stepped into the living room and I saw where everybody was. I said "hi" to everybody I knew. There were two couples on the floor dancing. Or should I say grinding, freaking like the dance should've been sponsored by Trojan. A dice game broke out in a corner of the dining room; young punks talking loud and waving money around. The sofa and loveseat were jammed-to-the cram with heifers and punks drinking and smoking. One of the roughnecks wearing a Detroit Tigers baseball hat and an oversized sweatsuit was regaling the others, with his index and thumb taking the shape of a gun, acting out his shooting of some boy in front of a movie theater. He even fell to the floor and played the role of his victim who obviously begged for his life. I couldn't believe that they were all laughing about it.

"Ay, homie, ain't that that ol' broad who run the beauty shop on Greenfield and Grand River?" I heard one of the guys say to the other.

Old broad? I thought. You know I was smoking. Pissed and disrespected.

"Yeah, man, I dropped my bitch off at that joint a few times. Not bad for an ol' broad," his baldheaded boy responded.

I almost said something to them. And just when I was about to go ghetto, Flash, Geechie's bodyguard, walked up.

"Yo, Geechie waitin' on you upstairs." He noticed the uneasy look on my face. "What's ya problem?"

"Just a little disrespect down here!"

"Which one?"

I nodded my head in the direction of a big, light-skinned guy wearing a baldhead and one of those long, hairy goatees. Baldhead was big, but Geechie's man was enormous. Flash was a black-hole color with huge hands and feet with a neck the circumference of a Tyranno-saurus rex and barbarian-sized biceps.

Flash called for the music to be turned down before figuratively jumping into the bum's chest with both feet. He stomped right up to Baldhead and whirled him around.

"If you disrespect her again," Flash threatened through clenched teeth. "I'mma break both of yo' jaws and have you sucking your woman's pussy through a straw for months."

For a point of emphasis, Flash bitch-smacked the hood in the mouth with an open hand and shoved him in my direction. Nobody said anything. They got out of the way to make room for the beat down. The guy walked up to me with a petrified look on his face.

"I didn't mean any harm," he apologized with his eyes cast toward the floor as if could see his manhood melting into a puddle at his feet.

Flash snarled at the rest of the baggy pants hip hop-pers, and then said: "Geechie handlin' some bidness. I'll take you upstairs to the room and he'll get up with you." Before I left, as the music was being turned back up, for a brief moment, I envied all the kids here—and I could say "kids" because I was the eldest here. Unlike my stringent upbringing, they were up in here sampling freedoms. Had I been able to partake back then, I probably wouldn't be selling myself short right now.

I did what Flash instructed. I walked into the room and took a seat on an older wicker chair. I considered sitting on the bed, but decided against it. I didn't know what kind of germs resided on those sheets.

Flash closed the door, leaving me alone to deal with my conscience. He was scary. There were rumors circu-lating about Flash killing for a living. I believed it. And the respect that was given downstairs only confirmed his deadly job.

I sat there fighting good, trying to rationalize the evil that I was getting into. I had a nice business, a nice husband and all the love in the world. Any other woman would have been happy, but not me. I tried not to think of my mother's condition. Didn't want it to ruin my mood. I was developing a small headache from the strong smoke and the alcohol that I had consumed earlier.

Twenty minutes later, Geechie strolled in. He didn't even offer an apology for holding me that long. His beady little eyes devoured my figure. I could see an erection bulging from his baggy jeans. He offered a toothy grin, almost sinister-like. I was violently grabbed.

I liked it.

Without words, he threw me harshly onto the nasty sheets. Before I could object, he had my dress up, panties down and was working it like a young gangster was supposed to. I was having a good time but somehow I understood that God would have the last laugh. If you lie down with dogs, you get up with fleas. I didn't realize what I had gotten myself into. All I knew was that every good ride came to an even faster stop. I was down...dirty and awaiting judgment.

✪ ✪ ✪

It was almost four in the morning and the party downstairs showed no signs of letting up. 50 Cent's vocals were crystal clear and the bass was vibrating underneath my bare feet. It seemed as if I was standing right on top of a speaker. I don't know which one I hated more: how I felt after my sexual appetite had been fulfilled, or washing up in this nasty bathroom that resembled a trucker's rest stop. Fresh piss collected in small puddles on the toilet seat. The floor was filthy and the dull light from the sixty-watt light bulb revealed a God-awful, deep dark ring around the bathtub. The sink in which I was bathing wasn't too much better. The finish had long since seen the days and rust settled around the drainage flange.

Geechie entered without the courtesy of a knock.

"Yo, ma," he said. He never smiled. Ruthless men like him had no time to smile. "I need to go to the dealership but I ain't got no credit. I need you to put a ride in yo' name for me."

I might've been whipped by this young buck but I wasn't stupid. I recognized the risk associated by irresponsibility. If he got caught by the police on a drug possession, the repercussion would be devastating to my business and family.

"I don't think I could—"

Geechie violently grabbed me by the throat. He shook me so hard my naked breasts painfully slapped against my arms.

With clenched teeth, he said, "You will do what the hell I say do." He released me. As my naked body dropped to the floor, I grabbed for my throat and inhaled deeply. "Do we understand each other?" I said nothing as I continued to struggle for air. He bent at the waist and grabbed a handful of my hair. "I said...do we understand each other?"

"Okay," was all I could manage. I'd brought this all on myself. I had to oblige. If I didn't, there was no telling what Geechie would do. I was horrified. I didn't know what had come over him. Didn't know if this was side-effects from the Ecstasy pills he always popped. He'd never acted like this before.

He looked at me with an evil grin. "Now if you be a good little girl, I might, just might, let you ride in my new 'Vette." A more malicious grin ripped across his chin. "Get dressed and get out."

My heart was beating like the drums belonging to that of a rock band. I could still feel his hand around my throat. On the drive home, I checked the messages on my cell phone. There was one message from Wisdom and one message from Momma, but I couldn't understand why there were no messages from Darrius. I drove at break-necking speeds, trying to flee from the ghetto. I was on the freeway now, thinking about my life, Momma's illness and how I hated Yazoo's guts. I don't know if I hated him for adding to Momma's stress or for really knowing the truth about my trampish ways. I had no kids. I was only responsible for myself. Thank God I had no little girls. I didn't have the morals of an alley cat, so I definitely wouldn't have been able to teach them a thing about life.

Silently, I drove toward Bloomfield Hills Township. A right and two lefts and another right put me into the driveway of my fabulous column-style home. I hit the button of the garage door opener and as I watched the garage door ascend, I thought about Geechie. Over the first part of our little affair, he had been well-behaved. I realized he was violent, but up to now, he had never shown any aggression toward me. I figured he thought that he had this old lady hooked. And now he was able to use me at his calling. The undying truth was that I *was* hooked. I needed that thug in my life. I needed the lawyer, too. The horror was that I needed different men to fit all of my desires for flesh.

I pulled in right alongside my husband's black Denali Yukon, thinking of an excuse that I could give for being so late. I walked into the kitchen through the garage entry, removing my heels. This part of the house accommodated stainless steel appliances, complete with a nice-sized marble island. I walked through the kitchen, my bare feet slapping against the marble floor and up our spiral staircase right into the master bedroom.

Darrius was a covered-up lump in our California King. He didn't move. He didn't do anything. I cut on the lights to get some response. He sluggishly stirred but never woke. I wanted him to wake up and hold me. Kiss me. But instead, all I heard was snoring. I threw a silent hissy fit on my way to the bathroom, closed the door, and turned the shower on as hot as I could bear. I sat on the toilet watching the steam rise, still thinking about all my skeletons. I sat for a moment before I shed my clothes. I glanced at my naked body through the steam-filmed mirror, hating the whore that stared back. I started crying as I jumped into the shower, trying like hell to scrub all my sins away.

REVEREND POPPA JONES

After I left my wife's bedside, one scripture came to mind: *Romans* 3:23: *All have sinned, falling short of the glory of God.* I'm a man of the cloth who's supposed to wear the full armor of God. The helmet of salvation, breast plate of righteousness, gird loins of truth, feet shod with the preparation of the gospel of peace, the shield of faith and the sword of the spirit, which is the word of God. I found out the hard way, no matter how much armor I wear, there's always a small hole for infiltration by temptation. I was now staring at the temptation that had managed to seep through the small hole inside my armor in the form of a curly weave, nice smile, and a big, fat behind.

Sister Lawson was a young widow who'd been a faithful member at my church going on ten years. Her husband had been gunned down by the Detroit police. The sister was now awaiting a seven-figure settlement from the city. One of my duties as the pastor of a prominent church is to make sure that the flock understands God's concept of tithing. It's 10 percent of one's pay before taxes. The sister stood to inherit a tidy sum and I felt obliged to remind her of the word. Her husband's death had left her stressed, distressed and now she lay before me, undressed.

We were helping each other relieve some serious stress. Her husband had been dead three months now and my wife was staring death in the face. I wasn't happy with the way that I had used my ministry to bed some of the most developed women in my congregation. I had taken advantage of my position. God was sick of my mess. I was even sick of it. I wondered why He would make the female's sexual organ so addictive to make us men double-cross Him. I was a victim. Felt like Satan's puppet. I had a big black Cadillac, a diamond Rolex and a whole closet full of high-priced suits—all from sleeping around in my flock. I was supposed to be guiding them, equipping them with knowledge to partake of the glories of the millennium kingdom.

"It's something else to know that you came from one my ribs," I joked. Sister Lawson reminded me of Pam Grier. She giggled like a young schoolgirl. And I loved the way her breasts jiggled when she laughed.

"Pastor, I love your sense of humor." She had that look like she was hiding something. Like a bit of useful information. I pressed her.

"You can continue. It's all right."

"I think I'm falling in love with you."

It took everything in my power not to crack a smile.

"I like your personality, your knowledge of the word. I love everything about you—from the gray beard, to your firm belly, on down to your feet."

I glanced at the clock on the wall. I had two hours to go before Wednesday night Bible Study. But I had to lock down and secure a piece of her settlement before I left.

"I realize this is a bad time, but the church is going through a financial strain. Now your husband, Ross, would want you to do the right thing when you receive your settlement. Shall a man rob God? That's what you'd be doing if you didn't give your ten-percent tithe." I looked at her with concerned eyes.

She looked confused for a second—that was until I gently kissed her forehead. The smile on her face reappeared.

"I would do anything for you, Pastor."

I kissed her on the forehead again, standing from the bed. I grabbed my clothes.

"I have to get ready to go. I'll see you in Bible Study." I kissed her one more time on the mouth. My Pam Grier giggled and purred. I put on my clothes. Carefully, I opened the door to our hotel room. I was sure I wasn't going to run into anybody way out there in Brighton, but I still wanted to play it safe. I eased into the parking lot, jumped into my brand new black Cadillac, and headed for the church. A shower and shave in the privacy of my bathroom study would be relaxing.

Once inside the car, I inhaled deeply. I pulled off

thinking about the fat slice of pie that I would be receiving once Sister Lawson received her settlement check.

I went into my glove box and removed my cell phone. As usual, I had a mountain of messages. You'd be surprised at the crazy stuff church folks leave on my voicemail. I know I'm flock leader but some of these people were pure retarded. One of my mothers at the church was calling me to tell me that she wouldn't be attending Bible Study because her hound dog was constipated; another message from Sister Payne wanted me to come over and chase a ghost out of her attic. I had a message from Deacon Smith telling me that some bum was sleeping in the corner of the church's parking lot. The next message made me think about the covenant that I'd made with God. My wife wasn't aware that I had a five-year-old son on the east side of town. His mother had gotten pregnant and I had to give her a fortune to find another church home—far away from my church.

I made a few stops along the way before I pulled into the church parking lot. I rushed right into my office before anybody could see me. I needed to wash away the sex smell. Inside the huge walk-in closet in my office, I removed a pair of slacks, a white crisp button-down shirt, and a pair of black shoes.

Before I entered the bathroom, I glanced around my office. I was happy. My congregation had taken good care of me. I had a mahogany desk. My two huge bookcases were also mahogany. I had a top-of-the-line Dell computer system and a twenty-seven-inch, widescreen flat panel monitor. Exquisite paintings of Jesus looked down on me from all four walls. Every step I took reminded me how good plush carpet felt to my bare feet. A huge model of the entire church sat in one of the corners in a nice glass case. I walked over to it and looked down, giving thanks for where I had come from, a broken-down church right in the middle of a crack-infested neighborhood. It seemed like the more I had fixed on that church, the more crackheads stole out of it. I was all in favor of doing mission work, bringing the word of God to that area. Being stuck up two times caused me to seek higher ground. It didn't take me being shot to know that those bastards in that area didn't want to be saved.

I marveled at the model. My church wasn't humongous but in no way was it small. Unlike the little storefront church that I'd come from, this one had a nice size parking lot. The thing could easily accommodate five to six hundred cars. A wrought-iron gate enclosed the whole facility.

I had stripped down butt naked when my private phone rang. I thought twice before answering it.

"I've been waiting on you to call me back," the female caller said sarcastically. "What the hell is wrong with your phone?"

I recognized the voice right away. It was a mistake from the past. And now it was stalking my present and threatening my future. "Didn't I tell you not to call here?" I said in a hushed voice as if someone was outside my door listening.

"Pastor Do Wrong, you have three days to do right. After that, I'm letting the dogs loose." By the powerful way she slammed down the phone, she almost left me deaf in my right ear. That threat left me chilled to the bone. My body broke out in goose bumps. I didn't know what to do. I couldn't keep brushing off this voice from the past. Couldn't keep treating it like it was a joke. Before I took my shower, I said a little prayer. I got up off my knees and walked into the bathroom. My reflection in the mirror caused me to face it head on. I didn't like who I was. How I was doing things. I had to tighten it up. I'd allowed too many demons in my life. I kept hearing the caller's threat in my head. This person was definitely Satan's helper. This was the one person who could ruin my entire life. Taking away all I'd worked for. A confrontation loomed on the horizon; I didn't realize how close it was.

I jumped into the shower and felt a little tension ease up. The hot water was just what I needed. At that moment, my wife's face flashed before me. The steam from the hot shower rose, covering the bathroom. Like a silent movie, our lives played out. I could see my wife in a healthier body, a more energetic body, a sexier body. Then just like that, her sexier body was transformed into a broken down, unhealthy, defeated wreck. Her ill health had devastated our whole family. All my kids were at each other's throat. Wisdom didn't care too much for me. Yazoo hated me. Jordan probably didn't know he was still in existence. And my baby girl, Tempest, had taken on my sex addiction. She didn't think I was aware of her activities, but I was. I had friends in high, and low places.

I didn't have a bad body for a middle-aged man. There were a few things I needed to tone up, but I wasn't bad. That meant that I had to require the services of Brother Frank in our state-of-the-art exercise room. Brother Frank worked as a personal trainer. The new gym cost the church a pretty penny. My health was worth it.

I got out of the shower and started getting dressed. I had just slipped on my pants when I caught a glimpse of a huge family portrait that sat on the bookshelf in the corner. I didn't want my wife to die. Didn't want her to suffer either. I splashed on a little Giorgio Armani cologne, grabbed my black Bible and headed to the fellowship hall where I held Bible Studies.

"Hi, Pastor," Sister Long said, chasing me down. She was out of breath when she finally caught me. Sister Long was the church's gossip columnist. A real chatty lady. She was in her sixties and looked every year of it, too. The sister wore a horrible ponytail weave, was slightly overweight and always talked down about the younger women in the church. I hated to see her coming—God forgive me.

"Pastor, did you hear what happened to Sister Black?"

I popped a mint into my mouth.

"No, I didn't."

She didn't wait for me to say anything else. "Her son shot and robbed her for money to go feed his crack habit." Sister Long was a real animated talker. She talked with a loud mouth and hands. So, whoever she talked to, it looked like an unfriendly, one-sided confrontation.

"You don't say," was all I could say. "I guess I'm the last to hear anything. Is she all right?"

"He shot her in the leg. She crawled outside and collapsed on the sidewalk. The neighbor called the police. They took her to Henry Ford Hospital."

I looked at my watch. It was about time for my session to start. Before Sister Long could say anything else, I excused myself from the conversation. I continued to walk toward the fellowship hall with Sister Long attached to me as if she were my shadow. I greeted everybody who crossed my path, stopping a few times to chat briefly with members. Being a pastor meant being a psychiatrist, also. The things I knew about these people. I could write a tell-all book.

Standing in front of the class, I could tell who was missing, who was new, and who was going to be running late. Sister Gibson always sat at the head of the class. She also slept in any man's bedroom that would let her. Right behind her sat Brother Griggs. He had lost his wife, his house, his car and his children to gambling at the MGM casino, downtown. Sometimes the poor brother slept in a room upstairs.

More people walked in with Bibles in their hands. The fellowship hall was pretty big. It was made up of sections. We had a nursery, and also a room where Sister Samson taught Bible study to young adults.

"Pastor, did you hear about Sister Black?" a lady's voice piped from the back. After a brief conversation about Sister Black, I led with a prayer for Sister Black and her son. Then, I opened with the lesson.

Two hours later, I was back in my office. I was sitting at my desk going over a sermon when my secretary came in. Sister Green was young and extremely attractive. She had a schoolgirl smile, long pretty black hair, a shapely body and long, luscious legs. The only thing that stopped me from propositioning her was that she was a yellow gal. I didn't like yellow women.

"Hi, Pastor. Here's your list of speaking engagements." She placed a sheet of paper in front of me. Sister Green always wore an enticing fragrance. And she flirted with me every chance she got. She made an effort to rub any part of her body against me whenever she could. "I don't know how you're going to keep this schedule. And offers are still coming in for you to speak at other churches. You're going to wear yourself out." The phone rang and she reached over me to grab it. She made sure that I was exposed to her neck, the very spot where her perfume was the strongest. "Pastor's office, Sister Green speaking." She listened for a second. "It's Deacon Clay." Sister Green handed me the phone, making sure that her hand brushed against mine.

I looked at her while taking the phone. "Doing God's work is never tiring." I gave her that "give me a minute" look. She left the office with an extra twist in her hips. The sister winked at me before she closed the door.

"Praise God. What's going on, James?" I said into the phone.

"Pastor, you know I have your back, right?" My silence was clue for him to continue. "Deacon Slydale and some of the other deacons are starting up on you again. They're trying to bring up those old sexual allegations, as well as some new ones."

Deacon Slydale was the chairman of the deacon board. He was short, so black that he looked blue, and wore a mini Afro that was plagued by a receding hairline with a bald spot. This guy was ugly and I could see why he was one of the hounds from hell—the man had no woman in his life. The old goat also hated me with all the animosity in the world. He was jealous and was the type that wanted to be in charge of everything. But he forgot one thing: I was the pastor at Infinite Faith Baptist Church. I couldn't see how he had become head of the deacon board. But he still was my most worthy adversary. He had a strong influence on a majority of the board. He was shrewd, crafty and very persuasive.

"I'm not worried about Slydale's game. We both know

that they want my job. Slydale has a hidden agenda; he's very good friends with Minister Pullman. He ain't slick; Pullman doesn't have a church. He's unemployed and would really like to be the pastor here at Infinite Faith. And you know allegations means lies. Satan has been trying to take my church from me for the longest." I popped a mint in my mouth and rubbed on my chin, a habit I'd formed whenever I was frustrated.

"Pastor, I'm just giving you the four-one-one. Please be careful. Slydale means you no good."

"I can handle Slydale. Don't worry. Start getting ready for Men's Night Out." After I got off the phone with Deacon Clay, my secretary stuck her head through the cracked door, telling me to pick up line seven. A pastor's work is never done.

Sister Lyons was calling. Her phone call reminded me that I had more work in the field. She and her husband were a middle-aged couple with a troubled marriage. Brother Lyons was an alcoholic who always physically took out his frustrations on her. He had come home in a drunken rage and jumped on her. She told me that she had called the police and they had come and taken him to jail. She felt sorry for her husband and asked me to go down with her and post bail.

I wanted to say no because I had an appointment to see Sister Walker later on that night.

So I went down with Sister Lyons to pick up Brother Lyons. When I first saw Sister Lyons' face, shock registered immediately. Her left eye was almost closed and she had a deep, dark bruise underneath the right one. Her bottom lip was split, and she had scratches on the right side of her face. My first impulse was to grab her and bathe her in scriptures. I gave her scriptures from *Psalm 23:30*. I also gave her another from *Psalm 46:91—125:* God's protections.

In the parking lot of the station, Sister Lyons told me about the demons that had taken possession of her husband. We picked up Brother Lyons. He kept going on about how sorry he was and how he needed to clean the demons out of his life. I was anxious to get them both home. The appointment with Sister Walker was deeply rooted in my mind. Sister Walker was in her late-thirties but looked early-twenties. She had the 3B's: brains, body and beauty. Her 3B's added to the growing lump in my pants, fueling my appetite for another 3B's: bed, breast, and booty. I pulled the Caddy in front of the Lyons' house. In a hurry, I gave them some courageous words of wisdom. I whipped out my cell phone and called my secretary. Had her make them an appointment with me for some marriage counseling. Shame on me, but I burned rubber leaving their street. Sister Walker was awaiting my assistance. The Lyons would be all right. I left them hugging, crying and kissing each other. I had to admit, if I was Sister Lyons, I would have gotten me a gun and relieved Brother Lyons of all his demons the old-fashioned way. He had beaten the snot out of her.

She probably wouldn't be to church for a while. A beating like that would require a lot of home healings, but still shouldn't stop her from sending in her tithes. The sister was committed to her church.

It was seven o'clock in the evening and the traffic was heavy going out to Sterling Heights, Michigan. I had to give the penis-pounding visual of Sister Walker modeling her skimpy outfit a rest and call my wife. I felt ashamed because this was my first time talking to her that day. Wilma understood that my mission work came first. I asked if she needed anything. She felt a little weak but aside from that, she was feeling fine. She told me that her doctor would be releasing her to come home in a couple of days. I could hear Wisdom's voice in the background. I told her to tell Wisdom hello. I could faintly hear him grunt something like "hi." I hated that I had fallen out of my middle son's graces. He didn't understand. I was not gonna let anybody come before my ministry.

I hung up from my wife and went into my glove box. It seemed that the older I became, the more sexual stamina I was losing. The Viagra pill bottle was a sad reminder of my impending bout with the geriatric erectile crippler. I didn't have any bottled water so I swallowed one dry. I figured it would take the pill forty minutes to an hour to work in my system. And judging from the heavy traffic on the I-696, it would take me that long to get to her place.

I thought about I Timothy 6:5. *Perverse disputing of men of corrupt minds, destitute of the truth, supposing that gain is godliness: from such withdraw thyself.* It's funny, when I was first called to preach, I downed all those pastors who used their ministry to gain worldly action. I hated those ministers that slept around in their congregations, yielding to the appetites of the flesh. I didn't want to think of myself as a false teacher. Some ministers would be quick to argue "that all have sinned and come short of the glory of God." There was a dangerous risk going against God, satisfying the flesh. The Bible spells out the baleful consequences.

During the rest of the drive, I begged for forgiveness, and asked for strength to resist temptations. But it wasn't that easy. I wondered why Sister Walker's body was designed to look so good in Victoria's Secret.

Sunset had descended upon the area. It was now time for shadows to lurk. Time for evil deeds to be hatched. I parked in her circular drive and gathered my Bible.

Time to go and perform an exorcism, I thought. I needed to relieve Sister Walker of those nasty underwear demons. I didn't need to knock on the door; she had seen me pull up through a huge bay window. She opened the door, looking enticing and as radiant as ever. The Sister wore her hair down around her shoulders; that drove me to crazy acts of intimacy. Her plump, kissable lips were a Satan-colored red. Her body was wrapped up in an expensive silk robe. My imagination was running wild.

I couldn't see through her robe, but the way the thing clung to her backside left me with little doubt that she was wearing panties. I pictured her beautiful backside wrapped up in a lovely thong. The robe hung around her knees. The stilettos pimped out her calves. I was a sucker for beautiful feet and hers left my mouth watering. No doubt that by the end of my mission, I probably would have flakes of her cherry red nail polish sprinkled throughout and caught up in my beard.

Something happened to me when I stepped over her threshold, right into her lavish den of iniquity. There were strange jolts of electricity surging through my body as I stepped out of the sweltering heat.

"Hi, Pastor." Sister Walker greeted me with a nice, warm, but very seductive, smile.

I was always in awe of her beautiful home. Literally took my breath away. My wife and I lived in a condo in Farmington Hills but it was nothing like the spread stretching out before me. And I was just standing in the foyer.

I shook off the strange feeling. "I have to say, Sister Walker, you are a very beautiful woman." I looked back as she closed the door. My face was one big question mark. "Where is your husband?"

She grabbed my hand and offered a huge grin, revealing evenly spaced, pearly white teeth. Her beauty was intoxicating. Her smile made me forget her husband, Wellington.

"He's out of town on some very important business. Pastor, don't worry about him; he's in L.A. for a couple of days."

I was able to breathe a little easier. Wellington was always out of town on business. Out of all the times that I'd been to their house, he was never home. I'd never seen him at church either. Matter of fact, I'd never met the man. Never had seen him physically. Brother Wellington was a mystery man. Sister Walker never mentioned anything about his business and there were no wedding pictures anywhere in the house. I began to think that Brother Wellington was a figment of Sister Walker's imagination. But I didn't really care. All I wanted was penetration and pleasure. No matter how relaxed Sister Walker tried to make me feel, I couldn't let my guard down in another man's home. I didn't care how much of an overactive imagination the lovely woman possessed.

She led me by the hand on an unbelievable journey of marble floors, ritzy furniture, glass pieces and a chandelier that looked like diamonds on top of diamonds.

"Pastor, I heard about your wife. How's she doing?"

"The First Lady is tough. The grace of God'll see her through."

We were in her kitchen now.

"Pastor, would you like some coffee?" She waved her hand in the direction of the coffee maker.

I couldn't keep my eyes off her very nicely shaped rump

roast. Didn't know if I said "yes" because I wanted to watch her booty jiggle while she walked across the kitchen. I didn't drink coffee at all.

"How do you want it?"

She didn't ask me that! No she didn't ask me that! My mind was in the gutter. At the moment I thought of many positions in which I wanted it.

"Black," I managed to say, loosening my tie. The minute she set my cup down, I grabbed her around her waist. I couldn't take the teasing another moment. In all the action, I'd forgotten that I was still holding my Bible. I laid it on the countertop, kissing her on the lips wildly, but passionately. Her body was stiff at first. But after I offered my tongue she let out a little kinky sound, relaxing into my grip.

On cue, I could feel the Viagra kicking in. Our bodies were pressed tightly together. The glow from her eyes told me that she appreciated what I had to offer. We were both breathing heavy. I pushed her away so that I could gaze upon her beauty, full-frontal. She shot me a playful smile, doused by naughtiness. The temperatures of our bodies rose to a dangerous level of lust. But no matter how hard I tried to concentrate, the struggle between good and evil were waging war inside of me. It seemed kind of funny. I could actually see an angel who looked like me sitting on my right shoulder, pleading for me to refrain from this immoral act. Sadly to say, the little devil on my left shoulder resembled me as well.

Unlike the angel, this little imp had pom-poms and was putting on one helluva cheering exhibition. The little bastard was winning, too.

Sister Walker stepped away from me and flashed open her robe as though she was letting me sample her goodies. Her curvaceous body was enough to shut down anything the angel had to say. I would have to ask for forgiveness later. Sister Walker had started undoing the buttons on my shirt with her left hand, and with her right, she was undoing my belt buckle.

In a moment of heated passion, I shoved her on top of the kitchen table. It was hard, but I finally shut off the powerful voice of reason, all while sliding off her thong. I wasn't going to get completely naked in another man's house. I finished undoing my slacks and pushed them down around my ankles. I wasn't wearing any underwear. I hated to say it, but I had prepared for this moment of sin. I had her shapely legs parted with one leg draped over my left shoulder, supporting the other with my right hand. As I did my business, she moaned passionately, cursing me out, using sweet terms of endearment. I was bareback, rolling around in her juicy tavern of love. It was feeling good but I couldn't get into it like I wanted, fearing, anticipating an untimely intrusion by Brother Walker.

I kept looking over my shoulder, having fatal visions of Wellington chasing me around the house while I stumbled over my pants, trying to get away from his shotgun. The more I pounded, the more sweat poured across my body as she screamed for it harder. I was in that zone. Sister Walker had disappeared. I could still hear her, but I couldn't see her. My strokes increased. I was on the verge of the granddaddy of all climaxes. I guess Sister Walker was, too, because she grabbed me around my waist as if signaling me to go faster. But the old man was stuck at one speed. Over the years, I'd heard of many older gentlemen checking out, trying to perform like a younger man. My last stroke unleashed everything: all my troubles, my declining sex life with my wife because of her health problems, my dysfunctional family, a dangerous voice from my past and my personal battles with the evil Deacon Slydale.

We sat around after our pleasurable session. I was sipping on bottled water while Sister Walker was smoking her funny cigarettes. I hated when she offered me marijuana. She knew that it was against everything I stood for. She said it gave her some kind of escape from the burdens of everyday life. As I looked around her extravagant dwellings, I couldn't help picture her with too heavy of a burden. I looked at my watch and it was time for me to go. She tried to get me to spend the night. Though the offer was tempting, I couldn't picture myself waking up staring into the barrel of a loaded gun. When she found out that she couldn't change my mind, Sister Walker informed me that she wasn't coming to Sunday service. She gave me her tithe and I was on my way.

I walked out into the darkness of night, wondering about my wicked life. I was looking punishment in the face. I wondered how long God would let me go on before He rendered His version of extreme justice.

I looked up at the sky and it seemed as if I could feel God turning His back on me. From what I could see, Sister Walker lived in a quiet subdivision. It was ten o'clock at night and no one was out in this awful summer heat. I drove along without looking back…I feared if I looked back, I would go back.

Playing with God was like playing with fire, wearing gasoline underwear. I began to feel hot. I was expecting the kind of hotness that my Caddy's air-conditioner couldn't cool down. At that moment, I expected to explode by spontaneous combustion. Felt like I was going to die. Felt like I was going to fall out behind the wheel. I kept thinking about how I was going to explain passing out on Sister Walker's street, smelling like sex to my wife, Wilma.

I pulled over to the side of the road to gather myself. I was somewhat familiar with my symptoms. I was having a panic attack. My heart was beating, pounding against my chest like the heavy bassline belonging to rap music.

The vibration of my cell phone left me thinking God was calling. But when I answered it, I heard Satan's voice: "Two more days," Satan said, using a female's voice. "You will experience my wrath in two days."

She hung up, leaving me even more breathless.

JORDAN

The grocery store was somewhat crowded. Customers milled around in search of that much needed bargain, trying to stretch the almighty dollar. Even though President Barack Obama was in the driver's seat, the economy wasn't expected to make a full recovery right away. Although Osama Bin Laden had been killed and most of his top lieutenants with him, or captured, there was no sign of the war letting up in Iraq and gas prices were still hanging higher than giraffe testicles.

A choking economy made for an even tougher time on senior citizens' pocketbooks. Higher prices made for smarter shopping. And that's why Old Lady Patterson was perusing the stocked shelves for budget buys. She was a regular customer at the Shop-N-Pick supermarket on the city's West side.

Old Lady Patterson was more than fed up with the country's economical problems. Cost cutting here and there in an effort at stabilizing the economy was pure bullshit to her. The fucking country printed money.

She couldn't, for the life of her, figure out why the United States was slowly siding down the ranking for the richest countries. Now the slick-ass bureaucrats were really starting to rub her ass raw. They were reaching their greasy hands into her pocketbook by freezing the yearly cost-of-living increase for those receiving Social Security benefits. She simply dismissed the country as going to hell in a handbasket. That's why she shopped so regularly at the market. The owner, Teddy, knew the elderly lady well and often gave her good discounts on all her meats. Not to mention that she cashed her check with him on a monthly basis. Old Lady Patterson couldn't care less for most of the Arabic merchants in her neighborhood. Most of her dealings found them to be callous, rude and pushy, but Teddy was an exception. He was an incredibly handsome man. Average height and build, partnered with a full head of complementary black hair gave Teddy that extra sex appeal that warmed the old lady in areas long forgotten by the sensual touch of intimacy.

Old Lady Patterson was going about her normal routine: squeezing bread, examining fruit, thumping the watermelons and checking the tops of canned goods for rust. She was a retired schoolteacher who spent her days doing whatever retirees do—shopping for the most part.

Old Lady Patterson pushed her cart along aisle five bothered by an unsteady wheel. The thing was shattering the silence and seemed to get louder the more she pushed. In aisle seven she could no longer ignore the nerve-pinching sound. Old Lady Patterson could've simply returned to the front of the store and selected a new cart but ruled it out. She was one or two items away from finishing. Distracted by her situation, Old Lady Patterson stopped right in front of the cereal display. Captain Crunch was on sale, two for one. She gave the wheel a swift kick while taking her attention of the other patrons, breaking her first rule: Never take your eyes off your surroundings. Her son was a narcotics cop who'd burned personal safety tips into her subconscious.

But it was too late. A silent predator had already zeroed in and separated her from the rest by physical weaknesses. She was an elderly lady, way below average height and build. The walking stick that hung from the cart's handle spoke volumes. She needed the thing for balance. The evil eyes picked apart the simple black leather purse she had set in the smaller compartment of the shopping cart. The hunter followed her from aisle to aisle, pretending to blend in with the environment. The stalker didn't look out of place because hundreds just like him frequented the market. The old lady's purse looked to be made from strong leather. That meant he would have to use brute force to relieve her of the bag if she put up resistance.

Old Lady Patterson laughed and joked with Teddy and a few of his cashiers as they rang and bagged her groceries. After the last bag had been placed in her basket, the old lady flirtatiously winked at her Arabic knight-in-shining-armor.

Oh, what a handsome man, she thought as she walked out into the parking lot. It was a scorcher of a day. Life on the street was going about normal activity. The parking lot was pretty huge. And in black neighborhoods, people parked as they pleased. The parking lot and a dirty alley ran parallel to each other. Old Lady Patterson had parked on the borderline, which put her in harm's way. The alley smelled like a septic tank had exploded; monstrous-sized trash dumpsters loomed every fifteen feet.

Her car in sight, she was still thinking about Teddy and all the kinky things she could do to him if she were twenty-five years younger. The old lady hadn't put her key securely in the lock of her older model Ford Escort when the predator made his move, springing from behind the Dumpster nearest her car. He looked like death, too. The old lady saw him coming through the reflection inside her driver's-side window. She was frightened. She was terribly frightened.

"Bitch!" screamed the attacker. "Give me the damn bag and I won't cut you!"

With crackhead-type reflexes, the attacker took out a switchblade. With one crusty hand, he whirled her around to face him. The old lady was shaking badly but never uttered a sound. The fear had closed up her throat. She urgently glanced around for help.

Nobody!

She held her right hand held over her heart while the

left clutched her strap tightly. Old Lady Patterson wasn't giving any ground. She wasn't about to give this sonof-abitch her bill money. The Devil was a lie. Her I.D., all her information, and the money left over from her cashed check was inside. The money was her last. She wouldn't part with it. No matter what the attacker would do, she simply couldn't part with it. So she struggled that much harder.

She made the mistake of looking into his eyes. They were blood- stained, his teeth were rotten, and his breath smelled worse than the foul stench emanating through the alley. He was grinning, savoring his power over her. At the moment, he was life or death. He was God.

"I won't give you my bag, you bastard! Take all the food, but you can't have my bag!" she screamed loud enough for somebody to hear. The old woman was feisty and stubborn. Her resolve to fend off this attacker matched the adrenaline coursing through her body. Not even the intro of the knife was enough to shake her.

The glint from the blade reflected the sun's rays. The look on the attacker's face turned into a snarl as he snorted like a bull. They grabbed for the purse strap at the same time. He struggled with the old lady for a moment until he remembered the knife in his right hand. With it, he cut through the strap with so much force that he cut through her white blouse. The blood flow from the deep puncture turned the left breast of her blouse red. With a mighty yank the purse was gone, and with it, the attacker did a Usain Bolt down the alley and out of sight.

The old lady fell to her knees, clutching the wound, and her ailing heart. She lay sprawled across the hot tarmac, praying and pleading with God not to let her die. Her life was flashing before her eyes, along with many different shades of colors. She thought about Teddy. She was so many feet from him, yet so far away. She couldn't believe that nobody had seen her. The old lady made a life-saving attempt to crawl toward the street. She was determined not to die in the alley. With renewed strength, Mrs. Patterson got to her knees. Wobbly, she slowly crawled out the parking lot, collapsing on the curb. An oncoming bus almost finished the job of the attacker but came slamming to a tire-screeching halt. The bus driver hopped off the bus and rushed to her aid. He checked her pulse, whipped out his cell phone and called for help.

Old Lady Patterson was rushed to the hospital, clinging to life. She would never forget her attacker's eyes and his awful-smelling breath. How ironic, her husband had died in the same similar fashion. A carjacker had taken his car, and his life. A part of her wanted to die. The other part wanted to live so that she could see her attacker put behind bars. She would live. She had to—at least long enough to give her son the description of her attacker.

✪ ✪ ✪

Hours had gone by since the mugging. The first hit of the pipe had turned out to be just what he needed. He needed to relieve himself of the demons from the past. They'd been nipping at his heels all day and alcohol wasn't doing the job. He sat alone in his rundown apartment. He'd usually smoke with his friend, Creeper, but today he didn't feel like being sponged off of. Creeper was always looking for him to do the hustling. Then he would sit back and wait until Jordan came home with the goods. But not today. Jordan needed this and more. He didn't picture himself as an addict. To him: he was a man caught up in the harsh grip of time. The crack was used in transporting him from the past to the present. The *high* part was a bonus.

Jordan took another hit of the pipe as he looked around, surveying his tattered and torn dwelling. Plaster was falling from the ceiling. Roaches were crawling everywhere. They were caked up in the corners of the place. Open tuna cans littered the dirty floors, casting a foul fish smell.

The only furniture he had in the place was a urine-stained mattress that he had found in an alley in back of his building.

He needed to put space between him and the past. It seemed as if every hit of the pipe placed him deeper and deeper into the middle of the lake where his life was spared and his brother's father's life had been taken. For years he'd blamed himself. Indeed, Frank had died that day saving Jordan's life, but Jordan mentally died, too. His brother, Yazoo, blamed him every chance he got. Yazoo just didn't know. Jordan had silently wished he had been the one to die that day. So much weight! His shoulders were burdened with so much weight!

As he kissed the pipe once more, he fell into darkness. The darkness that had robbed him of the childhood that his peers had enjoyed. Being a preacher's kid only added to the burden he was dragging around. Back then, he wasn't permitted to experiment with life, which robbed him of valuable experiences. Maybe if he hadn't been in church seven days a week, he could've dealt with the guilt of Frank's death a little better than he had. He probably would not have had to resort to using drugs. Where was God when all of this misery was happening? The same God he'd heard his father preach about every Sunday. His beliefs were getting him nowhere. The thought of his father caused him to break out into uncontrollable laughter. Reverend Poppa Jones preached one thing and did another. It seemed like every other Sunday, some bimbo was claiming to be pregnant by him.

The sun shone brightly through his curtain-less window. As a true sign of disrespect, Jordan held the crack packages up to the window. He held them there as if to say: *This is my god.* He thought about his mother's health, but the crack wouldn't let him fully commit to the thought.

His childhood wasn't a happy one at all. He felt that his father had declawed him and thrown him out in the world to do battle with good and evil. A fight that he was in no way, shape or form, ready for. He vowed to not be like his brother. Yazoo had a love-hate relationship with God. In fact, he loved to hate Him. Yazoo was the closest thing to an Atheist as you could get. The brother had totally lost his faith.

Jordan looked on the floor and picked up the Michigan driver's licenses. He shook off a few roaches before he read the name. This was the first time he'd paid attention to his latest donor. Jane Patterson was the old broad who he'd stiffed and slashed at the market for not giving up her purse.

The nerve of that old broad, he thought as he took another hit of the pipe. Up until now, he had never used any kind of brute force in his little purse-snatching spree. He wasn't the violent type. In fact, he was rather surprised by his predatory instincts. His will for completing his mission had been stronger than his compassion for human life. He pulled the knife out, flicking the blade. The old lady's crimson red blood still stained the tip. He was taken aback by his actions. The old Jordan would not have hurt anyone.

He popped in another milk-colored rock, and began filling his lungs with smoke. He couldn't believe the awesome power of his little white god. For years, black people had believed that God was of color. Hair like wool—and all that other stuff.

He looked at his last little package. This was the best stuff in the land. This could give you anything that your past life failed to provide. You could be anything you dreamed. Yes, he had found his god. And his god was indeed white. He would prove to all those backward, black churchgoers that God was white. His proof simmered inside the pipe. No, he didn't want to hurt the old lady, but she was trying to be a hero.

He laughed loud, wicked. Unrestrained. It was as if his god was trying to mutate him into a savior of some kind. He kissed the face of Jane Patterson. Then he threw her into a huge pile of I.D.'s belonging to previous victims. Victims that had supported paying tithes to his god.

Without a second thought, Jordan put the pipe on the floor and positioned himself in a bowing motion. He bowed to his god, and then took another hit. He cracked a grin, a fiendish one. He looked at the clutter of purses—and some wallets—and then thought to himself, if his apartment was raided by the police, a lot of robbery cases would end in his living room/dining room/bedroom. He would be up the creek without a paddle. He kept the purses and I.D.'s as a sacrifice to his god. He looked down at himself. Jordan couldn't believe he had let himself go. People used to say that he favored the superstar recording sensation, Usher Raymond.

Those looks had sadly faded into a puff of smoke. His body had once been regarded as his temple. And after hearing about his Usher Raymond comparison, he'd hit the gym to hone his body in meeting the exact specifications as his R&B hero. He'd become a complete replica. A real sweet clone. Even had the dance moves down to a science. He had talent, too.

After all, he'd spent enough time leading songs in the church choir. For years, he dazzled church members with sweet, praising hymns. But in one wink of an eye, that damn Pontiac Lake had taken it all away. At that moment he was filled with enough hatred for a lifetime. He cursed Frank for saving him. He cursed his brother, Wisdom, too. He felt that Wisdom had stuck his nose into the Grim Reaper's business. The wrong man ended up dying.

He lit up his last pack of crack. His left eyebrow arched in a questioning motion. He wore a "not bad" look on his face. If he couldn't meet death one way, crack would surely finish up what the lake had started. He hated his father, the good reverend. He hated his brothers. He couldn't stand that tramp of a sister. And he really hated this hell-hole in which he lived. He was wallowing in the depths of self-pity when a light knocking sound caught his attention. Even though he was higher than giraffe testicles, Jordan managed to pull himself out of the cellar of pity.

"What?" he growled.

"Jordan, are you okay?" A soft female voice resonated

from the other side of the door. Jordan was so high he stumbled, trying to get to his knees. After killing a few roaches and sweeping them out the way with his foot, Jordan fumbled to the door. With one hand on the doorknob, he looked back as if to scrutinize his studio apartment. All of a sudden, he was worried about his place being presentable.

Jordan examined himself as well. The crack had him feeling pretty sexy. He cracked the door a little. A pair of hard eyes stared back.

"Monique, what are you doing?" She pushed the door hard enough to make him stumble backward.

"Just came to tell you that the police have been snooping around!" She examined the filth that his place had to offer. A look of disgust stained her pear-shaped face. "You should try cleaning this place up."

Jordan closed the door, locking it. "The police, Monique—get to the police." Hearing the word "police" had blown his high.

She screwed up her face after a few roaches popped underneath her shoes. "This detective gave me his card to give to you." She went into her back pocket and removed a white business card. Detective John King was the name printed on the card. Jordan took the card and looked at it wide-eyed. Were the police catching up to him? How the hell did they know where he lived? Had Monique given him up for a hit of the pipe? Monique was his lover, and one of his many smoke partners. Although she'd never participated in any of his purse snatching escapades, Monique had her own scams she cashed in on. By working together, they were a couple of crackheads on a mission. They'd managed to always feed their addictions and come up with different ideas to clothe, feed—whenever they ate—and keep a roof over their heads.

Jordan had saved Monique from the wrath of another crackhead that was beating her because she wouldn't share her drugs with him. Acting fast, Jordan grabbed a two-by-four and split the deranged lunatic's skull. They'd loved each other ever since. Jordan saw past her flawed skin, through to her inner beauty. Monique's crack addiction had caused her to abandon her will to care for herself. Her once beloved, beautiful dark skin had taken on a life of its own. Monique's skin had turned rough, ashy and plagued by an unsightly scaly condition. Most men would have found her hideous to look at, but Jordan embraced it. She'd touch his heart, blinding him to her appearance. Her face was gaunt, her jaws sucked in. Not one gram of health existed inside a face that looked like skin tightly wrapped around a skull. Monique's once-promising, beautiful black hair had come out in patches. A worn baseball cap always concealed her baldness.

"Popeye wouldn't tell me what he wanted. All he told me was that they were following up on a lead."

"Why would he be looking for me? Damn, that's all I need is for this clown to be on my tail."

Popeye had been a rogue narcotics cop turned detective. Old habits die hard. He was just a crook with a different title. Back in the day, Popeye had made his name because he had huge forearms and puny biceps. In a drug bust he had gotten shot in the right eye. Miraculously, he had fallen into the hands of a brilliant, young surgeon. His eye was saved, but he was left scarred. Popeye's right eye was smaller, and he had to squint to see. The forearms and disfigured eye made him resemble the spinach-munching cartoon character *Popeye*. He put the boots to any crackhead or dealer who referred to him as such. He was feared throughout the ghetto. Besides shaking down drug dealers, Popeye was known as a gun for hire. He'd killed his share of young black drug dealers also.

Jordan appeared shaken. The last thing he wanted was this lunatic kicking in doors looking for him.

Monique looked at the empty pipe that sat on the mattress and got instant attitude.

"How the hell you gonna cop without me?!" Monique screamed, stomping over to the mattress. She picked up the pipe and hurled it against the wall. The thing splattered into a thousand, tiny, jagged pieces. Jordan didn't even flinch. He kept mumbling something about Popeye.

"Jordan, did you hear me!" Monique yelled again.

Jordan ignored her. He moved over to the window to peek out.

"We've got to get rid of the wallets and purses." In panic-mode, Jordan went inside the coat closet and emerged holding a black satin duffel bag. He crammed as many purses and wallets as he could fit into the bag.

Nervous sweat poured off his forehead as he stared at a mountain of bags to go.

After Monique pulled herself together, Jordan ordered her to go up to her apartment and grab anything that they could use. Popeye was a rough character and Jordan didn't want no parts of him. Monique returned with a few pillowcases, some grocery bags, and one large black garbage bag. They were done packing within twenty minutes. The two would carry out their operation using the cover of night.

They did manage to have some comedy in their dramatic episode. The purse belonging to old lady Helen had come open, spilling some of its content. Among her many properties was a small box of ribbed Trojan condoms. They had a good laugh as they stared into the seventy-two-year-old lady's face. After the last laugh, Monique tossed the old lady's drivers license into one of the open bags. It seemed that old people still possessed the will to get freaky.

That was it for the laughter. There was no telling how violently Popeye would deal with him if he found out that Jordan was behind all the senior citizen robberies. Jordan had heard rumors of torture, maiming. He had to get some help for his addiction. He couldn't picture himself being zipped up in a body bag—compliments of the dirty cop. But for now he had to concentrate on moving the purses. His life was at stake. He was determined not to get caught holding the bag.

WISDOM

Fall was my favorite season. A brotha got a real kick out of the colorful leaves. This was the only part of the year that I adored driving the mail van. There was something relaxing about the bright orange leaves falling to the ground. It brought to mind my childhood. How I used to rake up all the leaves in the yard. I would gather them in one colossal pile and play for hours. As a kid, I made a tremendous amount of money from rendering my services to the elderly. It was those same elderly people that were now being preyed upon by some twisted crackhead. The news of all the purses being snatched around the neighborhood wasn't enough to make the six o'clock news, but word got around. The neighborhood was in an uproar, screaming for justice. A lot of the elderly women were afraid to venture outside their homes. There was nothing that got underneath my skin more than a dope fiend who made a sport out of the elderly to finance habits.

If I had my way, I would gather up all the predators who prey on the weak and beg the top brass for national television airtime. Thirty minutes would be all I needed. The torturing methods I would use would bring about change in the community. After I got through pulling out fingernails and pubic hair with pliers, criminals would know that the elderly were off limits.

The doctors had released my mother. Whoever said that responsibility was placed on the head of the strong wasn't lying. My unreliable family had abandoned their responsibility in helping Momma get to dialysis. I was told that Momma's remaining kidney had failed and that she had to have her blood cleansed. Her health was failing badly. She needed a donor quick. It was scary that she was being kept alive by the aid of dialysis machines.

I didn't know too much about the procedure, but what I did know was that the machinery cleansed the blood of dangerous impurities. I silently prayed for a miracle. The routine was brutal. Momma had to go for treatment three times a week at three-to-four hours a pop. She was drained, I was getting tired, and Malisa was raising all kinds of hell.

I had to find time in my route to fit in Momma's treatments. That left me putting the pedal to the metal, trying to make deadlines after dropping her off. I couldn't believe that my no-good daddy was never home to help. I hated him even more. Words couldn't describe my hatred. I expected as much from Yazoo and Jordan, but even Tempest wouldn't make time to help, and she was the only girl. I felt all alone.

My eyes burned from the absence of sleep. If it wasn't Malisa complaining on every end about me helping Momma, it was my supervisor, Stanley Focus, hounding me about every little scratch he found on my mail van. I had no personal vehicle. Mr. Focus was kind enough to let me keep my van to take care of all my personal business. I drove for a mail delivery service. Mail On Time was the name of the company. Stanley was a good man but sometimes he let his position go to his head. By him being a big-boned man and extremely fond of eating, food was sometimes used as bribery. I couldn't count the number of times that Wendy's had saved my job.

The day was cloudy. Scattered rain showers. I whipped the van in the parking lot of the dialysis center. Momma was almost ready. I got out of the van and headed for the lobby. It seemed that kidney disease had no discrimination. It struck both young and old. White, black, yellow, red—it loved all ethnic groups.

The automatic doors of the lobby opened and closed, beckoning all. Some walked in, some were carried in, and others were rolled in by wheelchairs. But all had to come. One common quest: purification.

There was a female security guard sitting at a booth in the far corner of the lobby. She reminded me of Mable King. Something hysterical caught my mind. At the moment, I didn't know whose uniform fit the tightest. I was a big guy but all Stanley managed to issue me was a 2X uniform shirt. I needed at least 3. The thing fit

tighter than a straitjacket. You could see my heart beating
on a good day. My shirttail seemed to stop right above
my butt. With a shirt that didn't cover my manhood, I
desperately tried not to think nasty thoughts. My pants
fit so tight that one good fart would rip the seat out of
them.

Mable King looked even funnier in hers. Now there
was a tight shirt. Her junk was so tight that her round
mounds looked for any sudden moment to spill out.
Her first four buttons looked stressed and ready to pop
like toast.

I nodded slightly as I walked past her. Momma wasn't
sitting in her normal area so I sat there and killed time
by reading a *Sports Illustrated* magazine. LeBron James
had tucked tail and took his talents to South Beach. He
was on the front cover, posing in Heat gear with Dwyane
Wade and newly acquired Chris Bosh like they were
going to win not one, two, but ten championships.

Almost instantly, I was engulfed by a raging inferno
of jealousy. I glanced down at my damaged knee. I was
once a top-ranked college prospect, a standout in my
class and slated to be the next Charles Barkley. My
NCAA championship ring and MVP were validation. My
face was supposed to be on the front of the magazine.
But now I was a twenty-seven-year-old mail-delivery
schmuck, holding on to dying hoop dreams. My NBA
clock was ticking. I had to start now if I was going to
make a run at the pros. Orthopedic surgeons were not

always right. Even though my faith had been rattled by my old man's exploits, God had the last say about my condition. I had to do something. I needed money and this job wasn't getting it done.

The lobby was pretty busy. Still no Momma, but I saw plenty other people dragging in and out the door. Mable King wasn't exactly the picture of friendliness. The coal-skinned sister snarled at everyone who entered. She struck me as the type of person who took her job title too seriously. The broad was acting as if these sick people were gonna steal something. My chest tightened suddenly and I dropped the magazine. I could barely breathe. I clawed at my pants pocket, desperately trying to retrieve my asthma inhaler. My asthma activity had drawn a fan base. I caught stares from an old man in a wheelchair, an elderly lady struggling with a walker, and Mable King. I finally located my inhaler and took a deep, deep breath. As quickly as the symptoms came, they retreated. Hadn't had an attack in a while.

"Wizzy?" My mother crept up on me, holding my left shoulder. "Are you all right, son?" I stood up, trying to get myself together.

"I'm all right." My mother had deep distress lines embedded in her forehead. She looked tired.

I held on to her. We walked side by side with her arm interlocked in mine. I opened the van door and assisted her getting in.

"Be careful, old woman." I laughed. "Don't want you

to fall and that security guard version of Mable King come out here and sit on me for momma-abuse."

"Wizzy, leave that lady alone." Mamma chuckled weakly.

It was these times that I wished I had a car. Momma struggled to climb into the van.

On our way home we talked about her health problems and other family issues. She complained about this sassy-mouthed tech. Said that the heifer didn't know how to respect her elders. That only enraged me. Nobody disrespected my mother. So I made a mental note. The tramp would be put in check on my next visit. Momma also told me that she hadn't heard from Jordan in days. His crack addiction was getting the better of him. She said Yazoo was also missing. And Tempest was acting extremely funny whenever she talked to her. Momma said that Pops was up to his old tricks. He never stayed at home and when he did manage some time, he would snap at everything she asked him, and then he would go lock himself inside his study.

When we pulled up in the parking lot of Momma's condo, the rain started coming down in buckets. I ignored the angry ring tones of my cell. I knew who they belonged to. I was late picking up Malisa from her monthly pre-natal visit. Judging from the way she rang my phone, I was in for an earful once I answered.

I grabbed an umbrella from the bay of the van and sprang into action. I hid underneath and walked around to the passenger side. The rain beat at the pavement, sounding like little firecrackers popping off, and it poured off my umbrella like a waterfall.

I opened Momma's door. "Watch your step, Momma," I reminded her, grabbing for her hand. It was a rumble in the angry sky. A bolt of lightning brightened the horizons. Malisa was on my mind heavy, causing me to hurry Momma along.

"Watch what you're doing, boy." Momma grunted as if signaling to me that she was out of breath. I felt ashamed. My burdens were heavy on my shoulders. Now I was allowing Malisa the avenue to hurt my mother.

"I'm sorry. You okay?" It was chillier than normal. Not to mention that the breeze felt like ice on my skin, chilling me to the bone.

"I'm fine," she said.

I escorted Momma in the house. It was nice and warm inside.

"Wizzy, I need some bottled water and a few cans of New England clam chowder soup." With the remote control, she turned on a forty-two-inch flat-screen. The Lifetime channel was on. She was a religious follower of all the drama that the channel offered.

"Yes, Momma. Your wish is my command," I joked.

"You better be getting out of here to pick up that gal. You know how evil she can get." She walked me to the front door. One thing that was working in my momma's favor was that she lived in a ranch-style condo. Everything she needed resided on one floor. Buying this condo was the best investment my dad had ever made. Nobody predicted that my mother would be in the condition that she was in.

"I'll bring you that water and soup after I take Malisa home." I looked into her eyes. Didn't like what I saw. I hated to admit it, but it looked like I saw defeat. A weary soul willing to give up the ghost. Momma tried to offer an encouraging smile.

"Wizzy, don't worry. Momma's gonna be here to see that little rugrat of yours." I kissed her on the jaw and made my way back to the van. It wasn't until I got in that I found I was soaked to the bone. It dawned on me that I had left the umbrella in Momma's condo.

My cell rang again. I wasn't gonna answer. Instead, I pulled off, headed to get the witch from the doctor's office.

My cell vibrated but this time it went straight through to my voicemail. I could imagine the hot-mouthed profanity that Malisa was using. I threw the phone into the passenger seat, cutting my windshield wipers on high. Visibility was poor. I jumped on the I-696 Freeway and headed west. It surprised me that the traffic was flowing. I rode in silence, thinking about Momma. I couldn't live without my momma. It hurt me to think of life without her. Seeing her family back together again was her only wish. Somehow, I had to make that happen. I put everything on it.

I was on the Southfield Freeway now. That's when I made him. Some cat in an O.J. Simpson Ford Bronco. I had picked him up driving along the Lodge Freeway. He was quite obvious. The white man with the buzz cut stood out like a sore thumb. The guy had on sunshades, but there wasn't a ray of light in the sky. Just to see if he was following me, I exited the freeway at Grand River. As luck would have it, I pulled up into a parking lot of traffic. I don't know how he did it, but my mystery man pulled his truck right alongside of me. His driver's window was next to my passenger's. We sat there for what seemed like eternity, staring at each other, but it was only a minute. The traffic was bumper to bumper and no one else was moving.

The rain was coming down faster than my windshield wipers could work. Then it was as if something clicked inside his head; his smile inflamed wickedly. The fool looked out his passenger window. There were no cars on his left side. He backed up, and then his truck forcefully leapt forward, clipping the rear end of a Taurus. As jagged pieces from the Taurus' plastic taillight cover fell to the ground, I watched the white Bronco jump the curve and recklessly drive through a Coney Island parking lot. He clipped a few more cars before he found an open lane, gunning it. I sat there stunned. If that had been a brotha cutting up like that, I wouldn't have been fazed. But just knowing that a white man had come to the 'hood and clowned, had me trippin'. That, and the fact he had the plums to stare at me like he had some kind of beef, fueled my suspicion to no end.

"Buzz-cut had balls to come to the 'hood and clown the way he did," I said.

The owner of the Taurus was out, jumping around, pointing at her mangled taillight. Even with my windows closed I could clearly hear the dark-skinned sister yelling hot-mouthed words of profanity. The damage was done and the perpetrator was probably miles away. A crowd of black folks stormed out of Coney Island, cussing, yelling, and pointing at their damaged vehicles also.

Something was seriously spooking me about Mister Buzz cut. I couldn't see his eyes, but the darkness of his shades had delivered unto me a hot rush of chills. There was nobody in the whole world that could do that to me. This guy was serious. But I had no enemies, so I brushed it off. I was a big guy. A giant who wasn't scared of jack. Nobody from this world.

I looked at my Timex. *Gulp!* I was running thirty minutes behind. I had to rephrase my previous thought. I wasn't scared of nobody…nobody, but Malisa. The broad was wicked with vindictive ways. If I wasn't afraid of anything else, her daily threats of introducing me to the Friends of the Courts had me terrified. I wasn't making a grip on my job, but the child-support bull dogs wouldn't take that into consideration. And if it was up to my baby-mamma, I'd be given just enough to keep me alive so she could kill me slowly.

I pulled the van in front of Dr. Gilbert's office, forty-minutes late, five new messages laced with profanity—courtesy of one Malisa.

The heavy rain had fizzled out, tapering into light showers. The white man was still riding my shoulders. The smug cheese he'd given me before he turned into a vehicular maniac was playing Tiddlywinks with my poor ability to recall faces. I'd done dirt to quite a few brothers, but I couldn't remember doing any to a white man.

The devilish look that Malisa wore on her caramel grill as she stormed out of the door of the doctor's office made me put an end to matching the white man's face with the many faces I'd seen "wanted" on the post office walls.

Malisa crawled into the van. And with all the strength she could muster, dumbo slammed the door with enough force to rock the ride.

"Damn!" I shouted, feeling the van rock from side to side.

Without further embarrassment, I pulled out of the parking lot. I guess I should've been scared when Malisa pulled a fashion magazine from her bag and started reading. Her silence unnerved me. Didn't know if she was trying to flip the script. Used the old Jedi mind trick. I hated to say that it was working.

Five minutes into the drive, I muscled up enough nerve to ask, "How was the visit?"

She said nothing. Didn't even mean-mug me. She just continued reading. I wasn't going to play her game. I met silence with silence.

We were halfway to the 'hood when mighty mouth exploded into an argument. "What sorry excuse do you have for being so damn late?" Her pear-shaped face was twisted into a million ugly frowns.

I didn't say anything. Just kept on driving. I recognized the rules of engagement. Knew 'em all too well. A few times before we had verbally sparred off while I was driving, only to end up with the police separating us in the middle of traffic. Coincidentally, the same two police officers had come to both of our sparring sessions. After the last one, they warned if it happened again we would both be hauled in. Some people say that it takes two to argue, but those people didn't know Malisa. The girl could start an argument by herself in an empty room.

"You ain't got no excuse, Boo-Boo"—she snapped her fingers. "And don't use that 'momma' excuse because you got brothers and a sister to help." She put a fist up to her devilish smile. "Oh, I forgot about your sorry-ass family."

I angrily rolled my eyes, letting her know that that was going to be enough. There was no need to go there. Malisa was a hothead. She didn't care about breaking the rules. Crossing combative boundaries.

"Whatever! You ain't goin' to play me and my baby cheesy. I don't care about the arrangement you have with yo' *momma*. My baby comes first." She dropped the magazine and turned her entire body in my direction. Malisa raised from her seat—all up in my face now, baptizing me with her spit.

My temper soared. I lost it. Steering with my left hand,

my enormous right hand ushered her back to her seat. But that turned out to be the wrong move.

"You done put yo' hands on the wrong one, Boo-Boo! We'll see what the police think about yo' ass when I call them and tell 'em you're manhandling a pregnant woman."

Without word or warning, she hauled off and punched me in my right eye—temporary blindness—causing me to lose control of the van. Malisa might have been little, but the girl had some power. The red and blue lights flashing around inside my head were true testaments to her strength. The horn of an oncoming motorist snapped me out of it. When I got myself together, finally working the bugs out, all I could see was the front end of a Dodge Ram pickup truck gunning straight for us—I'd veered over the yellow lines for oncoming traffic. All my years of professional driving were about to be tested. Without a second to spare, I cut the wheel hard to the right. The rear end fishtailed, but I managed to slide back into the right lane. The rear of the van swerved right. I flowed with it, cutting the wheel hard to the left. All through the ordeal, insane laughter was resonating through my head. At the moment I gained control of the vehicle, I found out that the wicked laughter belonged to Malisa. I couldn't believe that this broad was enjoying this craziness.

"What the hell is wrong with you, Malisa?" I yelled, stopping at a red light.

In a calm, creepy demeanor, she answered, "Yo' dumb ass is my problem, Mister Basketball-Superstar. Frankly,

I don't see why God's gonna let you father children. You ain't nothing but a dying hoop dream. I hope my baby don't take after your side of the family—all ya'll crazy."

I looked at Malisa. She had been a booty call gone wrong. A booty call that had turned into my baby momma. She had been a dancer when I first met her. A dollar in her G-string then had turned my present upside-down and set an asterisk in front of my future.

"That was pretty cold, dissing my dream. And it ain't like your family is all that."

We were pulling into our driveway. Malisa popped her lips and rubbed her four-month-old stomach. "Whatever, Superstar. All I know is that if you put me last again, you will be paying child support."

I cut the van off. "Is that a threat?"

She winked her eye at me. "No, Boo-Boo…that's a promise."

My first mistake had been letting her quit her job. After she'd hung up her thong, she worked as a bank teller for almost a year when she up and quit. My poor paycheck wasn't enough for the both of us. Here I was about to have a third mouth to feed. We were almost an empty soup can away from poverty. I couldn't wait for the little bundle of joy to arrive, but the baby was gonna bring major stress to my already stressed-out world. I could've asked my father for a loan, but I didn't want anything to do with his kind of money. Pride was all that I stood for. Being a man who could stand on his on two feet was all that I had. I was determined to make it. Determined not to crack under pressure. On the basketball court, I was the go-to guy. Mister Clutch. The same philosophy I displayed on the basketball court, I had managed to incorporate in my personal life.

"Wisdom, you're a loser," Malisa ridiculed as she popped open the door and started for the steps of our wood-framed colonial.

After I got out of the van, I took one long look at my block. My once-beautiful block was slowly decaying from the plague of rental property, crackhouses and vacant lots that held every discarded object you could name. Kids were out everywhere. Some indulged in frivolous games, a few teens were playing basketball in the street on a portable hoop and a few were standing around drinking beer and servicing the local crackheads. This was not the neighborhood that I wanted my child growing up in.

Malisa was still hot-mouthing me as she disappeared through the front door. I stood on the sidewalk almost feeling sorry for myself. How could I slip so far down on my knuckles? Hell, I was blaming the plague of rental property for the downfall of this neighborhood, but I was renting myself. One pick-up game had ejected me from the lavish seat of a promising life and dumped me off inside of a nightmare for the living-damned.

The more I stared, the more I became reluctant to go

inside the house. Malisa's hot-mouth was waiting for me—along with a nasty house. The broad might've been a lot of things, but a cleaning lady she wasn't. I mean, com'on, just because your house is a broken down eyesore, don't give you the green light to keep it nasty.

I counted to three before I went in. The house was HAM, a hot-ass mess. The carpet needed vacuuming, dishes were piled up to the ceiling, the kitchen garbage was overflowing and a couple of large empty pizza boxes were still on the kitchen table from three nights ago. I naturally detested when she cooked and left the stove greasy.

I stood amongst the mess, shaking my head.

"I don't know what you shaking your head at, loser," Malisa blazed.

"That's all the name calling I'm gonna take from you," I said, pointing.

She stripped down to her thong and left the clothes where they dropped. She smiled at me, fake shivering. "I'm soooo scared. Wisdom, you so stupid."

I drug my hand down my face, trying to ignore her. I didn't want to go there, but I said, "Why don't you clean this place up? Why do I have to come home to a pig pen every day?" I waved my arm around the room, letting her see the mess. "You don't work; why can't you clean?" She ignored me, walking right into the kitchen. Malisa opened the refrigerator and grabbed a wine cooler.

"So what does it feel like to be close to millions of dollars and piss it down the toilet on a pickup game?

D'Wade, LeBron James money could've been yours. You stupid, Superstar. Fucked it up for e'erybody." Then she popped the cap and took a small sip, her eyes daring me to come take it.

Another verbal jab dodged. I was becoming pretty good with the restraint whenever she went for the nuts.

"Didn't you just come from the doctor? How you gonna mix wine and pregnancy?"

"You not my daddy."

I knew what I was about to say. I felt helpless to stop my mouth. "Do you know him?"

The last word wasn't out of my mouth when the bottle met the wall I was standing in front of, bursting into itty-bitty pieces. The throw had been swift, smooth. The bottle had whistled, passing my head. Now my face and uniform shirt smelled of blackberry wine. My psycho switched flipped. I didn't see anything but her pregnant behind.

She took off running, yelling, "Yo daddy is a corrupted preacher!"

I went to grab for her. The girl might've been four-months pregnant but she moved with the gracefulness and speed of an Olympic sprinter. Malisa faked me out so bad that I tripped, falling to the dirty carpet. I grabbed my knee in intense pain. My old basketball war wound was back with a vengeance. I shrieked in pain, clutching, rolling back and forth. The horrible pain was trying to force me to call her every cuss word in the book.

I tore myself away from my pain, witnessing a tragedy

unfolding in slow motion. My eyes were filled with the terror of my most valuable possession clinging for safety. My fall had caused a re-verberation in the room and now my NCAA tournament trophy for most valuable player was tottering back and forth on the edge of the mantel. Then, it was as if time did a 'fast forward' thing and I had the sorry displeasure of watching my pride and joy strike the bricks of the fireplace floor, breaking in two pieces. My heart sank deep into my stomach. Tears welled up in my eyes. I let go of my knee and crawled over to my broken baby. A lot of hard work had gone into this. My award was all gone now. I held it in both hands, listening to Malisa chuckle pleasurably.

"It's broke, just like you, Superstar. You didn't make it to the pros, loser." Malisa stood over me. "Look at you. Crying like a big punk over a trophy. Such a sorry sight. I hate that I even let you get me pregnant. The baby's probably gonna turn out to be a loser just like you." With that said, she walked up the stairs. I sat there cuddling my ego. Malisa's malicious laughter taunted and teased.

After ten minutes, I got myself together and limped out the door. I didn't even change my uniform shirt. Just left the liquid there as self-punishment. A painful reminder that I'd gotten the wrong girl pregnant. The blackberry wine cooler was beginning to dry up. Stanley Focus was going to take money out of my check for this damaged shirt.

I hadn't hobbled out the house two minutes when an unmarked police cruiser pulled in front. I recognized Popeye right away. I couldn't stand this cop. If you ask me, the powers that be had given this nigga a badge to dispose of young black men.

Little Mini Me limped up to me.

"I'm not gonna waste any time," Popeye snorted, wiping at his semi-closed eye with a tissue. "Lookin' for your brother, Jordan."

Because of my size, Popeye had to look up at me. He was a short drink with a big mouth. It seemed that he was highly bothered by that small man complex.

"Can I ask why you're looking for my brother?" I could tell he didn't like me asking him questions. He got all huffed in the chest and I could see his little beady eye pulsate. A snarl ripped across his grill.

"Nigga," he said in his very best Dirty Harry, tough man voice, "you don't ask me no damn questions—I ask you all the damn questions. Now...where's your brother, nigga?"

"I ain't got him in my pocket. Do it look like I'm my brother's keeper?" I said, slightly raising my voice.

I could see his fist balling up, like he was getting ready to do something foolish. "I got me a bad ass nigga here! The fool that was too dumb to sit his ass in front of the television on draft night! The same fool that ended up injuring himself and missing out on millions in the NBA! My brother, you shouldn't ask me crap until you can answer why the hell you were so stupid!" he yelled, trying to outdo my tone.

Damn, that hurt like a kick in the nuts. A real cheap shot. I bit down hard on my lip, suppressing my anger.

Our heated exchange had drawn us a nice-sized audience. Everybody was present except the teenage dope dealers. They knew Popeye was the shark in the water. I didn't blame them for scurrying for cover. The cornball cop pointed a bony finger at me. He turned to speak to the crowd.

"See, this is why niggas end up dead in the alleys."

The cop was in his arena. He realized that everybody was familiar with his reputation. He had to keep them scared. Popeye looked to be going for his weapon. He spat on the ground, and then pulled his Glock. He didn't aim it; just let it dangle menacingly by his side. His action drew a couple of loud gasps from the crowd. I didn't flinch. I expected as much. Besides, I feared no man.

"What? You gonna shoot me in front of a crowd?" I guess that statement had jarred some sense into him. He holstered his pistol.

"This ain't finished." He smiled as though he were the devil himself. He was backing away when Malisa stumbled onto the porch, wearing a T-shirt and jean shorts.

"What's your crackhead brother done did now?" she shouted. I gave her a "not right now" look.

Popeye had a hand on the door handle. He was still wearing a devilish smile. "Nigga, I know yo' old man is a preacher. He's gonna have to preach Jordan's funeral." He jumped in his car and sped off. Malisa flipped me the bird. She walked back into the house, leaving me and my blackberry-stained shirt to wonder what the hell Jordan had gotten himself into. My burdens had become that much bigger.

The crowd that had expected to see a high-stakes scuffle hadn't fully dispersed when Kirk pulled up in front of the house in a brand new Chevrolet Impala. It was black with twenty-two-inch rims. The ones that cost a chunk of change. Kirk claimed to be Malisa's second cousin, but I didn't really believe it. They were a little bit too close for my taste. I had no evidence of anything to make a claim. Kirk was the first brother that I'd seen that stayed fresh from head to toe and driving a brand new car without having a job, or slanging dope. He was a pretty boy, standing six feet seven inches, tipping the scales at three hundred pounds. While shaking his hand, I glanced down at his new Nike Air Jordans. He was wearing a sweet Nike sweatsuit, too. But what impressed me was the bling that brightly sparkled from a medallion on the brother's necklace.

Kirk looked around puzzled. "Whassup, Wisdom?" He pointed in the direction Popeye had sped off in. "What was that about?"

"You got it, Kirk." I looked at the slowly dispersing

crowd. "Popeye came around, playing the role. But it was nothing."

"Malisa in the house?"

It was something about the way the brother's eyes glittered when he asked about my woman. It had me a little unnerved. I couldn't let that bug me; I had bigger fish to fry. I dapped Kirk and was out. Five minutes later, I was headed up I-96, on my cell, trying to track Jordan down. Popeye never issued a threat he didn't follow through on. So he was dead serious.

I stopped by the grocery store and picked up Momma's water and soup—all the while still trying different phone numbers for Jordan. I kept coming up empty. I called Momma and told her that I was on my way. If I knew Popeye, the clock was ticking. Young black men—especially drug dealers and crackheads—had a nasty habit of coming up dead around him. That moved me with a feverish urgency. My game plan was simple: first, I would take Momma her supplies. Secondly, I would hunt down Jordan, even if I had to knock on the door of every crackhouse in the city.

TEMPEST

I was at my beauty salon, trying to figure out how the City was getting away with charging me a small fortune in water and sewage when heavy bass from rap music killed my focus and was threatening to shatter my expensive custom windows. The bassline was sharp and crisp, but Tupac's lyrics were crystal clear. He was rapping something about him going to every other city and seeing the same hoes.

I didn't mind the music being loud; a couple of my stylists had that loud music equipment in their cars. But this bass was different. It was much heavier. It even set off a few car alarms in my parking lot, which, by the way, was able to accommodate thirty vehicles.

From where I was sitting, I couldn't really see the parking lot that good. I yelled, "Do anybody know who that is in the parking lot?" I wasn't yelling to anyone particular. I was hoping that one of my stylists was nosy enough to go see. Toy went and looked out, yelling back that she didn't know. Said that she'd never seen the truck before.

After that, I didn't think much of it. I had a pile of paperwork on my desk and a lot of products to order. I was waiting on Darrius to walk through the doors with supplies for the vending machines.

I wasn't aware of who I buzzed in. When I looked up from my paperwork, my eyes almost popped from their sockets. My mouth ran dry. My heart, I had to pull out of my shoe. My palms were moist and my mind kept on repeating: *Please God. Please, not me…not here.*

I opened and closed my eyes as quickly as I could, hoping the image would fade away. But every time I opened them, his naughty smile grew naughtier. Geechie stood in my office doorway as bold as ever. As usual, I felt weak in the knees whenever I stared at his deep dimples. His wavy hair. His chocolate skin. What the hell was he doing here? Darrius was due back any second. I thanked God that this wasn't a busy evening. The rainstorm had kept a lot of customers away.

"Wha'dup, Ma?" he said, grinning like he had done something taboo. "Why you ain't answering my phone calls?"

I was praying that he wouldn't start anything. "Can you step in here, please?"

He slowly stepped into the office, his True Religion jeans sagging well below his waist. I had family pictures in frames on my desk. He picked one up and shot a sly smile.

"So dat's him, hunh?"

"I thought we agreed that you would never come here. What are you doing here, Geechie?" I nervously finger-combed my hair.

"Like I said, you ain't returning my phone calls." He took my silence as a signal to prattle on. "I've been waiting on your answer."

I arched my eyebrow like I didn't know what he was talking about.

"Ma, don't act like this is all brand-new. 'Member that little discussion about you cosigning for my 'Vette?"

It was at that moment I cursed my pimp of a father for my crotch's promiscuous activities. Yes, it was a curse. My preacher-father had handed down to me his lustful demons. God was now cursing me for my father's inability to keep His covenant. I wanted so bad to shun these demons, but every time I'd ask God, it seemed that He wouldn't answer.

I continued to nervously play with my hair. "I...I need more time." I was lying. I always played with my hair when I was getting ready to lie. Geechie sensed my hesitation.

"Don't lie to me," he said, slightly raising his voice, approaching my desk. He looked around my well-furnished office. "This sure is a nice office you got." He ran a finger along the fine finish of my mahogany desk. "Ma, you got it going on. This is the bomb." He opened and closed the lid of my copier machine. "I hate to see, or come between a married couple." He picked up the picture of my husband and me again. "You guys look so happy together. What would he think if I told him that his wife had done thangz to me that homeboy has only dreamed of?" He grew strength from the worried expression on my face. He was smiling like he'd won the lotto and was now getting ready to accept the cardboard check. "I don't think you would get much from the divorce settlement, being that you're a lying, deceiving whore. And to top it off, I'll provide your husband with a DVD of our sexcapades." He was definitely smiling now. He had every reason to. I knew nothing of a DVD, but I didn't put it past him. Geechie was a conniving, manipulative, evil bastard. I might as well had put the gun up to my own head and pulled the trigger.

"Please, Geechie," I begged, "please don't do this." He laughed even harder at the pitiful expression on my face. It was as if this was freaky foreplay for him.

He was thoroughly amused at this game of power. A mischievous look flashed across his face. He looked at the closet door in my office.

"I might be able to cut you some slack. We can go in that closet and you can really show me how much you love your husband, and value your marriage." The punk rubbed his hands together, staring lustfully at my body. "Damn, Ma, the way that brown skirt is hugging yo phat ass got my dick hard as diamonds. The come-and-fuck-me heels you got on is taking a nigga there. What do you say?" He grabbed my hand.

The evil bastard! Satan. I had gone to bed with Satan. My soul had been sold. I had sold it cheaply. Sold it for the measly price of a few hot minutes of cheap pleasure. The temperature rose hellishly. I was expecting flames to burst through the walls, and an evil voice welcoming me to hell. Tears were trying to escape from my eyes. Satan already had the upper hand, but I didn't want to supply him with pitiful tears of pleasure.

I snatched my hand away. "Geechie, you're putting me in an awkward position. My husband should be walking through that door any second. How's that going to look if he opens the closet door and finds your dick in my mouth?"

"That's not my problem. It's either cosign…" He nodded his head in the direction of the closet. "…or sucky, sucky."

"What kind of trade-off is that?"

One of my nosy stylists peeped her head through the doorway.

"Boss lady," Tammy said. She looked surprised to see Geechie in my office. She was waiting for a nod of approval to continue on. I nodded and she asked, "Can you order me some flat irons? I dropped mine on the floor, breaking the handle."

I tried not to look nervous, but I don't think Tammy bought it. She gave me an 'are you all right' look. I shamefully nodded, telling her that I would put an order in. Then she was gone. Geechie was standing there looking like a gargoyle statue.

"Time's ticking," the hood said, cheesing, playing with his watch.

That was funny. It seemed as if I could actually hear the second hand. My greatest fears had come true. The door opened without me buzzing it. The jig was up. Darrius was rolling in a dolly, stacked high, with potato chip boxes. I quietly awaited the moment.

Hi, honey. Darrius, meet Satan. Satan, meet my husband, Darrius, I sadly amused myself.

Upon entering the office, Darrius had a startled look in his eyes. Like he could sense some chemistry between this strange man and me. He looked handsome in his black slacks, Cole Haan loafers and button-down matching shirt.

I tried to look happy, but was failing miserably. Darrius stared at me, then at Satan. To ease the tension in the room, I said, "Darrius, honey, this is Sat—" I caught myself. "This is Geechie. He was inquiring about the available booth." I tried to coax Geechie to play along, using my eyes. "Geechie is a barber with an impressive clientele."

He gave me that devilish smile, then he looked at Darrius. "Yeah, my boy was telling me about how off the hook your salon is. I stopped by to put my bid in."

I immediately blew out a sigh of relief. Darrius still look suspicious. Like he had entered into a "no fly" zone. He wheeled the dolly to the closet, opening the door. What struck me as funny was his lack of energy.

Like he was nonchalant. He went into the closest to stack his boxes.

"Welcome aboard," he uninterestedly said from inside the closet.

Geechie gave me a satanic smile. "Thank you. I'm gonna leave you good people to it." He rubbed his hand across his crotch. "I got to get over to the dealership. My boy wants me to cosign for a Corvette." He blew a kiss at me, then, without another word, Satan went back to the hell that he'd come from.

This Geechie situation was becoming intense. Coming up to my place of business was a real bold move. The young creep showed me how much he cared about himself. This was as close to stalking that I'd ever heard.

Darrius came out of the closest, carrying a couple boxes of potato chips and a few boxes of candy bars. I think one of my reasons for marrying Darrius was that he favored Michael Jordan. He walked right past me without a word. Didn't even look at me.

This was the first time I noticed that I had sat through the whole Satan ordeal. I stood up to stretch, and rub out some wrinkles in my chocolate brown skirt. I should've had enough by now. But my crotch kept calling, enticing me to put out its sexual fire. God had showed me tonight that if I kept playing with fire I would eventually get roasted. I couldn't help myself.

I grabbed my Christian Dior bag and headed out the office. Darrius was filling up vending machines. He was on his knees filling the last rack when he paused and looked down at the floor. I took it that I had his full attention. I looked down on him.

"I have some business to take care of. I'll see you at home." I waited for my words to sink in, but he started back filling the machine. Like I hadn't said anything at all. He didn't even ask where I was going.

I wheeled on my heels in frustration, headed for the door. Before I opened it, I looked back at my husband, trying to catch the essence of what we used to have.

A part of me wanted him to jump up and come to my rescue. To put his arms around me and chase away all my demons. Make me feel secure. Be the man that I always wanted him to be. Somehow, I sensed he felt me looking at him. He didn't bother to look up. If he had looked up, he probably could've saved me from running into the arms of my big, strong lawyer.

YAZOO

Geechie opened the truck door and jumped into the driver's seat of his silver Yukon Denali, and within seconds, was peeling out of the parking lot of my sister's salon. Tempest was a tramp. She blamed everybody for her loose crotch problems; everybody but herself.

Geechie was hyped. I had been hanging with him for five months now. He still didn't know that Tempest was my sister. I was looking to get paid. Knowing that I was her brother would be a huge conflict of interest. But not knowing that she was my sister came with some stomach-turning moments. I really didn't want to hear about how her lips work, or how good she felt when he entered. That didn't concern me at all. Just knowing that she was about to risk her business and marriage was all the ammunition I needed. Something to hold over her head. It was good crap to know. Tempest would be my back-up plan. If I couldn't get paid running with Geechie, blackmail would be another avenue.

I listened to Geechie run his mouth about being the

Don of the city. I couldn't forget about the big nigga sitting in the back seat. Flash was scary-looking. Big round head, muscles on top of muscles, plus the nigga wore a size seventeen shoe. Flash was tar-baby black. And because of it, he was able to do his dirt at night, transparent to mortal eyes. He didn't talk much, but when he did, it was something threatening. When I'd first started hanging with Geechie, I was thinking about robbing the nigga. That was until I found out about Flash. I didn't want to butt heads with that big joka.

Geechie turned up the bass and headed for Dearborn. To me, Dearborn was nothing but a poor suburb of racism and hatred. The city was split between two cultures. Dearborn was dominated by Arabs. White folks colonized Dearborn Heights. It didn't matter to me. The punk-ass police still didn't want black people in Dearborn, period! So when I found out that Geechie had a safe-house in the heart of KKK-ville, I thought he was crazy. Drugs in a bungalow in Dearborn Heights?

When we crossed the Dearborn city limits, Geechie turned the radio off. There wasn't a word said. Other than the hum of the powerful engine and patter of rain-drops on the windshield, nobody said nothing. Geechie was alert. One wrong move could get us life in jail. Two kilos of cocaine and a few pistols were hidden inside the truck. The kush that I'd smoked had me floating in the ozone. It was funny to me that my stepdad, Reverend Poppa Jones, had called me today, trying to reach me.

After I told him that I was an Atheist, and what he could do with his collection plate, the good reverend hurried up and got off the phone. The nerve of that corrupted bastard. The jackleg had tried to give me the old fire-and-brimstone sermon when he was out chasing every skirt that would lift up for him.

I'd talked to my moms earlier and she told me that Wisdom had been carrying her back and forth for treatment. I hated Wisdom. I hated him with every fiber of my soul. Wisdom *this*, or Wisdom *that*. That's all Momma talked about. She was sick and I was supposed to be helping. Money was first, though. If I didn't have the loot, how could I help?

Night had settled over the city. Geechie drove, smoking a cigarette and talking business on the cell. Up until this point, I thought Geechie was the smartest drug dealer around. Talking prices over a cell was stupid. I knew a couple of people who'd caught basketball-type prison sentences yapping business on a cell joint. Not smart at all.

I felt eyes on me. Eyes that were searching for the truth. My neck started to burn. I glanced over my shoulder and met Flash's eyes. They were as cold as ice. Eyes that had stared into many a victim for the last time. Creepy. He said nothing. I broke contact. I couldn't stand to look into the eyes of the Reaper any longer.

We drove on for another fifteen minutes. Drove past a huge man-made lake. And right next to it sat an enormous cemetery. That was a helluva combination. It was water that had taken my father. The grave collected the remains.

These days, sleep was few and far between. It seemed every time I closed my eyes, I had nightmares of my dad drowning. Risking his life to save the life of somebody that had turned into a junkie. And you ask me why I hate God? He knew how Jordan was gonna turn out. Yet, He let the whole thing go down. Now I'm without a dad. I'll never step foot inside a church again. My knees will never bend in prayer. Seems like all that time I spent in church should've counted for something. But it didn't.

Five minutes later, we pulled up in the driveway of a bungalow. It was a plain-looking house with no lights on. Geechie put the truck in park, ending his phone conversation. He looked at me like he had something funny to say.

"I got word from the Ghetto News Center that Popeye's momma was hit by some crackhead," Geechie said, opening his door. He laughed again. "I guess we can relax a little bit. That nigga shakin' down the neighborhood, trying to flush that fool out."

I didn't know the guy, but I felt really sorry for his family. There were things in this life you just didn't do: cheat the government, or cross Popeye.

We entered the house through the side door; the basement steps were right off the entrance. A few steps led up to the kitchen. I stayed right there while Geechie and Flash went through, cutting on lights.

"Yazoo," Geechie said, smiling, "go downstairs and cut the lights on." I found that to be kind of strange. I'd never been to this house before. Didn't know the layout. He had something up his sleeve. A test?

I said nothing as I started my dark journey, descending into the musky smell of dampness and mildew. I took it one step at a time, trying not to trip and fall on my face.

Once downstairs, I blindly felt on the walls for a light switch. There was a scent that kept playing with my senses. I had smelled it before. I moved along the wall slowly, feeling, touching. In the darkness, I could hear Geechie's sneaky sniggering. The mysterious odor grew stronger as I entered into the washroom. The smell of washing powder had betrayed my position. My steps were halted as my left foot struck something solid.

The growl started low at first, something akin of a car struggling to start. I stopped in my tracks. It seemed that Geechie was getting a kick out of this strange situation. As the seconds passed, the growl grew louder. My instincts told me to run. But the darkness asked, where to? Then it seemed like pandemonium broke loose. The growl turned into insane barking and I was knocked off my feet by the animal. I didn't know what kind of dog it was. I covered my head and face when I hit the ground. Balled up into a tight knot so that the thing couldn't get to me. The animal viciously attacked me, tearing savagely at my windbreaker.

"Leave it!" Geechie's voice commanded. The lights went on and a light-brown Pit Bull sat at Geechie's feet.

The dog looked like nothing had happened. Tongue wagging.

My horror quickly turned to rage. I bounced off the floor.

"What the hell is wrong with you?" I yelled. The dog started barking again and Flash stiffened up. Attack mode. But I didn't care. Adrenaline was pumping through my body. I could take on the whole basement. Didn't give a damn about the dog or Flash. These niggas had taken a joke too far. Put my life in jeopardy.

"Chill out, Cowboy," Geechie said, laughing. "Just testing your heart out. I wasn't gonna let him go far."

"Go far...man, your dog could've killed me!" I looked down at my mangled jacket. "This how you treat your friends?"

Geechie laughed nonchalantly. Like he was laughing in my face. "Ease up, homeboy. Like I said, I can't have no punks in the crew. Now, you can be down with us, or you can take a walk."

I nodded my head to be down. Right then and there, I realized that Geechie would pay.

REVEREND POPPA JONES

I had two hours to go before Sunday service. I usually went in for Sunday school, but not today. Although I had a ton of pastoral obligations, I had to make a little time for Wilma. My wife didn't look so good these days. She was bloated, and her face had taken on a chubbier form. Her blood pressure was up, plus she was suffering from sporadic bouts of dizziness. Dr. Webb had informed me that her symptoms were directly related to her condition.

I was fixing Wilma breakfast. Was just getting set to add her eggs onto the breakfast tray when I heard a loud crash come from the bedroom. Naturally, I called out to her. When I got no response, I almost broke my neck as I headed toward the bedroom. Wilma was lying on her back on the floor, her legs and arms flailing around. She looked like a turtle on its back, trying desperately to right itself.

"Wilma, what in God's name," I rushed to her side to help, "possessed you to get out of bed?"

"I was going to the bathroom," she struggled to say, almost out of breath.

I gently shoveled her up into my arms and placed her back in the bed. Her extreme weight loss made it easy for this old man to handle her. I tucked her into the bed, propped her head up with pillows so that she could receive a meal, and pulled the covers up to her waist.

"You stay put." I waved my finger in a "shame, shame" motion. "I'll get anything you need." I rushed into the bathroom and grabbed a bedpan. "I don't know why you don't want to get a bedside commode."

"Because I can walk to the bathroom myself," she said in a voice filled with pride.

After I got her set up with breakfast, and emptied her bedpan, I ran off to my study to put the finishing touches on my sermon.

At my desk, I was supposed to be focusing on the Lord's Word, but instead, I found myself recalling the unpleasant scene from the night before. I had gotten a cell phone call from a lady that I hadn't heard from in years. Robin had been a lady that I'd met in Starbucks. She'd flirted with me. I'd flirted with her. And over two cups of expensive coffee, she'd poured out her heart to me. About how her loser husband would gamble all the money away at the casino, then come home in a drunken rage and beat her. She started crying when I told her that I was a pastor. I'd made her and her husband an appointment with me for some marriage counseling. It never got that far, because Robin and I had fallen into a motel room and I laid hands on her. Over, over, and over again. Was at her place last night. Robin was thirty-six. A big bubble-eyed, brown-skinned, deliciously built sister. I was weak for tiny waistlines and huge booties. Robin had both. So when I'd gotten the phone call, I forgot all about my rule: never go over a woman's house that had a seriously deranged husband. But my little head was no more rational than a drunken man locked in a store filled with liquor.

So in the middle of a serious lovemaking session, Robin's crazy husband burst into her apartment. He was yelling, cursing, and threatening her life. I hated to know what he would've done to her if he had known I was in her bedroom. We jumped up out of the bed, fumbling and stumbling, trying to find clothes and shoes. Robin found her bra and panties and threw on a house-coat. Before the lunatic could kick in the bedroom door, Robin walked out, shutting the door behind her. I could hear my heart beating a tune in the darkness of the bedroom.

With a pleading voice, she managed to calm him down. Then just like that, he nutted up. I could hear him slap her so hard that she crashed into something that sounded like glass. His voice was masked by alcohol. I didn't know what to do. It was as if the Lord was trying to tell me that I was running short. I wasn't trying to listen to the voice in my head. I had to get away. The nut showed no signs of letting up. The fleshly smacks were loud. Behind every smack, the maniac would talk to her. Tell her about how much money she'd made him lose at the casino. Like she'd put a gun up to his head and made him pull the lever of the one-armed bandit.

In the midst of the chaos, I somehow located my clothes and shoes. I had put on my last shoe when I heard, "John, what are you doing with that gun? Please don't shoot me."

I went to the door. The dining room light streamed underneath. It was the only light that I could see.

Had to think, and quickly! I was up two floors with a drunken idiot who was, no doubt, waving a loaded hand-gun in his wife's face. I headed for the bedroom window and quietly lifted it as far as it could go. I stuck my head out into the night air and looked down. It was a long way to the ground, but I figured I'd rather break a leg instead of a bullet in the head. I scooted out on the ledge and that's when I heard the gun go off. After that, I was airborne, saying prayers all the way down to the ground. Praise the Lord, the bushes broke my fall. I got a few scratches, but I was alive. It was more than I could say for Robin. When I was safely in my car, I called the police and reported a gunshot. When they asked for a name, I hung up. I said a prayer for Robin and disappeared into the night. I was getting too old for this crap!

My wild ways were catching up to me. I was fifty-three and still very much sexually active. I hadn't had sex with my wife in a year. I was a man of God. And my ways were wayward, very wayward. I was being tested. Tests that I was failing badly. God knew about my sexual stamina. Why had He put me in this position? I wasn't blaming Him; just wondering what plan He had for me. I was growing tired of creeping around in the shadows. Lying to my wife, but most importantly, lying to the Lord.

I sat at my desk in thought, drumming my fingers. I thought about when Satan first tempted Jesus to cast himself from the pinnacle of a 600-foot mountain. Said if he was the Son of God, the Angels would catch him before he dashed his foot against the stone. Jesus quoted: *Thou shalt not tempt the Lord Thy God.* But when I was confronted by Satan, I jumped out of a window. Picture that—a pastor of a well-known church jumping from a window, trying to escape a homicidal husband.

Enough thinking. I got up to get dressed. My home office somewhat resembled a smaller version of the office at the church. Some of the same furnishings. I went into my walk-in closet and came out as sharp as a tack. Black Gucci single-breasted suit and a pair of Gucci loafers, white Gucci button-down shirt and a slick Gucci tie. I was wearing about four thousand dollars worth of merchandise.

I went into the bedroom. Wilma hadn't touched her food. She just lay there with her eyes closed, almost like she had been made ready for viewing at the funeral home. My heart was beating savagely. I didn't know if she was sleeping or had gone home. She looked so

peaceful. So still-like. I called her name from the doorway so that I wouldn't scare her. She opened her eyes
and moved around a bit.

"You on your way?" she asked.

I walked into our spacious bedroom and removed the
breakfast tray from her lap. Our California king made
her look like a small child.

"I got some things to do before service."

"Poppa, why don't you stay home with me today? Why
don't you get one of your ministers to cover today's
service?"

I pinched the bridge of my nose. We had gone over
this dozens of times. Nothing frustrated me more than
missing services. God was my first priority, and she
knew when we first got married that she would have to
share me with Him and the congregation. Besides, I had
to get out of the house. It upset me to be around Wilma
in her condition.

"God is counting on me to be there for His sheep." I
leaned down and caught her chin between my thumb
and forefinger. "God sacrificed His only begotten Son
so that I could go and teach His Word. Sometimes we
have to make sacrifices."

Tears welled in her eyes.

"Are you sure they're sacrifices benefitting Him or
benefitting you?"

"If you have something to say, say it."

She adjusted herself in the bed as if searching for a

comfortable position. "It was all your sacrifices that have our children so messed up now. You were not there to spend time with them. Because if you were there to spend time, Jordan wouldn't have gone to that lake. No one would be dead and my baby wouldn't be"—she sniffed—"a crackhead."

I looked at her as if she had turned into a venomous snake in the bed. I stood up straight. "You're blaming me for that? God has a time set for everybody. It was Frank's time to go. Now, as far as our kids...they're rebelling against God. Jordan has a demon, Yazoo has a demon, and Wisdom hates me because he *thinks* I'm a demon. We brought those kids up in the church and I don't see not one of them in the congregation—"

"You walk around here like you're representing God," she said, interrupting me. "But I know what you're doing. How quickly we forget about those kids you fathered in that storefront church down home in Bentonia."

I went to my nightstand and sprayed on some Cartier cologne. "I don't have to hear this. I'll see you when I come back home."

I was almost out of the room when she tearfully yelled, "You reap what you sow!"

I walked into my office and grabbed my briefcase. I left before I said something I would regret.

✪ ✪ ✪

The order of service was as follows: devotion, a hymn of praise, Benevolent offering, A&B music selection, announcements, tithes and offerings, followed by my sermon, altar call and benediction.

We were in the devotion part of the service. The deacons were praying. It was Deacon Slydale's turn. I had spoken to him numerous times concerning his lengthy prayers. I'd asked as politely as I could for him to shorten them. And each time he would give me a dirty look and nod his approval. But he would do something entirely different in service. Now here he was—his black, crusty, rusty self, engaged in almost a ten-minute prayer. He should've known that his prayers were going up, but coming back down, hitting him in the top of the head, widening his bald spot.

After ten minutes, he got up from his knees and gave me another dirty look. I smiled brightly at him. I would deal with that gorilla later. I stood in the pulpit behind a fiberglass podium, overlooking a few hundred members. Most pastors had the wood podium and wore robes, but me, I wanted my congregation to see me. To identify with me. To let them know that it was all right to wear the Lord's wealth. That it was all right to wear pricey clothes. Not to mention, a few of the sisters had told me that I reminded them of Laurence Fishburne.

As the service wore on, we were now at the giving portion. This was the part of the service when everybody could participate. This was the part of the service that we locked the doors. There was no such thing as being too careful. After the church down the street had gotten robbed a couple of weeks ago, I immediately had a meeting with the Usher Board. For the immediate safety of the congregation, the Usher Board had been instructed to lock the doors and not let anyone in during tithes and offering.

On cue, the choir director stood the choir to its feet. The music ministry started with a musical selection. I watched hatefully as Deacon Slydale and Deacon Todd retrieved and set the tithe box directly in front of the pastor's podium. The choir belted out a beautiful rendition of "Jesus Keep Me Near The Cross." I watched with open admiration as the Jr. Usher Board worked the congregation, passing the collection plate down every row.

My church was beautiful. The ceilings were made of cedar. All the pews were done in cedar as well. The strawberry cushions were the same color as the carpet. Huge stained-glass windows were set in rows on both sides of the church, leading right up to my lovely pulpit, and the enormous choir stand and musician area.

I saw Sister Walker deliciously running her eyes in my direction. She sat under a very colorful, but tasteful Sunday hat. She had taken position in her usual place on the left side of the church in the third row. She told me she wanted to sit that close so she could be closer to the Word of God. Sister Lawson was sitting in the opposite direction, but same row. I could see Brother and Sister Lyons sitting way in the back. Sister Lyons sat under a nice, stylish Sunday hat as well. She was also wearing dark sunglasses. I guess my marriage counseling was falling on Brother Lyons' deaf ears. I hated to admit, the only way that Sister Lyons was gonna get her husband to stop beating on her was to leave, or outright kill the bastard. Either way, I couldn't see her staying in their marriage.

The collection plates came to the front and evil Slydale eyed me once more before saying a prayer over the money. He had to go! I didn't want this thing to end in a fistfight in the church parking lot.

After a couple of "Amens," the service moved on to the sermon. The title of my sermon was, "Are you stuck in Egypt?" I went on about how God had brought the Children of Israel out of Egypt. But their sinful ways had earned them a walk in the wilderness for forty-years...

"Are you stuck in Egypt?" I asked halfway through my sermon. Beads of sweat started to trickle down my face as I worked the congregation into a frenzy. "Come out of your wicked ways. Stop putting money before God, your house before God, your children before God and even your dog before God. Because God is in the blessing business." I huffed, jumping up and down. "Cast off your wicked ways, pick up your cross and follow God..."

"Amen, Reverend!" the congregation shouted.

"...He'll bring you out of Egypt..."

The congregation was feeling the wrath of the Holy Spirit. They shouted and danced the dance of the Holy Ghost.

"...they stretched your God and my Lord wide. Hung him on the cross. The sun refused to shine. He said: 'Father forgive them for they know not what they do.' He hung His head in the locks of His shoulders and gave up the ghost. They took my God down and buried Him in a borrowed tomb, but early Sunday morning. My God, and your Lord, rose with all power in His hands." I danced while the Holy Ghost took control of my body, sparking the congregation. They were on their feet praising, worshiping and talking in tongues. There was a real controversy about tongues. The Bible stated that tongues were a gift. You couldn't teach that. But there was money to be made in selling gifts. Sister Sanders taught the tongues class. She had come from another church where she taught. When she joined my church, Sister Sanders brought it to my attention that she taught tongues, and how successful the class was over at Pleasant Day Faith. We naturally adapted and kick-started a program that offered a morning, afternoon, and night class. And just like Sister Sanders projected, the program was a success.

As I looked out into the crowd of worshipers, I could hear that sweet sound of tongues. After my sermon, I called for the doors of the church to be opened. Deacon

Slydale rendered me another malicious scowl as he set the chairs out for potential members. At that moment, I was struck with a devious plan for his removal, a plan so wicked, so diabolically clever that I'd expected to be struck down by lightning at any moment.

Keep smiling, bastard, I thought as I devised my plan for his elimination. There were no new members. Without further hesitation, I went into altar prayer, calling all with problems to come forth and be prayed over. Half of my Mother's Board had to be wheeled up.

The benediction closed out the service. I shook hands with members and visitors as I made my rounds. The church cleared out in fifteen minutes. All but one man remained. I didn't know this man, but I had seen his face on the news a lot. A few scandals. The man was short and wore a clean-shaved head. He moved toward me with a noticeable limp from the back of the church. As he got closer, I could see that his right eye looked to be half-closed.

"Pastor Jones," the man said with an extended hand, "I'm Detective John King."

I shook his hand firmly.

"How can I help you, Detective?" I asked. I already knew what this man wanted. The sarcastic look on his face told me that he was looking to do somebody serious harm.

"Nice sermon," he said. "Is there some place we can talk?"

I glanced down the long aisle way to see Sister Walker waiting for me at the entrance. She looked to have a worried expression across her face. I wanted to attend to her needs, but I had to help the arrogant detective. "We can talk in my office."

Detective King sat in front of my desk with his legs crossed and a smug look plastered across his grill. I'd told Sister Green to hold all my calls.

After toweling down and putting on a fresh shirt, I stepped out of the bathroom and smoothly sat down at the desk.

The detective looked around my office as though admiring, but judging at the same time. "I must say, I can see that you're doing very well for yourself."

I saw that he was gonna be a pistol. "God takes care of His servants. Now, how can I help you?"

He shook his head in a judgmental way. "Pastor, I'm not gonna beat around the bush. We have reasons to believe that your son, Jordan, is responsible for a rash of robberies; my mother being one of them."

"If that's so, don't you think this case is a conflict of interest? I mean...if my son is guilty, are you gonna have enough presence of mind to restrain vengeance?"

"Pastor, this is a matter for the law. I'll treat your son like any other criminal I've ever apprehended."

I removed the glass lid off my candy jar. "Would you like one?"

"No, thank you."

I popped a mint into my mouth and placed the lid back on the jar. "*Revenge is mine*, says the Lord," I quoted. "Detective, I find that very hard to believe."

"I didn't come here to hear a sermon. Where's your son?"

"Haven't seen him in four months."

"This thing can go smooth, or it can be rough." He pulled his badge from inside the neck of his shirt. "I'm the law. Out in the streets, I'm God. The criminals are judged by *me*."

"Detective, there will be no blasphemy in the house of the Lord."

The detective thundered from his seat. Became unglued. Like he was going to attack me.

"Your son is a junkie. And that junkie attacked my mother, stabbing her in the shoulder. Then the little prick took her social security money and ran off down the alley like the filthy scum that he is!"

I was gazing at the man like he'd lost his mind.

"My job is to take the scum off the streets; sometimes by any means necessary."

"It seems like you've already made up your mind. You have no concrete evidence that my son is your man. I believe all you're working with is hearsay. That's not enough for me. Detective, if you find and hurt my son, I will have you prosecuted to the fullest length of the law."

"My mother identified him. But do I hear a threat somewhere in there, Preacher? You are in no shape to threaten me. I'm the law." He glanced down at my watch and smiled. "A Rolex, hunh? All you preachers are alike. You're all parasites, feeding off the congregation. And preacher, I know about you. You might be a big man around town, but I'm the *m-a-n*."

"Detective, I think we're done here. I have church obligations to attend to. If there is nothing else, close the door on your way out."

The muscles in his jaws seemed to relax. A sneaky smile outlined his face. With his hand on the doorknob, he said, "The only obligations you have to attend to involve laying the pipe to some man's wife." He laughed his way out the door. I could hear his sick snort all the way down the hallway. I had to find Jordan before the detective found him. I had failed my son; my family. But it would kill me if I had to deliver the eulogy at my son's funeral.

Then it seemed like my day had gone from bad to worse. Without knocking, Sister Walker entered my office, crying.

"Pastor, we need to talk."

Sister Walker took my puzzled expression as the green light to continue. She removed a tissue from the box on my desk and began to wipe her tear-stained cheeks.

"My husband's firm called and told me that my husband was killed in South America."

What was he doing in South America? I asked myself. I wrinkled my brow in confusion.

"I might as well come clean. Wellington was working for a private investigation firm. Going out of town to work was the norm for him." She released more tears. "They never sent him out of the country, though. They have special field investigators for that. I got the call this morning saying that Wellington"—her chest heaved uncontrollably—"Wellington was eaten by some animal in one of those jungles down there." Sister Walker lost it, falling to the floor in a sniveling ball of tears.

I aided her into the chair where the heathen detective had sat. I put a hand on her shoulder.

"We do not know at what time or place we'll be called home. We have to be ready." She clutched my hand, holding on for dear life. "God has called Brother Walker home. He gave him to us for a little while. Rest assured that he is smiling down upon you right now. Grieve right now. Weeping may last through the night but joy comes in the morning." She balled heavily. Like a wife who had lost everything in the world. "To be absent in body is to be present in spirit with the Lord." I consoled her as best I could. I don't know. It was something about the whole thing that didn't sit right with me. My senses were telling me something was foul. I couldn't put my finger on it.

"Pastor, I really need to see you today. Can you stop by my house later?"

I looked around the office as though it had been bugged by Deacon Slydale. I had to get her out before she said something further incriminating.

I bent down and whispered, "Be expecting me around eight. Now go home and try to get some rest." She stood up, kind of shaky. The Sister tried to kiss me on my jaw but I was quick with a handshake. Rejection registered in her face, but her eyes told me she understood.

Right after she closed the door, my private phone rang. I didn't have time to form a single thought. I picked up the phone and got my third surprise.

"I called myself trying to be nice. But you don't understand what that means. I didn't go through with my last threat. I was kind of hoping that you would give in before I went there. But bastards like you are hard-headed. Big-headed nigga. Now I got to spank you for being so damn naughty."

"Judgment awaits you. My sins have been forgiven. You were one of them. God pardoned me a long time ago for you. You have to get on with your life now. Don't call me ever again," I retorted.

The caller's tone went from docile schoolgirl to a psychotic pitch. "Who the hell do you think you're dealing with? I am judge and jury, and your ass will be executed."

The phone was slammed down in my ear. The harsh hum of the dial tone sent bad vibes through my body. My dirt was catching up with me. I didn't know how long it would be before God would lay out full vengeance. It seemed as if everything was being served up on my plate at one time. A full course meal of trouble. I believed that dessert would leave a bitter taste of God's wrath in my mouth. I should've been on my knees, but instead, I was beginning to succumb to anger. I was angry at myself for not following God's word. I was angry at Wellington for being devoured by an animal, leaving me with his grieving widow. I knew the direction Sister Walker was headed with this. With her husband out of the way, she would be looking to be the next Mrs. Jones. I was also furious with committing adultery with a vindictive tramp. A tramp that was now threatening to reveal all. I couldn't afford to lose control of my empire. I had worked hard to get here. Had too much riding on wealth. I couldn't go back to being poor. I had a sweet condo, an exquisite wardrobe, a classy Caddy and the church was paying me almost two-hundred grand a year, plus donations and anniversary offerings. I couldn't lose that. Just to think somebody was trying to take this away peeved me to no end. I had to vent. Had to unleash this anger upon somebody.

I picked up the phone, pressing the button for Sister Green's intercom. "Sister Green, get Sister Smith in here!" I yelled, almost surprising myself.

Within five minutes, Sister Smith knocked and walked through the door. She was a plain-looking lady, head of the Nurses Guild. Her body was horribly proportioned. Her breasts were too big for her small frame, and her legs were skinnier than giraffe legs. For a lady that looked to be in her middle twenties, Sister Smith's body was jacked up.

I could tell that she was startled by the madness in my face.

"Yes, Pastor, did you call for me?" she meekly answered.

I went right into it. I had expected to talk to her under normal circumstances, but she was the type that wanted to do things her way.

"What did I tell you about serving me the plain tap water?"

"But—" she tried to interrupt.

"Gatorade, or bottled water"—I pointed—"you get that? Gatorade or bottled water!" I yelled, using a nasty tone.

Sister Smith stood there with a frightened look on her narrow face. It seemed as if she was paralyzed.

I decided to give her a little help. "You may go."

She almost broke a heel hustling out my office.

Minutes later, Sister Green entered. She was wearing a cautious look.

"Pastor, is everything okay?"

"Don't I look like everything is all right?" I sat down hard in my chair.

"Well, judging by the way that Sister Smith ran out with tears in her eyes, I would say that there's a problem."

"It's nothing that God can't fix. I have to be alone. So can you close the door on your way out?"

She was almost out the door. "Sister Green...hold all my calls."

My ship was sinking, and I felt helpless to stop it.

✪ ✪ ✪

As weeks went by, Wilma's mood swings were getting on my nerves. She felt depressed, then angry, then guilty, and then came denial. She had gotten so bad that I started sleeping in the guest bedroom.

And if that wasn't bad enough, Sister Walker was blowing up my cell phone. I had spent half the night with her after she'd found out about the swallowing death of her husband. The lady was visually shaken. She kept yelling his name and asking me how she was gonna live. She told me that Wellington was a very private person, and he never talked of an insurance policy. Said that she would look to sue his firm. After one of her funny cigarette things, a couple of Valiums and a pint of Remy Martin VSOP, she got off to sleep. I had tiptoed out the house. Sister Walker was beginning to be more trouble than she was worth. With no husband now, and no sure way for financial support, she was of no use to me. But the lady had good loving. And I was a sucker for the poor and needy. I thought it was kind of depressing to know that Sister Walker probably would have to move out of her nice mansion. She would have to trade it all in for meager dwellings.

It was around 11 p.m. My oldest trustee had been involved in an accident. Trustee Otis Blake had been finishing up church business. He'd left the church headed for home when a stolen car broad-sided him. His unconscious body had been extracted from the wreckage by using the Jaws of Life. Otis was now clinging to life at Mercy Memorial Hospital.

I had gotten a call around midnight and was requested for consolation and prayer. I hated hospitals. Hated the smell. Hated the doctors. Hated everything there is to hate about hospitals. But it was my job as a Pastor to bring faith and hope. A Word from the Lord.

When I got to my trustee's room, he was in bad shape. His wife and a few of his children were bedside. I hugged his wife and gave his kids words of encouragement. Otis was surrounded by a ton of machines. Some beat, others distributed fluids and monitored vital signs. He was in a body cast. His head was capped by white bandages from forehead to neck. Otis was brown-skinned but he had a pale look to his face. I guess the airbags were to blame for his black eyes. Otis was in bad shape.

I said a silent prayer before summoning the family around the bed for prayer. I stayed there for three hours before I left for home. It was now 2 a.m. I was going home to try and get some sleep before I got up tomorrow morning to deal with the Deacon Board, and the evil Deacon Slydale.

WISDOM

"I don't want to hear that crap!" I yelled into my cell. "Tempest, have your ass over Momma's Saturday at four!" I hung up on all her excuses. Things were getting way out of hand. We had no family unity; no order in the family at all. And since my weak ass old man didn't have the balls to call a family meeting, I was calling one. Tempest thought she was gonna get off. Thought she was excluded because her old man was out of town and she had no one to run the shop. I didn't give a damn if Saturday *was* money day. She knew I didn't play. I would drag her out of her office kicking and screaming.

I sat in my mail van, getting ready to deliver to my last stop. The month of October was a memory. The biting cold November winds were now upon us. I sat in the parking lot of my last stop, scrolling through the list of contacts in my cell phone. I was trying to find a number for Yazoo. The dude never kept a number for more than three months. He constantly changed it, like he was trying to stay one step ahead of the FBI.

The heat in my van wasn't working so well. I'd phoned my supervisor and told him that if he didn't get my van into maintenance, his free cheeseburgers would be a distant memory. The fat punk put a work order in right away.

I played with my phone book until I found my brother's number. I was saving my old man for last. He would have a ton of excuses.

I dialed the number and sat back, listening. He picked up on the third ring.

"I need you to listen to me," I sternly spoke into the phone. "I need you at Momma's Saturday at four."

He sounded like I had awakened him from the best sleep ever. "Fo' what?"

I knew this Negro didn't want to get rowdy. The way Malisa had me wound up lately, I was ready to take it out on somebody. Didn't give a damn if it *was* blood.

"Don't question me. Just have your ass over there."

"Wisdom, I don't know who the hell you think you talking to? The last time I checked, my daddy was resting six-feet under. No thanks to you and that junkie we got for a brother."

"You a gangsta now? I ain't gonna waste my time commenting on your madness. But if you don't be at Momma's, I better not ever see you around town!" I pushed the END button, letting him know that I meant business.

It seemed that the colder it was becoming, the worse

my knee began to hurt. I was scheduled to begin therapy. I got tired of looking and thinking about what could've been. Tired of picking up a sports magazine and not seeing my face. I was broke. Didn't have a car of my own. A cent to my name. And worse than that, Malisa was in her sixth month of pregnancy. I was determined to work my way back into playing shape.

I got out of the truck and headed for a plain-looking building with "Speedy Mail" plastered over the top of the entrance in big white letters. I hobbled through the door.

I spoke to Janet, kicking it with her for a few ticks. Janet was the plain-Jane type. She was highly intelligent, sweet, and always had a kind word to say whenever I was feeling the blues. Kind of tall for my taste, but her sweet chocolate skin, big brown eyes, lovely thick lips and big old booty were enough to change my mind. Talking to her almost made me late plenty of times. This girl was dangerous. The chemistry we shared was off the charts. The way we flirted with each other made me daydream about the good life. Taking my dream girl and running off to paradise.

After a few moments had gone by, I reluctantly pulled myself away from her tasty conversation, picked up two mail tubs and headed out the door. The hawk reminded me to buy a new winter jacket. But the scene that was playing out in front of my eyes made me want to kill. A newer model black Cadillac had rolled up in the parking lot of a Red Roof Inn across the street from where I stood. Out jumped my sorry-ass old man and some bimbo. My first impulse was to drop my mail, run up on them, and Rambo both of them. My momma was lying near death and this schmuck was going into a room with one of his cheap whores.

I played it cool. Didn't want to do anything stupid. Had to maintain my composure.

I jumped in the van and rolled over to the motel where Pastor Slick-Talker was posted. They had a ground walk-up. It was the end of the day so the parking lot was empty. How convenient. I had to talk to this bastard anyway.

Like I'd just rented a room, I limped to room 666. The mark of the beast. I found it kind of poetic. I guess the horny schmuck was paying more attention to laying the pipe instead of the unholy number. The numbers stood against everything that he wasn't supposed to be. It was like Satan had the room reserved for the damned. My old man's soul was as filthy as a highway rest stop.

I cursed him for the way that our family had turned out. Jordan was on the run because of my Pastor-father. A fury was raging, trying to escape from me. With no hesitation, I banged on the door. The laughing on the other side hushed immediately. The room had a bay window right next to the door. The curtain moved slightly. Like somebody was trying to get a peek at the visitor. I could hear him say something to her in a moderate tone.

A few seconds later, the schmuck opened the door. His face held a tamed look of surprise. He didn't want to look like he'd been caught with his hands in the collection plate. The moron kept trying to look like he was in control.

"Wisdom, what are you doing out here?"

"I'm working. Are you working as well?"

"You never know where God's work will take you," he said, trying to smile, but his frightened inner child was as scared as a soul going to hell. I could see that in his eyes.

"Don't talk to me about God. Right now, the only thing stopping me from pounding yo' ass into the ground is that I don't wanna be late getting back to my job." The hawk went up my pants leg, freezing my manhood.

The ol' dude tried to say something smart, but I brushed right past him, limping into the motel room. The bathroom door was closed. I was assuming that his tramp was hiding behind it.

"Is this why you can't help with taking Momma to dialysis?" I asked, pretending like I was gonna open the bathroom door. I could see the old man tense up. He shut the front door and turned around to face me. I could see that the schmuck didn't have an answer. I pointed to the bathroom door. "Is this why you can't spend any time with Momma?" I sat down on the bed just to be funny, folded my arms, preparing for the suitcase of lies he was about to unpack.

"I know this looks bad," he said, still standing at the door. "The sister was having problems. Her husband recently died and I was ministering to her." He pointed to his Bible sitting on a nightstand. "We were getting prepared to go over scriptures."

"Then what were you gonna do? Lay holy hands on her? You see, you dime-store minister. My mother is laying a plot away from death. And you and this tramp up in here, playing church. You've cursed yo' whole family. Your wife is dying behind your mess. Your baby girl is a harlot behind your mess. And your youngest son is a crackhead—all behind your mess."

He said nothing. Just stood there like a kid being chastised. He nervously shifted his weight from one leg to the other. I looked toward the bathroom. The lady was as quiet as a church mouse. Not a sound. The thoughts that had to be going through her mind were priceless to know.

"Son, it's not what you think." He had his hands up in a pleading motion.

I waved his words away. As much as I wanted to, I couldn't bring myself to hurt one of God's servants. His treacherous soul would have to answer for all his mess on Judgment Day.

"Has Jordan called you?" I asked, still glancing at the bathroom door.

I could see the tension ease from his face after my question. "I haven't seen him. But a detective came by the church—"

"Popeye. His name is Popeye. He's a dirty cop from our neighborhood."

"I don't know where Jordan is but we have to find him before the detective. He let me know that once he finds Jordan, he'll dispense his own brand of justice."

I looked at my watch. The evening traffic had just begun. I would be late for the office if I didn't leave now.

"I'm gonna find Jordan and I'm dragging his behind to the family meeting we're having Saturday at four." He questioned with his eyebrow. "The meeting is over your house so you will have no excuse." I limped to the door. He finally unglued himself from the spot in which he had been standing, moving aside. I looked toward the bathroom door. "Preacher, we have a lot to talk about. Make sure you have your ass there." I didn't give him a chance to respond. I opened the door and was met by a blast of bone-chilling wind. It was beginning to get dark out, but I could still see the white man in the dark-colored Mercury. He had what looked to be a camcorder up to his face. I didn't think nothing of it. I figured that this was a sleazy motel and he was a gumshoe hired by one of those reality shows, to catch unfaithful spouses and lovers. I jumped in my van, headed for the office.

The traffic on I-96 East was gridlocked. I was simmering in thought. I'd caught my old man in the beginning stages of adultery. To know was one thing, but to actually see firsthand was unfathomable. Way beyond understanding. There were so many things that I wanted to do to him. I wanted to take out all my frustrations on him. Straight pile-drive him through the ground. If I had been a kid seeing his father in the act of defilement, I probably would've been scarred for life. But I was a grown man and had been through far too many traumatizing moments. So this was another chapter of madness in my life. I could deal with it. I thought about my mother and how she had put up with my father's trifling ways as long as she did. Now she was down and he wasn't there for her.

I always hated the drive back to the office. The last official drive of the day. Cars were moving a few inches at a time. There was always some idiot trying to cut in, and out of lanes. Always somebody that was in a rush to be somewhere. I thought nothing as I cruised right by an accident scene. Some idiot that had passed me up five minutes ago now sat on the left shoulder in twisted carnage. The whole front clip of his small SUV had been torn off. It looked like he'd rear-ended a red Lincoln Navigator. There were two State Trooper cruisers on the scene. One of the troopers was setting down flares and the other was directing traffic. They had somebody in the back of one of the police cars.

Always in a rush, I mumbled as I made eye contact with the face of the silly-looking white man in the back of the trooper car.

Seeing the trooper car painfully reminded me that I had a fugitive brother on the run. I had to find Jordan.

He wouldn't be given a fair shake if that hitman with a badge found him. I didn't have any idea where he was, but he hung out with a rashy-skinned crackhead. The heifer lived two floors up from him in an apartment building that was considered condemned. The place would serve as the start for my first unofficial manhunt.

The traffic decided to open up and I floored it. To avoid further traffic complications, I took the express lane. My cell rang. My home number displayed on the caller ID. I didn't feel like dealing with a pregnant, angry woman. Didn't feel like the hassle. So I let it ring while turning up the volume on the knobless radio. Anita Baker's soulful voice was soothing. I was so happy that Anita was back on the scene. I severely missed her much-needed ballads.

I was flowing with the traffic now—Ms. Baker and me. My Metro PCS sat in the passenger seat, ringing like it had a mind of its own. Taunting me to answer. But I decided not to add to the rest of the stress riding on my shoulders. I was twenty-seven and had been forced to be patriarch of the family. I figured I was too young for this crap. This was an old folk's position. My soul was tired and my mind was exhausted. It seemed to be no stopping this merry-go-round of madness.

The constantly ringing cell was a testament to insanity. I got no rest at the job, and I definitely didn't have peace at home. I thought home was a place where a man could escape the madness of the world. Could shut his door on all the chaos; kick back in his recliner while watching his big screen with a bottle of suds in one hand and himself in the other. But my world was hell and Satan lived in my house.

In good faith, I was hoping that all my siblings willingly participated in the family meeting. I didn't want to act ugly.

I was almost back at the office when I picked up the white Bronco in my rearview mirror. Mister Buzz Cut was back. The white man lagged me seven car-lengths behind.

Who is this schmuck? And what the hell did he want? I came up on the Tireman exit. The office was a couple of blocks away. I didn't want to let this creep know where I worked. Then I remembered the name of my company and the phone number were plastered on the side of my van. I took him the long way, hoping that the traffic on Tireman would snare him. To my surprise, Mister Buzz Cut kept on coming. I had five minutes to go before my supervisor would put out an APB on me.

I made a pair of right turns, then a left. The office sat on a residential street in a non-descriptive building.

I pulled in the driveway, exited the van, preparing for an altercation with Mister Buzz Cut. Instead of my usual mail tubs, I jumped out with a tire iron. My van sat right before the closed overhead door of the garage. I limped to the curb. The Bronco was two cars away and slow-rolling. Like he was getting ready for a drive-by. The adrenaline surging through my body had put me in harm's way, totally uncovered and vulnerable for a deadly blast of gunfire.

What if this white man had a gun? I didn't give a damn. Since our last encounter, I had racked my brain trying to figure out who he was.

It was freezing cold out and no one was on the street. It surprised me that there were no other drivers checking in. It was just Mister Buzz Cut and me. He slowly rolled right by me without a word, wearing the same dark shades from our previous encounter. The jerk smiled at me. Not the friendly smile either. His smile told of a final encounter. One where he would finally reveal his position.

I stood there poised in a throwing stance, not knowing how foolishly stupid I looked until I came down from my anger. Felt real dumb. All the white man had to do was pull a pistol and I would've made the eleven o'clock news the hard way. I looked at the tire iron and smirked foolishly. It was like bringing a knife to a gunfight. I watched as the back of the Bronco disappeared.

This was yet another chapter in the book of my troubled life. I guess it wasn't supposed to end right there.

✪ ✪ ✪

"What the hell is this?" I screamed at the top of my voice. I had opened an envelope from Posey and Posey law firm. I couldn't believe my eyes. I was staring at a letter for a Request and Writ for Garnishment. I blinked my eyes quickly, trying desperately to make this newest bad chapter in my life go away. But try as I might, the piece of paper in my hand stared boldly at me like it was a stick-up man, robbing me for an empty wallet. In reading the letter I learned that Western Motors Credit Company was suing me because my ex had defaulted on a car loan that I'd whole-heartedly cosigned on. Caliba had been my college sweetheart. Marriage material. We started as freshman at Michigan State University. She majored in Law, and I played ball.

We had dreams of her becoming a hot-shot lawyer and me becoming a superstar in the NBA. Fantasies of a family, big house, white-picket fence and Rottweiler patrolling our home. Those dreams had sadly melted behind my unfaithfulness. Had a one-night stand with some girl in North Carolina. The NCAA tournament of my junior year was held in Tar Heel Country. After my squad knocked off the Tar Heels, we had a wild party that night to celebrate winning the championship and my MVP earnings. She was a willing groupie and I had consumed a massive amount of alcohol. That had been my one and only one-night stand and I wasn't proud of it. The guilt ate at my conscience like battery acid eating away human flesh. So one night, I'd broken down in tears and revealed my treachery to Caliba. She didn't take it well at all. The girl tried to cut me with a box cutter. Her flunking out of law school was my fault. Drugs and alcohol became a way for her to escape academic and relationship failures. With a full-blown habit, Caliba couldn't afford to make the payments on the car.

The letter that I was now holding reminded me of my painful shortcomings to a beautiful lady that should've been my bride. I had destroyed a life and now the punishment for my sins were coming to bear.

Where I could've married and had a prosperous future, I was now cursed with a life of strife and misery. Malisa was the fire and my knee injury was my hell.

Western Motors was now suing me for five thousand dollars. I stood in my living room in total shock. Malisa was gone with Kirk. Thank God. If she would've gotten to the mail before me, I would've heard it for the rest of my life.

I walked around the house, trying to get my bearing. I had to call and see if a payment arrangement was feasible. I was hoping that they would accept an arrangement. Couldn't afford for them to garnish my wages or take my tax refund.

Right now, I couldn't afford to worry about myself. I had bigger fish to fry. Jordan was running around with a bounty on his head. I had to find him.

I changed into more comfortable clothing, picked up my boy, Rico, and headed for the first stop of this manhunt. Rico wasn't as tall as me, but the boy was a bruiser. A former Golden Gloves Champion. I'd seen him smack up three men in the parking lot of a movie theater. When it was time for this type of work, I didn't go nowhere without him. Rico was black as coal and looked a little bit like Wesley Snipes. Born Figgy Dale Lemon, Rico absolutely abhorred the humiliating birth name. The name Rico had come from a Puerto Rican bully who picked on Figgy constantly. But boxing lessons defused the situation. Figgy had beaten the crap out of Rico, and to add insult to injury, assumed his name.

We parked the van around the corner from Jordan's apartment building entrance. There was no security system in place, no bell to push, so we entered. One time Jordan had told me that he lived on the third floor. I think apartment 305. I wasn't sure, but if need be, we would knock on every door of that floor.

The place looked worse on the inside than it did the outside. The hallway smelled like piss. Litter claimed the floors. Plaster was crumbling all around us, and the ceiling was plagued by holes. We took the stairwell up to the third floor, could hear rats scurrying for cover. It was dark and the smell of piss was strong. I could see Rico slip his hand under his coat, embracing the handle of his pistol. He almost pulled it when some wino tumbled down the second-floor steps, landing at our feet, snoring, dead drunk.

We foolishly smiled at each other. The third floor smelled like vomit and it looked worse than the first floor. We walked right up to apartment 305 and knocked on the door. A few unanswered knocks told us that Jordan wasn't in. I tried the doorknob, and luckily, it opened. I wanted to vomit when I stepped inside. I put my hand up to my mouth.

Oh my God! I thought, as I stepped over a platoon of roaches. I couldn't believe my brother was living like this. Garbage was all over the floors. Crack pipes could be seen in a few of the corners. The only furniture he had was a piss-stained mattress in the middle of the living room/bedroom floor. And that was covered with roaches as well. My bet was that Jordan was in hiding. I would be damned if I was gonna wait here for him to come home.

"Man, I can't believe this. I'm having a hard time trying to keep my dinner down," Rico said, almost gagging. I was embarrassed, but felt pity for the way my brother was living.

"Rico, I got an idea."

He asked no questions, just followed me back out of the apartment from hell.

I remembered Jordan talking about the ashy-skinned broad, two floors up. If the lady's place looked any worse than Jordan's apartment, I was gonna lose *my* lunch.

We took the nasty stairwell up to the fourth floor. Hallway lighting was dim. This floor looked a little bit more decent. Looked like somebody had actually taken it upon themselves to clean the dirty red-colored carpeting. The smell was a little better, too.

"Rico, this little broad that Jordan hung around supposed to live on this floor?" I was beginning to sweat inside the thick black leather jacket. I wasn't wearing a weapon. I hated guns, but I didn't blame Rico one bit for having his. Let's just say that I had a bad experience with them one time. He was a prizefighter, but he wasn't a fool.

"Let's do this," he said. "Jordan's like my brother, too."

"There's one thing," I said, "I don't know which apartment number she lives behind."

"Let's try the direct approach," he responded, going right up to the first apartment, and aggressively knocking on the door.

"Who is it?" the deep voice of a lady boomed from behind the door.

"We're looking for Jordan," I offered, giving her a deep tone to match.

"Don't know no Jordan."

We moved right to the next apartment and kept the same routine. The man in this apartment also told us that he didn't know Jordan. We got lucky on the fifth try, apartment 507.

"What do you want with him?" a lady hesitantly said. I didn't blame the lady's voice being filled with fear. This wasn't exactly a secure building in an upscale neighborhood. And it sure wasn't like Rico and I were Boy Scouts bringing hot meals to the elderly. The neighborhood was a warzone. The building was an eyesore. And Rico and I were two strangers asking questions about a man she obviously had contact with.

"My name is Wisdom. Jordan's my brother." There was no peephole in the door. One would have to take a chance and crack the door to view visitors.

I could hear the sound of locks tumbling open. The security chain was attached. The door cracked opened, traveling the length of the chain, stopping with *pop*. I could see nothing but darkness and a lazy pair of eyeballs peeping from between. I could tell she was looking for confirmation. I pulled out my wallet, removing my license.

"Ms.," I said, extending my license through the door, "I'm just looking for my brother. I have to find him." She looked at Rico, wondering about his position.

"This is Rico. He's my friend."

Rico gave her the homeboy-acknowledgment nod.

She handed my license back to me. "Wisdom, I don't know where your brother is. But I know one thing, you better find him before Popeye do."

Rico and I looked at each other curiously.

"How do you know this?" I asked.

"Popeye came around here, asking questions. He didn't look like he was playing either. He wanted to know where your brother's apartment was."

"What did you tell him?" Rico added.

She gave Rico a long study. It was as if to say that this conversation was between her and me. That he should butt out.

"I didn't tell him anything!" the sister said with attitude.

An apartment door opened three doors down. Rico slowly put his hand under his bomber.

"So you have no idea?" he shot back, matching her attitude.

A young man walked out of the open door. He started to walk in our direction but thought better of it after peeping out Rico's concealed right hand. The young brother stepped off in the other direction.

"If I knew where he was, I would tell you. Popeye had murder in his eyes. Your brother's in danger," she admonished.

I wrote my cell number on the back of a business card and slid it through the crack.

"If Jordan contacts you, call me and let me know his whereabouts. Let him know his brother is looking for him."

We were getting ready to walk off.

"Wisdom," her voice called out. She was still locked behind the safety of the security chain. "Please find him." There was a genuine concern in her voice. A concern that let me know that they were more than friends. Possibly lovers.

I said nothing as we disappeared down the dark stairwell and back out of the building. Rico and I drove through the dark city streets in search of my elusive brother, not sharing a single word. We were both locked in our own thoughts. I couldn't believe all this was happening. Couldn't believe that it had come down to this. Just felt like throwing my hands up and yelling, running out on all my troubles. Just felt like taking all the money out of my bank account and purchasing a one-way plane ticket to the other side of the world.

I couldn't go anywhere. Was too strong to run from trouble. I was a preacher's son. That meant I had survived all my father's scandals. All his paternity suits. His constant infidelities. Being a bad example for his children. Not being there for us in our hour of need. My knee injury. But most of all, my dying mother. All of this was enough to make me doubt my faith in God. Had He run out on me? Had He cursed my brothers and sister for my old man's broken covenant? I didn't know anymore. I wanted to pray, but what would it solve? Would God hear me? Or had my old man create a bad reputation for his family in Heaven?

My cell rang. I was expecting my house number to appear on the caller I.D. but instead, it was a number that I didn't recognize.

"Wisdom," the female caller said, "this is Monique. You just left my apartment."

"Okay?"

"I couldn't take no chances. Didn't know if I could trust you or not. Just because your last name is Jones, didn't mean that you're Jordan's brother. But I could sense your honesty. Jordan's favorite smoke house is ten blocks away from this apartment. It's on Lindalwood. Do you know the area?"

"Yep."

"The address is 55521. And, Wisdom, be careful. They don't like intruders."

I ended our conversation, committing her warning to memory. This was happening way too fast. Running up in a crackhouse was an act of desperation. It showed how much I loved my brother. I couldn't keep rescuing and rounding up stray members of my family. I had my own house to clean. Had my own life to put in order. Taking a bullet right now wasn't in the cards. Drug dealers didn't play that. I was putting my own life in jeopardy. My unborn baby needed me. There were so many things I had yet to accomplish. I was filled with the resolve at rehabbing my knee and regaining my shot at the NBA.

"Jordan's girl told me that he's in a crackhouse on Lindalwood," I informed Rico. He was playing with the climate control levers. The heat in my van was still coming out lukewarm. It was freezing outside and Rico was determined to fix the unit. ·

"The Cemetery, hunh?" Rico said with a stupid smile on his face—and for a good reason. The area in which the crackhouse sat was one of the roughest in Detroit. They nicknamed it "The Cemetery" because the area had the highest murder rate in the city. It was nothing to be walking through an alley and stumble upon a dead body. Just last month, I'd been riding through the area and saw a man gunned down in broad daylight.

"Yep, The Cemetery. If I didn't love my brother I

would leave that schmuck to Popeye," I said, turning on to Lindalwood.

"How we gonna find out if Jordan's in there?" Rico asked. "I mean, it's not like they gonna let us in to ask questions."

"I know," was all I could say. I didn't have an answer. Didn't know how we were gonna pull this off. Small-time crack dealers were known to be more ruthless than the drug overlords. They didn't like strangers asking questions. Many undercover cops had been shot and killed trying to infiltrate crack-dealing organizations. So it would be nothing to put bullets in two strangers.

I drove along the semi-dark street, trying to match the address that I'd written down to the address of the crack spot. This neighborhood made my neighborhood look upscale. Made my 'hood look like the suburbs. Every other house had been torn down, leaving a vacant lot behind. Two burnt-out cars sat in one vacant lot. The houses that were left standing looked vacant.

"We must be getting near the spot," Rico said, pointing out his window. Crackheads looked like zombies parading down the sidewalk. We parked three houses down from the spot and watched the young crack dealers serve fiends like McDonald's serving hamburgers.

Rico lit up a cigarette, inhaling deeply. The orange-reddish fire of the butt shattered the darkness inside the van. "You wanna try the direct approach?" he asked, blowing smoke from his nose and mouth.

I watched with growing disgust as the young boys sold crack in plain sight.

"You trying to get us killed?"

"Those are young kids," he said, taking another pull on the cancer stick.

"Kids with itchy trigger fingers, and no home training, or regard for human life," I voiced. "Just to think, we were that age once."

Rico lit up another cigarette. "Yeah, but we got our hustle on by cutting lawns, shoveling snow or pushing a paper route. The game has definitely changed. Pushing crack is the job of choice."

"Back in the day we played two-hand touch football, hide-and-go-seek, freeze tag and stickball. Today, every little Negro is trying to be a gangster," I stated.

"How are Malisa and the baby?" Rico wanted to know. It was hard for me to gauge Rico's emotions; my partner always wore a sneaky smile. Even in the face of mortal danger.

"They all right," I short-talked him. Rico had known me for years. He recognized my moods. Realized when something was troubling me. He was a nosy bastard.

He took another drag from the cigarette. "What's the problem, partner?"

The smoke was irritating my lungs. Had my eyes watering. Had me wanting to grab his unfinished pack of smokes—including the one he was smoking—and toss them right out of the window. But I put up with it; he was helping me find my brother.

I was about to break down and tell all when a scuffle broke out in front of the spot. One of the young rollers started smacking up a female crackhead that seemed twice his age. The bright light from a lamppost lit up the action. The young roller seemed to be average height, but the kid looked like he had put in some serious time in a McDonald's dining room. The punk was big-boned. Real robust. I could tell he was a Southpaw, judging from how fond he was of smacking the woman up with his left hand.

Rico's cigarette fell from his lips, surprised by the action.

"Man, do you see this crap?" he said, grabbing my right shoulder.

I was seeing it, but I couldn't believe it. "Rico."

"What?"

"Get your cigarette. And yeah, I see it."

The young punk began stomping the lady.

"Wisdom," Rico said, reaching for his door handle, "we can't let this young sissy get away with this. The lady's a crackhead, but she's also somebody's mother, or sister."

He had his door halfway opened when I grabbed a handful of bomber. "What the hell are you doing?"

He gave me a "nigga, get yo' hand off me" look. "You ain't gonna help this lady?"

At the moment, I didn't know what the hell to do. I hadn't planned for this at all. Matter of fact, I hadn't had a plan period. If we went over there to help, that would squarely put us on the wrong side of the gun. These young punks fed off violence. We would be taking on the woman's sins. Making us the objects of their anger.

"Chill out, Rico. I realize this is hard to stomach. If we go over there as heroes, we won't get a chance to find my brother."

I guess the magnitude of my words snapped him back to his senses. I could see the madness in his face ease away to sanity. He gently closed the door.

The shorter of the two rollers looked like he had seen enough. He went over and broke it up. The lady was visibly rattled but she was able to get herself together and limp off down the street. I was surprised that she didn't scream one time, but I wasn't surprised that no lights went on in the surrounding houses. I figured that there was no profit in being nosy. These people had seen a lot of shootings, so they probably made it a point to mind their own business.

"Let them young niggas cool down before I go over there, asking questions," I explained.

"You don't want me to go with you?" Rico asked, giving me a confused look.

"Nope. You're a loose cannon. And these punks got guns—"

He pulled his pistol out. "What do you think this is…a damned Snickers?"

"That's the reason right there," I said, pointing at the gun.

He put it away. "Whatever."

We let minutes fall off the clock before I got up enough nerve to go and kick the *million-question game* with the armed kindergartners.

"Promise me you won't do nothing stupid," I asked.

He hesitated before offering, "You got it." He pointed to the place where he'd stashed the pistol. "We'll be waiting right here."

I did something I hadn't done in a while; I said a little prayer before I opened my door.

All sorts of deranged thoughts ran through my mind as I limped up the cold streets. The more I drew closer to the rollers, the more I prayed. I begged God not to let anything foolish go down. I had a whole life to live and I was determined to grow older.

I could see the thugs' posture stiffen at my presence. I could tell by their hostile appearances that I hadn't given them enough time to simmer down.

"How many you want, Old School?" asked the Cro-Magnon-looking kid that had smacked up the woman.

"Lace..." the other one said, craning his neck to look up at me. "We ain't never seen this nigga before. And he definitely don't look like no head."

The kid named Lace put his hand in the pouch of his hoodie when a black car slowly rolled down the street.

"What's yo' bidness here, Old School?" asked Lace.

It was colder than an ice-bath out and I was trying extremely hard not to lose my patience with the two schmucks standing before me.

"You some kind of pig, Old School?" the shorter one said. This punk had a grotesque-looking mole on his chin. I couldn't believe how ugly these two kids were. For the sake of a good condom this much ugliness was added to this world.

I looked back in the direction of the van, hoping that Rico stayed put.

"Just looking for my brother, Jordan," I said, visibly holding both my hands in the air.

The two punks looked at each other and laughed. I could see the cold smoke escape their sarcastic laughter.

"Old School, you might as well turn around and take yo' ass out of here. Ain't no Jordan in here." The turd pointed at the house.

I could tell they were lying. The deceitful smirks on their ugly faces gave them away. I pressed. "Listen, I got some business with my brother. So won't you be good boys and run and get him." I was trying to restrain my sarcastic tongue but I was losing the battle. My time was winding down. I had no time to play with BeBe's kids.

Lace pulled a pistol. "Listen, nigga…" He pulled back the slide of the Glock. "I ain't scared of yo' big ass." He pointed the weapon at my chest. "This lead will chop yo' ass down to my size."

I showed the little fella with the pistol a smirk that displayed my manhood. Had to let him know that I wasn't wearing a skirt. There was no fear in my heart whatsoever.

"Easy, Youngblood," I said, staring down the barrel of death. "I didn't come here for beef."

"Like he told you," the little creep with the ugly mole on his chin said, "take your Bigfoot-looking ass up out our spot."

"Raise the fuck up," said Lace.

I had to use extreme caution here. The kind of caution a snake wrangler used when handling dangerous serpents. These little Negroes looked startled. My size was intimidating. In today's society, the bigger you were, the more likely the shorter opposition wouldn't fight fair. Why waste time with a moose when you can shoot it and get home in time for dinner?

For over three minutes, I tried to reason with these two crack babies. I explained to them why I needed to talk to my brother. I tried to persuade them to chill out. But when I turned in the direction of the van, my mouth grew drier than a sandy beach. Rico was nowhere to be found. I hadn't looked away for a split second when I returned my eyes to the thug holding the gun. He was wearing a dumb look on his face and his boy was looking stupid as well.

That's when I realized where Rico was. My partner had crept up behind the two stooges, placing his pistol to Lace's head.

"Looking for me?" Rico asked in a sinister pitch. He relieved Lace of the firearm. "Like the man said, you little niggas need to chill out and answer the questions."

The front door of the spot opened quickly, causing Rico to swing the gun he had arrested from the roller in that direction. Out walked Jordan. He slowly walked down the stairs. I wanted to murder him.

Jordan strolled up to us like the hardware Rico was holding didn't faze him. He had a carefree attitude. I could tell he was high. I asked him why these two punks were trying to cover for him.

He put his head down for a second. Then he looked up wearing a stupid face of embarrassment. "I'm their best customer." He looked from Lace to Moleman. "I told them if anybody came looking for me, tell them I wasn't here."

I cussed Jordan out for about five minutes. I escorted him to the van and almost threw him inside.

We stepped away from the rollers without another word.

"What about my damn gun?" Lace yelled at our backs.

Rico was getting in the van when he yelled back: "Y'all need to get y'all little ass in school! This is my pistol now, and unless you want me to pop you out, I'd forget all about this pistol!"

Lace flipped Rico the bird as we drove off into the night.

I'd found my brother. Now I had to figure out a way to get Popeye off his back.

I had dropped Rico off at his house. The drive to my house was filled with silence. When I had been on the wrong business end of the punk's pistol, I didn't have time to think. But since Jordan was in a crack coma and my radio was on the blink, I had all the time in the world.

I thought about the aftermath if the idiot would've pulled the trigger. The loss of my life would've devastated my wayward family. I was the glue holding the crumbling spinal column of my family together. My mother's life would have been greatly affected. My baby's life.

I looked over and saw all the destruction caused by my father. Jordan sat in the passenger seat, nodding. He had his head against the window. I was speechless. Jordan didn't look like the brother of old. Crack had ravaged his body. His face looked like a skull wrapped in a thin layer of skin. His lips were doughnut powdery white and his eyes had a sunken look. He wore a secondhand coat so I couldn't guess his weight. Crack was deadly. I believed it to be one of the most dangerous narcotics on the street market. I also believed that it was specifically designed to hunt down and decimate the black race from the face of the earth. Over the years, I'd seen many of my friends and family members made zombies by the stuff.

I was a couple of blocks from my home. My life had many twists and turns. Almost all bad. I looked out of the windshield toward the darker skies, wondering why God had placed all this burden on me. Sure, I knew that He wouldn't place no more than I could bear. But right now, my knees were buckling from the strain of an enormous boulder of problems that had formed between my shoulders. The weight of the world. The Polaroid picture of my father's freaky Red Roof Inn rendezvous still burned brightly in my mind, too.

Who could I tell?

I wasn't close to none of my family members. And I certainly wasn't about to run outside of the family circle to tell somebody else. I couldn't even tell Rico this crap. It was too embarrassing.

✪ ✪ ✪

"What the hell do you mean?" Malisa screamed. "That crackhead has to stay here, Boo-Boo?" Her belly stuck out longer these days. It looked like she was about to drop right there on our bedroom floor and give birth.

"Keep it down," I countered. "Jordan is downstairs in the basement. He might hear you."

"He's a CRACKHEAD, CRACKHEAD, CRACK-HEAD, CRACKHEAD! I don't give a damn about him hearing me! You bring this zombie into my house without asking me? Where the hell is your brain?" Malisa had that black woman mannerism working. Her neck snapped on every word coming from her mouth. I didn't pay attention to what she was wearing. And if I would have, I would've asked why the hell she was dolled up on a Tuesday night? She had on a nice maternity dress.

"Why don't you chill out and listen for a second?"

She had just come in, and was now shedding her clothes.

"I ain't gotta do a damn thing, Superstar." She slid out of the black dress. "Now, I gotta carry my damn purse around the house so that that crackhead won't try to stiff me."

I wanted to think that it was her pregnancy that was responsible for the vicious jabs at my brother's short-comings. But that would've been a lie. Malisa was downright ornery. She didn't have any money in her damn purse anyway.

"It'll be for just a little while. Jordan is in trouble and I can't turn my back on him."

Malisa went into the bathroom of our bedroom. "If that cop finds out that your crackhead brother is hiding out here, ain't no telling what he'll do. And I can't have that stress around me and my baby."

I could see that this was going to be a battle. Malisa was a tough nut to crack. So I had to enforce plan B. I had to put my foot down. I paid all the bills. The girl didn't have to come out of her pocket with a slug. I couldn't turn my back on Jordan. He was my brother. My blood.

To hell with Malisa!

"Listen here," I said, my tone aggressive. "My brother is staying here until this whole mess is settled!"

Immediately after my muscle-session, I heard the faucet turn on. I knew what she was up to. She was trying to drown my conversation out. That was her little childish way of expressing to me that the conversation was over.

I took my minor victory down to the basement to set Jordan up. He was lying on the couch with his eyes closed and his shoes off.

"Sorry for this, Wiz," Jordan said with his eyes still closed. "I don't mean to put you out with Malisa. I'm just in a bit of trouble and don't know what to do."

I didn't want to be funny, but Jordan needed a shower, real bad. He had that junkie funk. His body smelled horrible and the odor flowing from his shoes had me checking for dog crap under mine.

My basement was somewhat spacious. The last tenants that stayed here had finished it. I had a thrift store-purchased sectional, complete with sleeper. We also had an extra shower down there and a toilet. So Jordan wouldn't have to come upstairs. He could stay out of Malisa's way.

"You're not putting me out. This is what family is all about."

I gave him a reassuring smile, and then directed him toward the bathroom. I went into a chest of drawers and pulled out a shirt, pajama bottoms, and some underwear. They were too big for Jordan, but judging from the personal assault that the foul funk and ground-in dirt imposed upon my sinuses, I would bet the farm that Jordan wouldn't reject the super-sized drawers. When I heard the shower running I went back upstairs ready for round two.

Malisa was lying on the bed pretending to give Bernie Mac her complete and undivided attention.

"You know that you're going to be responsible for an unhealthy baby, don't you, Superstar?"

I questioned her with my eyebrow.

She sat up on the bed. "I'm gonna have to sleep with one eye open, which means I'm not gonna get any sleep. I told you that I was gonna make your life a living hell if you put one more family member ahead of me. Now listen here, Boo-Boo, you got one week to get that junkie out of my house. Or I will kick you to the curb and file child support papers."

It wasn't until Malisa threatened my paycheck with the made promise of a garnishment that I was reminded of the five-thousand dollars that I had to pay the finance company. I felt the walls closing in on my wallet.

"We have a family meeting in three days. Until then, Jordan stays here."

I was ready to walk out of the room when she yelled, "If anything comes up missing out of this house, I'm calling Popeye myself, Superstar!"

Jordan had just stepped out of the shower when I limped down the stairs. He had a towel wrapped around his waist. My eyeballs almost jumped from their sockets when I got a gander of his upper body. He had the physical form of a man that lived in a Third World country. His ribs were visible and his skin looked ashy. His chest looked birdish and I swear I could visibly see his heart beating. Death. My brother looked like death. The Grim Reaper was his smoke partner.

Jordan didn't see me because he was wiping his head with a towel. I had to force words from my mouth.

"So why is Popeye looking for you?" I started with the obvious. "And don't lie to me either."

He came right out and told me the whole story of how he'd robbed and stabbed Popeye's mother. He didn't find out until later. But the crack had his senses numb. I found out that it was my brother who was responsible for all the purses being snatched, sending senior citizens into a panic.

I could remember back to when I'd first heard about the purse-snatching spree. How I'd fantasized about getting my own reality show and torturing those criminals who preyed on senior citizens, not knowing that my brother would've been my first case.

Jordan sat on the couch with a defeated look on his face. I wanted to ask him why he had chosen crack in an attempt to escape the past. But I already knew the answer. My old man had played us all. The curse that he'd produced probably would run for generations to come.

Jordan laid his head on his knees and wrapped his arms around himself.

"I need some help, Wiz. Don't want to be like this anymore. This crack has got me hurting people. Next time I might just kill someone. I can't have that on my soul." He let out a deep, wounded sigh. Like he had relieved himself of some serious stress.

Not this rehab thing again, I surmised. Every time he

started feeling sorry for himself, Jordan would always pull the rehab card. The line had become so worn that I started to regard it as a con. Crackheads would say or do anything to get a rock.

"Brah," I started, "how many times have I heard this rehab con?" I sat down in an old armchair, crossing my legs.

"I'm for real this time. I'm ready to come out of the land of the dead. Just look at me." He threw up his hands so I could get a full view of his body. "I'm wasting away to nothing."

There was something in my heart that told me my brother was full of crap. But I wanted to believe him. Wanted to help. My brotherly instincts were overriding the warning whistles going off inside of my head.

I stared into his eyes. I couldn't read anything going on inside.

I scratched my nose. "Okay." I drug my hands down my face. "I'm gonna get you some help before you get yourself killed. But after our family meeting."

"What family meeting?"

"You've been M-I-A for two months. Your momma has gotten worse. And all the weight of taking care of her is falling on me. This meeting was called by me. I have two brothers and one sister. Ain't no way in hell I should be the only one who's taking care of her needs."

My last sentence brought tears to his eyes. The poor boy had been missing and didn't know that his mother was lying at death's door.

We got caught up on old times. I brought him up to speed with the present. Even though I was feeling the weight of the world, I wouldn't tell Jordan about any of my problems. He had enough of his own.

When I left to go upstairs, Jordan was asleep on the sleeper. He had cried himself into sweet dreams, or whatever his kind dreamed about.

I walked upstairs to the bedroom. Malisa had all the lights off. So I relied on my memory to navigate through the darkness. I was going to the closet to get myself a couple of blankets. At one point in time, my navigational system failed me and I hit my bare right foot on something hard.

"Ouch!" I yelled in pain.

"Dumb ass," I heard Malisa say from the darkness.

I limped back down the stairs and laid my big body across the couch in the living room. Although I half-heartedly believed that Jordan was ready to give up the rock, I wasn't gonna get caught with my drawers down. I didn't know if my brother would get sticky fingers late in the morning and take something out of there to fix his habit. I was positioned right next to the front door. Being a light sleeper, I could hear if the door opened. I was more scared of child support than Jordan clipping us.

I fell asleep, drifting off to a place where my worldly problems couldn't follow. My mother used to tell us that when you go to sleep, your soul went back to do some talking to God. I was in for one long discussion.

YAZOO

I was chilling at one of Geechie's stash spots. He had houses that were used primarily to sell the crack rock. His other houses were used to warehouse large quantities of cocaine. Weight houses—was what they called them.

Since I was coming up in Geechie's organization, he started me with a good job in a weight house on the northwest side of Detroit.

I was still somewhat fuming from Wisdom trying to strong-arm me into going to that damn family meeting. Only white people did corny crap like that.

Family meeting, hunh? I thought. The nigga was forgetting who was the oldest. But he got his nuts at being a bully boy. One day I would show that big bastard who was boss. I was going to have to show him that we were no longer kids. Had to prove to him that he was messing around with a grown-ass man. Wisdom's day was coming. But today I had to get money.

There was nothing to my job. Just had to sit here and serve some of Detroit's elite dope men. Some niggas would come pick stuff up driving hoopties. There were a few who chose to throw caution to the wind and drive up in flamboyant whips. Those were the dumb ones and they didn't stay in the game too long.

I was in the upstairs bedroom of a decent-looking colonial on a street called Hitsville. As I scooped up the cocaine, placing it on a scale to be weighed, I felt myself growing stronger. Self-supportive. Didn't need anyone, including God. I looked out the window and up to the clear blue sky. I hated Him. He had taken away my life. Taken away my childhood happiness. I used to listen to my sinful stepfather preach about God being on time. That He was never late.

Well? I grimed up at the sky. Where were You when my father was drowning? He was neither late, nor on time. I figured God to be one of those Italian mobsters, because He made my father sleep with the fishes. That's why every chance I got, I shot my pistol in the air, letting Him know that I was pissed off.

When I looked down from my hatred, I found that I had weighed and rationed almost a kilo of cocaine. We had a room with a secret stash spot where we kept drugs and money. Out of three other guys in the house, two of us had knowledge, and access of the secret stash spot.

That's where I was headed when I heard a loud crash come from downstairs. The noise sounded like wood breaking. I was almost in run-mode when I heard shouting, screaming and scuffling. The unfamiliar voices commanded the workers downstairs to lie on the floor. That put fire under my steps. I had the door of the secret compartment open when I heard a melody of metallic clicks behind me. I had been in a couple of police raids, and knew how they operated. But this was something totally different. This wasn't police procedure.

"Nigga, if you move another muscle, I'll pop you a new asshole in the back of yo' head," the gruff, but muffled voice said from behind. "Stand up slow and move away from the goodies."

I did what the creep commanded. I slowly walked backward until I was pushed to the floor. The foot on my head came afterward. From what I could see, the punk looked to be wearing Timberland boots.

The men joked and laughed about hitting the mother of all jackpots. These bold niggas even had the gall to start fantasizing about the cars that they were going to buy. The diamond watches they would cop. After all the bragging, I was snatched up by my neck, and with a pistol at my head, I was marched downstairs and viciously slung to the floor with other workers. It was only then that I found out about the quality of niggas I was working with.

One of the punks was named Pete. He was a big, cocky fool. He talked about nothing else but killing people. But the voice that he was using, begging for his life, left me to believe that he was a man in drag. Pete was the one that the jackers had the most fun with. They slapped him up with the gun and made him pull down his pants. They made him walk around the house in homo fashion. I looked up periodically to see the sad sight. That's when I realized the creeps were wearing masks.

When the jackers upstairs came down carrying bags, they stopped all the foolishness and threw Pete back to the floor. Without another word, the jackers walked out into broad daylight.

TEMPEST

If you dance with the devil too long, he'll eventually ballroom your soul right to hell. Here I was trying to change dance partners when my dancing shoes kept tap dancing back in Satan's direction.

Darrius was out of town on business and I was downtown with Geechie all up in my business. We were in the bedroom at one of his spots. I was so drunk, I couldn't really remember how we had gotten there. All I knew was that Geechie was working his stick like he was a professional driver on the NASCAR circuit. High gear. Low gear. Low gear, back to high. He was showing me why I couldn't break away from him. Why I couldn't shake Satan and leave him in the dust.

The full-sized bed squeaked as the headboard banged against the wall. This young buck was pulling out all the stops.

"Whose is it?" Geechie asked in a winded voice. His face was wet with perspiration. And his breath was 20-proof.

"Yours," I said helplessly. I tried to resist and say nothing, but he kept digging deeper, and deeper into my soul.

My legs were spread from east to west. And his nice ass was humping from north to south. We had to look like some freaky compass of sexual magnetic energy.

Geechie was young, and with liquor in his system, the boy could go all night long. Unlike Darrius. My husband had no sexual stamina whatsoever. He didn't do the things to me that my young thug was doing. Darrius treated me like a lady. But I was a freak and wanted to be handled roughly. I liked when Geechie pulled my hair harshly and smacked my butt hard enough to bruise. I loved when he called me out of my name, talking dirty.

The alcohol had my body numb and feeling pretty damn good. We had switched positions. Geechie was behind me with a handful of hair and banging my head against the headboard. I liked it rough.

I was caught up in the tasty taste of my third orgasm when somebody knocked on the bedroom door. I jumped because as far as I knew, we were there by ourselves.

"Boss," a heavy voiced boomed, "we got trouble."

Geechie seemed disturbed. Like he was getting ready to cum and someone had busted his groove.

"What?" Geechie yelled back. "Damn, man. What the hell is it?" He withdrew his package from me and rolled out of the bed, leaving me to feel like an unclean, filthy whore.

He went to the door and opened it, stepping out naked. I couldn't imagine the look on the intruder's face when he got a peek at the pole that Geechie was packing.

He wasn't gone a minute when he came back in yelling at me to put on my clothes.

Dusk had settled over the area. The dying day's light helped us to find our clothing articles that had been thrown around when we first began to freak.

Within minutes, we were dressed and speeding down Jefferson Avenue in my Lexus LX 570. Geechie was wearing a real serious mug, and his man, Flash, looked like he could kill somebody. Geechie said nothing to me as he drove my truck like a madman. They sat up front, giving me the backseat.

The SUV was silent as we blazed down the Lodge Freeway. All sorts of thoughts were flowing through my mind. I was scared. I didn't know what I was more scared of: finding out where we were headed, or one of my husband's friends or family members spotting Geechie, figuring out another man was driving my truck.

We came up off the freeway using the Wyoming exit. I fully sobered when Geechie cut a corner full speed, tossing me around. The man even ran a couple of red lights. That kind of urgency dictated to me that something was seriously wrong, and that frightened me even more. Geechie was a drug dealer with a bad temper. His business dealings were sometimes handled by gunfire.

We finally arrived, pulling in front of a decent-looking, two-story house on a street called Hitsville. I wanted to stay in the truck but Geechie screamed at me to come inside. I had on an expensive pantsuit and pumps. I looked totally out of place. Geechie and Flash were wearing jeans and Timberland boots.

The door of the house looked to be kicked off its hinges. I didn't want to go in. The savage thumping of my heart highlighted my fears. The door was splintered. This couldn't be good.

Inside, three men sat around on couches with their heads hung low. Almost like someone had died.

Geechie walked right up to the biggest one, pulled out his pistol and smacked the big guy off the couch and onto the floor.

"What the hell happened?" Geechie shouted, sizing up the men. His pistol hung menacingly at his side. His ghoul played in the background. Flash's presence was enough to invoke fear and dread. I took a seat in the corner.

God only knew what was about to happen.

Geechie put the pistol to the head of the man on the floor. "What happened, Pete?"

"Some fools jacked us—"

"Shut-up, Donnie!" Geechie hollered, slinging the big gun in the direction of a big-eared boy. "I didn't ask Donnie. I was talking to Pete."

Pete grabbed the right side of his head. Geechie had opened up a big gash. Pete tried to hold the area tightly, but blood oozed through the cracks of his fingers.

He was trying to catch his breath. "Like Donnie said, we were jacked and they were wearing masks. We don't know who they were."

The interrogation went on for a full hour. I felt sorry for the workers in the house. They were drilled with questions from Geechie, and Flash. And if Geechie didn't like the answer, he would signal for Flash to administer serious pain.

I found out that the jackers had gotten Geechie for ten thousand dollars and a ton of cocaine. I also found out that one man was missing. Some guy named Zoo. I guess the guy had gotten scared and left. That didn't sit too well with Geechie. He whipped out his cell phone and dialed some numbers. When he got no answer, Geechie picked up an empty beer bottle and threw it through the windowpane facing the backyard.

I didn't know who this Zoo guy was, but he'd better have a damn good answer as to why he left before Geechie could get here.

Time was the enemy. It was now ten at night. I had to get home. The ton of work in my home office beckoned for my presence. I wondered if I had any messages on the home phone or cell phone. In a horny rush, I had run off, leaving my cell phone on my office desk. I looked at my watch one more time, thinking about all of the drama that was unfolding. But this drama was nothing compared to the drama that would happen at our family meeting tomorrow. There was a lot of bad blood between members. A lot needed to be addressed.

REVEREND POPPA JONES

I was trying to have a civilized meeting with the deacon board. But there was nothing civil about it. Every time we tried to discuss church business, Slydale managed to get personal.

We were in a conference room next to the fellowship hall. The room was nice and spacious. A huge circular maple conference table sat in the center. I sat at the head. Deacon Slydale sat on the opposite end. We had been grimming each other since the start of the meeting. My friend, Deacon James Clay, sat to the left of me, along with Deacon White, Deacon Braxton and Deacon Shoe. Seated directly across from them were Deacon Long, Deacon Kelly and Deacon Robert, Slydale's crew of wicked holy-rollers.

My supporters sat on my side and Slydale's gang sat against us.

"Pastor," Deacon Clay said, "we were not going to tell you but we're trying to raise fifteen thousand dollars for your anniversary." Deacon James Clay was my right-hand man. He reminded me of what Morris Chestnut might look like in middle-aged skin. He had a head full of hair and a salt-and-pepper goatee.

"We already pay Pastor a generous salary," Deacon Slydale chimed in. "I don't think it would be fair to put that type of burden on the members." He administered me a sinister look.

"I second that," Deacon Kelly agreed with Slydale. Kelly was an old troublemaker with a terrible marriage. His wife wasn't putting out anymore and now his only source of pleasure was raising hell in the church. He was a tall, grumpy, fat man with terrible acne and a humiliating receding hairline.

Slydale looked at his flunky, rendering me a devious smile.

Deacon Shoe came to my aid. "This church was built around our beloved Pastor. Most churches run through Pastors like you change socks. We are indeed blessed to have Pastor." Deacon Charles Shoe was an elderly man. He was an old soul filled with infinite wisdom and never-ending knowledge. His eyes were those that had seen everything that the world had to offer. Anybody that saw Shoe automatically knew that God had hands on him. Tall at one time, but now stooped over by the weight of the world, Shoe's hair looked grayer than the color.

I smiled at Slydale on the other end of the table. He had lost this battle. Shoe was the elder and whatever he said usually stood.

Slydale bowed his head, accepting defeat this round.

"Any more new business?" I asked, looking around at faces.

I noticed Slydale leaning over and whispering something to Deacon Long. Whatever he said must've tickled Long's funny bone.

"Would you like to share with the rest of the board?" I challenged Slydale. He didn't like to be called out. But I didn't care. He was a playa hater without a life.

He cleared his throat, giving me another sly smile. "I said, if you left all of those women alone, we wouldn't have to burden the congregation with digging into their pockets. Our members are comprised of blue-collar workers. And they have bills, too." He exchanged hateful frowns with me.

At that moment, the old man was trying desperately to take over my body. Satan was trying to present himself as a barrier between rational and irrational thinking.

Silence was louder than quiet in the room.

"Deacon Slydale, you are totally out of line," Deacon Clay said.

"That's the kind of froggishness we don't need here," Deacon Shoe added, standing up.

"Hold on." I put my hand up, silencing Clay and Shoe. "I would like to hear proof of these outrageous allegations."

"People talk," was all he could say. He was fishing. And everybody else in the room realized it.

"You of all people," Deacon Shoe chastised. "You should know that we have a bunch of busybodies at this church. You are the Chairman of the Deacon Board. Let's start acting like it."

Slydale stood up quickly. Like he was getting ready to leave. This Negro wasn't about to get off that easy. He had served as a disruptive device for the last time.

"Fellow servants of God. This is my church. And anybody that don't like the way that it's run"—I pointed to the door—"there's the door. And furthermore, *Chairman*, let this be the last time I tell you to shorten your prayers in devotion." I knew it was nothing but the devil. I was having satanic visions of slitting Slydale's throat with a straight razor. I would watch him die as his worthless blood leaked on the cold ground, and then somehow, I would revive him only to kill him again. I couldn't believe I was having these thoughts inside of God's house. This moron had taken me there. The creep didn't know that I was a few French fries short of a Happy Meal these days. A ton of dynamite with a short fuse. I had Sister Walker in my study every chance she got. Her husband hadn't been dead a month and she was trying to get me to divorce my wife and marry her. Not to mention that my wife was crankier than ever lately. She was blaming me for all her health problems. Wilma had gone as far as calling me a predatory pastor. And on top of all this stress and pressure stood my son, Wisdom. I gave him credit for finding my estranged baby boy, but Wisdom could be worse than the Boogie Man himself. He'd caught me at the Red Roof Inn with Sister Lawson. Now, I didn't know what he had in store for me—with this family meeting and all. I couldn't help to think that this meeting would turn out to be a lynching. My character would be burned at the stake. But worst of all, my family members were being assembled under one roof. It was a powder keg waiting to happen.

"If there is no more new business, this meeting will stand adjourned," I said, standing to my feet. This was all the meeting I could take today. I was headed for the office to take something for my migraine. Another intense, stomach-turning stare down with Slydale only intensified the pain in my head and behind. He looked at me like he knew something I didn't. Like he was harboring information that would bring about my demise. His time was coming. Of that, I was sure.

I left the deacons mumbling amongst one another. I was halfway to my study when my cell started ringing.

"Hello, Preacher," my past spoke. "You will suffer ten times worse than I will while having your baby. It's coming." The transmission went dead, and so did my blood. My good presence of mind kept on telling me that my days were numbered. Not to mention the girl's window I had jumped from. I found out that Robin had been killed by her deranged husband. God could be a comedian at times. To show you how funny he was, Robin's auntie was one of my members. And since Robin didn't have a church home, her aunt asked if she could have the funeral at the church, and asked if I could preach the eulogy. My every step was blowing up in my face, uncovering skeletons I thought I'd buried decades ago. I was a tired soul, and my past was riddled by a mine-field of sin.

The hot shower I took in my office bathroom couldn't begin to dream about removing the crust of sinful dirt that was clogging the pores of my salvation. The Bible stated that man should be the head of the family. But at the meeting tomorrow, I wondered if my family would have my head on a platter, John the Baptist-style.

WISDOM

Before the start of the family meeting, we had been warned to keep it down. Not get rowdy. My old man told us that his white neighbors wouldn't hesitate to call the police. Farmington Hills had a no tolerance law when it came to black folks. So we had to keep it down, but I had a feeling things would get heated.

This meeting was for family members only. No girlfriends, no husbands, etc. And since my mother was in bad shape, I took her over to her friends. The stress of family bickering would be too much for her.

We had all made the set time. Everybody except Yazoo. I didn't know if he was having hooptie problems or he was trying to make a statement. The schmuck had been extremely pissed because of my demand. I could see him being late because he was trying to prove his independence. The Negro had a problem with people telling him what to do.

I didn't like Farmington Hills. I couldn't stand how the police sweated us; by us, I mean black folk. Before I came up with the idea of my momma's spot, I had kicked around different locations. I couldn't have it at my place because Malisa didn't know how to keep her trap shut. Tempest's crib would have been ideal, but she didn't want Yazoo to know where she stayed, and under no circumstances did she want Jordan at her place. She'd dismissed the boy as a sticky-finger undesirable.

So here we were, waiting on Yazoo. Besides simple pleasantries, the only language was unbroken silence. The tension in the air was thick and the anticipation of "the blame game" was heavy.

"Where the hell is Yazoo?" Tempest broke the silence. She looked stunning in her designer jeans and expensive blouse. That was one thing about my sister; the girl could dress.

Before anybody could respond, Yazoo's voice resonated from the front door. "Don't worry 'bout where the hell I'm at. Just worry about yourself." I guess that was the official start of the meeting.

Let the gut-wrenching, sibling-tear-down show begin!

"Let's be civil in here," Reverend Poppa Jones spoke up in a church-like manner. The way that the condo was made, the family room in which we sat was positioned all the way to the back. We couldn't see Yazoo yet, but we could hear his angry footsteps.

"I didn't call this family meeting to cause a brawl," I said, standing near the doorway.

When Yazoo walked in everybody but me was seated.

My old man was resting in a recliner. Tempest sat on a loveseat by herself. Jordan sat balled up on the couch in the beginning stages of withdrawal.

"Nice of you to make it," I said to Yazoo.

The punk grimmed me and shot back, "Don't start with me, Wisdom."

"Now that everybody's here, I want to bring this meeting to life." I stood center floor.

"I think we should open up with a prayer," Poppa Jones cut in.

"Preacher, save all that prayer stuff," Yazoo blazed. "Let's start this crap."

My old man looked silly-faced. He looked at Yazoo like he wanted to strangle him. "There will be no blasphemy under this roof."

"Blasphemy is what you be doing with them tramps you mess around with," Yazoo hissed, wearing a pleased look on his grill.

"Why do you always have to start stuff?" Tempest asked Yazoo.

Yazoo childishly stuck his tongue out at his sister. This meeting was headed in the wrong direction.

"Yazoo...Tempest," I snarled through gritted teeth, "if y'all don't chill out, somebody's going outside with me." I stood there mean-mugging my sister and brother. I wasn't gonna let them get on my nerves, ruining this thing before we could root out the problem.

"We have to find a way to get along. We can't open

the door for Satan." Poppa Jones stood up and went to the window.

Jordan hadn't said a word. He hadn't had crack for a couple of days. And the brother was hurting. He had told me that he planned to kick the narcotic cold turkey.

"I'm gonna get down to it," I said, taking a couple of steps back to the wall. "I need help with Momma. I shouldn't have to be the only one taking her to appointments and running errands."

The room grew quiet. Nobody said a word. They were all guilty of not sharing the load.

"I have a church to run and—" my old man said.

"Excuses," I cut in.

"I have a shop to run," Tempest added.

"And I have a damn job, too!" I shouted. "Y'all ain't no more than me!"

"Whoop-dee-do," Yazoo broke in. "Nigga, just because yo' broke-knee ass won a college champion and MVP you think you a saint? You ain't no saint. Always trying to make it sound like you do so much. That's a bunch of bull."

No this schmuck didn't? I thought to myself. The nerve of this Negro. He was guilty but now trying to disguise his guilt by attacking my character.

"Yazoo," I said, trying to get my thoughts together. I didn't want to pick the wrong words that could trigger chaos. "You know what? Matter of fact, I don't know why I even called you to this meeting. You haven't done a damn thing for Momma since she's been in this condition. So you should shut your mouth, and sit down somewhere, little boy."

I thought Yazoo was about to have a stroke. His face twitched with rising anger. He had been standing over where Jordan lay in a ball. I was halfway across the room. With cat-like speed, Yazoo closed our distance. He stopped on a dime, careful to keep out of reaching distance.

"Punk, I been waiting on this day! You better recognize the gangsta in me!" Yazoo yelled. These days he looked like a gangster. His style of dress had picked up. And judging from the way his diamond Rolex watch and bracelet blinged when reflecting the room's electrical lighting, it was safe to say that he was getting money. Illegal money. But he was overdue for an expensive butt-whuppin'. He was definitely barking up the right tree; I was in the market for unloading some serious stress.

The good reverend jumped between us. "Can't you two see that Satan is tearing our family apart? We need to learn how to talk to one another."

"Shut up, Satan!" Yazoo yelled, stepping back.

My dad was wearing a navy blue suit. He pulled on his gray necktie, looking Yazoo straight in the eyes. "Boy, you need Jesus."

"Don't you ever in your life bring God up to me." Yazoo pointed in the old man's face, spit flying from his words. "There ain't no God. Yo' trifling ass has proved that. Sleeping around with women in your church. Cheating on my momma. If there was a God, He would've struck you down a long time ago. You messed up this whole family. And this is one time that I'm proud to say that I didn't come from your nuts."

"I think we're getting off the subject." I pinched the bridge of my nose in burning frustration. "Let's everybody calm down." Everybody went back to their neutral corners. This could've been the end of the meeting. I had to keep better order if we were going to get anything accomplished.

"I have to go to the bathroom," Tempest interjected. She made her direction to the door, but I cut her off.

"Nobody's going anywhere until we get things settled." I stood in front of the doorway, my arms folded across my wide chest as though I were a bouncer at a strip club.

"I gotta go pee," she whined, doing the pee-pee dance.

"Hold it. Go sit down." I pointed to the loveseat.

"Mr. MVP, who the hell do you think you are?" Yazoo piped, his bling-bling almost blinding me.

I sidestepped my brother's blazing hot mouth.

"I can't continue to carry Momma's load by myself. Either y'all gonna step up, or we gonna have to go in our pockets to get her a caretaker." It was as if I had said the wrong words. Pop looked like he grabbed his pocket that held his wallet in a Full-Nelson. Tempest held her designer bag with a vise-grip. And Yazoo sarcastically popped his lips in my direction, giving me the feeling that he wasn't gonna budge one way or the other.

Pop had money, but when it came time to spend on somebody else, his pockets became deep and his arms shortened in length.

"Wisdom," Pop cleared his throat, "my schedule is booked solid. I'm the pastor at Infinite Baptist Church. That means: My Father's work comes first."

That statement burned my buns. I was wondering had this sucker forgotten that I'd caught him down and dirty with some tramp at the Red Roof Inn. I was looking to see if he would retract his statement. But my good presence of mind led me to believe that this Negro was starting to believe his own lies.

"You mean to tell me that helping Momma isn't considered mission work?"

"Mission hell," Yazoo snorted. "That fool ain't got no damn mission. He can't even keep his Johnson in his pants long enough to work a mission."

The good reverend looked at Yazoo with murder in his eyes. I was seriously relieved that there were no sharp objects in the room. God was a restraining factor in Pop not breakin' it off in Yazoo's crack but I was wondering what would it take to drive him to the brink of insanity?

Poppa Jones slowly turned back to me, ignoring his obnoxious stepson. "Wisdom, I'm not disputing your point at all. It's just that it would be hard for me to take Wilma back and forth to her appointments."

He was not getting off the hook that easy. "That's what assistant ministers are for. They are put in those positions to help the pastor."

Jordan quickly sat up with the creepy demeanor of the dead coming back to life. He went into a series of dry, hacking coughs and started scratching his arm like his skin was on fire.

"I see," Yazoo said, giggling, "the crackhead circus is back in town. It…is…alive."

"It won't work. Without the shepherd, the sheep at Infinite Baptist Church would run astray."

"The only thing that's gonna run astray is you, preacher," Yazoo spat. "You still don't get it, do you?"

I could've kicked myself for strong-arming Yazoo into attending this family meeting. The atmosphere was getting testy. And Yazoo's disrespectful humor wasn't making it any better. The boy was downright rude. He was only serving as Satan's pawn.

Tempest hadn't breathed a word. My girl was doing the pee-pee dance in her seat. She was rocking from cheek to cheek with a tight-lipped expression on her face.

"What about you, Tempest?" I asked. "You gonna tell me that you don't have any time either?"

She sat there for a second, glaring hatefully at me. Tempest had the look of a little girl that was not permitted bathroom privileges by her third-grade teacher. Ever since I could remember, Tempest always wore that look when she couldn't get her way.

"I can't!" she yelled at me, crossing her legs. She looked like she was about to *go* on Pops' leather loveseat. I could only imagine the muscle action that was working to squeeze off her pee. "Between my shop and my real estate, I don't have the time."

"Y'all not leaving me with no choice." I stared around the room.

"Preacher," Yazoo said, "why don't you admit that your whores come first, before your family, and yo' God? It was your selfish ass that broke up this family."

The room grew to a deadly silence. Yazoo was at it once again, and this time, he was going for the throat. Playing hardball with the bases loaded.

"Fifth Commandment, honor thy father and mother," Poppa Jones quoted, slowly walking over to Yazoo.

"Satan knows scriptures, too," Yazoo blazed, standing to his feet. I could see his fists balling with the anticipation of a physical encounter.

The slimy, grotesque-looking vomit that volcanically spewed from Jordan's mouth defused the impending scuffle. Jordan popped off the couch like toast from a toaster, running in the direction of the bathroom leaving a foul trail of smelly liquids behind.

I hadn't taken my eyes off Yazoo and Pops for a second when I noticed that Tempest had joined in, and was doing some finger pointing of her own. All three mouths were simultaneously running, trading "kick in the nuts" insults.

"You jailbird, gym-shoe rolling, simple-minded bum. How dare you attack my father!" Tempest yelled loud enough to be heard in the next condo. "You just mad 'cause you ain't got no dad—"

Tempest wasn't given a chance to mouth another insult. I guess it was safe to say that the pursuing violence that followed led to the ending of the meeting. All I saw was the blinding glitter of diamonds and gold. When Yazoo's right jab snapped back, Tempest's body had completed a 180-degree turn before falling face-first to the carpet.

It all happened so fast. I didn't have time to react. My mouth hung open. It was as if I was watching a bad episode of the ghetto version of the *Brady Bunch*. My sister was knocked out cold. I guess her bladder went on vacation because she pissed all over herself.

Dad went to grab Yazoo before he could do any more damage. He was surprised by Yazoo's right-cross. Pops fell beside Tempest, holding his right jaw.

The closet doors were open and skeletons were marching out in droves.

Yazoo was on the blink. I was kind of stunned that he had the balls to hit family members. But when the crazy Negro lunged at me, I figured him to be out of his mind. His face was twisted by hatred. He wasn't gonna fight fair because of my size. So he tried to deliver a kick to my groin. I blocked it, grabbing his foot and slinging his worthless carcass to the other side of the room. He was airborne a little while before slamming into the entertainment system. It took a second for him to get his wits about him. But when he did, the wimp picked up a lamp and threw it at me. I didn't want to hurt my brother. Had to stay in control. The slightest drop in my sanity and a strong increase in my blood pressure could prove to be fatal for Yazoo.

I dodged the lamp and rushed him, tackling him to the floor.

"Calm down, Yazoo," I instructed, pinning his arms to the floor under my powerful legs. "Why you always gotta cut a fool? Hitting women and everything. You're a punk."

I was sitting on his chest and had pinned his arms under my knees. He couldn't do anything but squirm and cuss. I was in control and Yazoo hated it. This moment took us back in time, a time where Yazoo had presented a physical challenge. When he was always eager to jump in my face. And the result would always be the same; the Negro would always end up like he was now, without a chance in hell at whipping me.

"Nigga," Yazoo screamed, "you better hold me down here for the rest of your life! Because if I get up, you are one dead nigga!"

I sat on his chest, looking at the carnage that Yazoo had left in his wake. My sister still hadn't awoken. No matter how hard my old man tried to revive her.

Yazoo must've looked over at my sister about the same time I did.

"That's the only time I like that broad. Too bad I had to knock her ass out to get along." The wicked laughter that echoed from his lungs spelled out disrespect for the family.

I wanted to treat this fool like I didn't know him. Give him the nastiest beatdown that I could summon from my big body.

His steady laughter only fueled my desire to shake this bastard from the branch of our family tree. Totally destroy his birth certificate. Satan had entered my body. He had fashioned my hands to accommodate my brother's throat. Satan was trying to tell me that if I strangled my brother, our family curse would be lifted. Vanquishing me of my pitiful brother would raise all problems off my back—Malisa's crack-braniac behind, the garnishment, all my money troubles, the burden of caring for my mother, my injured knee, and my white mystery man with the outstanding buzz-cut.

After running down my painful checklist of burdens, I snapped. Nothing could bring me back. Not even the wet gurgling noise that was resonating underneath me. I was choking the crap out of my oldest brother.

I was so tuned into getting rid of my burdens that I was totally oblivious to the platoon of footsteps coming from behind. Something grabbed me and I blindly threw a right cross.

"Ouch," the thing that I hit yelled and dropped to the floor.

When reasoning returned, the Farmington Hills Police had drugged me off my nearly unconscious brother. When they'd finally pried my death grip from Yazoo's throat, a paramedic moved to his side. It was then that I looked over at my sister. Fear was in my chest and butterflies flew around inside my stomach. When I saw her moving around, I felt relived. Slowly the paramedics sat her up.

I heard the white officer mention something about her making a statement. She spoke something softly to him. Whatever it was, the cocky cop removed his hand-cuffs from his belt and placed them firmly around Yazoo's golden wrists. The officer pushed the bling-bling up so he could cuff Yazoo properly. I swear I heard the macho punk mutter "niggas" before he stood my brother to his feet. I felt like challenging the pig on his racist comment, but there was no need to get nasty. Besides, my family had enough drama going on.

"That boy got the devil in him," the good reverend told one of the white officers, using his hand in describing different actions. "That's the only reason I could see him attacking us." The good reverend was still favoring his right jaw.

Despite all the pandemonium, Jordan was nowhere to be found. Both right and to the left, I couldn't find him. The boy was a ghost in the wind. I knew where Jordan had probably gone off to. That didn't frighten me, but the placid look on Yazoo's grill sent goose bumps up and down my spine. Just a minute ago, he was trying to kill everyone in the house, but now he stood as quiet as a church mouse. I couldn't read his expressionless face. Like he was stewing a silent caldron of madness.

They asked a few more questions before the paramedics placed Tempest on a gurney and wheeled her to the door. The officers brought the big bad man out last. It was a circus of white folks outside. The neighbors didn't care about the bitter cold temperatures. You could tell that they had already prejudged the black man's plight. Hell, some of them looked to be satisfied to see a brother going to jail. They had that look like they expected nothing more.

"Wisdom," Poppa Jones said before jumping up into the back of the ambulance. "Wisdom, take my keys and lock up. I'm going to the hospital with your sister." He threw his keys to me and I grabbed them with a one-hand catch.

The ambulance pulled away with lights flashing and sirens blaring, letting people know they were coming. The police stood around. I observed one of them on his radio, another was busy jotting something in a notepad, and two others looked to be working the crowd for more info. I could only imagine what some of those folks were telling the police officers. The slow murmuring from the nosy crowd was getting on my nerves.

I still couldn't believe this whole scene had gone down. Couldn't believe how violent my brother had acted. I looked sternly at Yazoo in the back of the police car.

We locked eyes for a minute. I glared at him with total disgust. He looked at me as though I were a dead man walking. I couldn't believe my brother was threatening me with his eyes. I shook it off and stepped back in the house to find Jordan. All I found was vomit all over the bathroom. I couldn't find the clown nowhere in the house. That meant that the boy had pulled a David Crackhead-field style-disappearance. God only knew what valuables were going to be traded for cash at one of the local pawnshops.

My cell buzzed before I could get in the mail van. I tried to ignore the thing and jump inside. I started the van and sat there for a minute, trying to let the thing warm up. As usual, nothing but lukewarm air was blowing from the vents. My phone buzzed again, reminding me to answer. I plucked the unit from my belt holster. Didn't quite recognize the number. Malisa crossed my mind, but instincts explained that it was much deeper than her simple behind.

"Wisdom, my man, how have you been doing?" a strange, but very familiar deep voice spoke. He took the confusion inside my head as a signal to continue. "You're breaking my heart. How can you forget my voice after all the years we spent together?"

The latter of his statement jogged my memory, matching a face to the sinister voice.

"Long time no hear, Highnoon," I said in a perplexed voice.

"How's your mother's health these days?"

"Fine." I kept it short.

His voice was low and eerie. It had the same creepy demeanor of an undertaker preparing bodies for one-way trips to dirt destinations.

"Now we both know that's a lie. Word has it that your mother is a very sick lady these days. Little birdies are telling me that if the old bird doesn't get a kidney donation pronto, her days are numbered."

"Why don't you make your point, Highnoon?" I let the dislike in my voice ring out. Had to let him know that his voice wasn't welcomed on my line.

"Your mother needs a kidney and I need some justice. I know where to get a donor, but under one condition."

He had my complete and undivided attention.

"I don't discuss business over the phone. You have to stop by the house. I think you still know where the place is." He hung up. I was still sitting in front of the condo.

My mother wasn't looking real healthy these days. Matter of fact, without a donor soon, she wouldn't make it through the winter. I had no idea what Satan wanted, but my mother's life was at stake. Without another word, I drove in the direction of Highnoon's place.

Like a bad rerun from a low-budget sitcom, the evening's events kept replaying inside my head. Everything from the vicious verbal assaults to the Mike Tyson mighty blow that cold-cocked Tempest, up to Yazoo losing his mind and trying to attack me, and the grand finale of the police replacing Yazoo's precious, golden wrist wear with silver, police-issued bracelets.

I've never known Yazoo to touch drugs or alcohol. But tonight his temperament was totally evil. Almost demonic. Like he'd been under the influence of some type of drug demons. The Negro was totally crazy. I could have expected that from Jordan, but Yazoo surprised me when he put his hands on the good Reverend. But one thing was sure about tonight, he was going to jail in Oakland County. A Black man's—and woman's for that matter—worst nightmare. A place where the legal system failed to show justice to people of color. In short, I hoped Yazoo was ready to trade in his shiny Rolex watch and bracelet in exchange for protection against the big, bad booty daddies of B-block.

The Negro had his nerve to put hands on a woman. I hoped my sister was doing okay. When I'd first pulled off from the condo, I'd meant to call my dad. That was before the devil gave me a cell phone call. Didn't know they had cell phone towers in hell.

As I drove through the night, I had a ton of burdens on my shoulders and a bag full of worries in my gut.

I had been to Highnoon's luxurious house of hell. The guy was real shady, a man who wore many corruptive hats. If you needed a kilo of cocaine, he was your man. If you needed a weapon that could bring down an airplane, he had it for you. From arranging bloody hits, to selling bootleg DVDs, this was the moron to see. Highnoon was the ultimate ghetto concierge.

As I moved through the silent, ghostly, wintery streets of Bloomfield Hills, I couldn't help to think about my mother. I couldn't face life without her. I wanted her to be there when Malisa gave birth to our baby, her first grandbaby. That's why I was now ignoring all the apprehensive feelings I was having about this meeting with the King Snake. For all I knew, I could be walking into a trap. I didn't trust this fool. I had no respect for a man who didn't respect his own people. He'd been exploiting black men ever since he was weaned from his baby bottle. Many a young black kid was wasting away on city street corners to finance this fool's elaborate crib. We had a dark history together, and that's why I was now dialing Rico's cell phone number.

My boy picked up on the first ring. He was breathing real heavy. Like he was getting his freak on and I had been the lame duck to interrupt. I explained to him where I was going. After a few "whys" and "what for's" I made him write down Highnoon's address and street name. He wrote down everything I told him, including directions. He also knew that Highnoon was not to be trusted. The concern in his voice frightened me. Rico didn't ask to tag along. He knew me. He could tell by the tone of my voice that this was a solo mission.

After a minute or two more, I ended the call and drove the rest of the way in silence, pondering. My life was becoming more complicated by the moment. I often looked to the sky as to why God had placed me with this family? A family where everybody was out for themselves. There were times I longed for family unity. My jealousy toward Rico's family was evident. His family didn't grow up with middle-class money, but they had each other. They had love. The togetherness I yearned.

As I made a left on to Highnoon's high society street, I broke out of my funk. When dealing with a poisonous snake, the snake handler's mind needed to be clear. There was no room for error. One slip-up could lead to a dastardly dose of deadly venom.

No matter how many times I had laid my eyes on Highnoon's estate I was left breathless. The man's crib was off the hook. It looked like a house that I'd seen from MTV's *Cribs*. His spread looked like it sat on a couple of acres. The nature in which he made his money caused extensive paranoia. The coward hid behind huge wrought-iron fences. The arrogant bastard even had a guard shack at the entrance to his home.

I drove right up to the guard shack, and some fat, dumpy-looking brother walked out holding a clipboard. When I rolled down the window, his putrid face stared in. I didn't know somebody could be that damn ugly. His face reminded me of a pig-faced human that I had seen on an episode of the *Twilight Zone*. I told him my name and he must've found it on his clipboard.

He grunted something that sounded like "go ahead." I proceeded past the checkpoint with a sudden urge to oink like a pig.

Darkness hovered over the estate with the eerie consistency of Dracula's castle. I almost expected to see that one storm cloud—with lightning bolts—that usually portrayed haunted houses in the movies.

As I made my way to the house, yard lights were enough to show off a well-manicured lawn and shrubbery. I could see that he had a thing for brush. They were all over the front yard. Huge ones, short ones, fat ones and skinny ones. It seemed like shadows lurked behind every bush, every tree.

I pulled up to the front door, putting the van in park. This was it, I told myself. The reasons why the snake had summoned me rested behind two enormous maple doors. I couldn't believe how big the doors were.

Before I could form another thought, one of the huge doors swung open, creating an eerie creaking noise. The sound was akin to that of a century-old coffin door swinging open. Some guy stood in the doorway. This Negro looked inhumane—he was so tall and robust. Frankenstein's monster came to mind. I walked up to the front porch. I could see that the monster was dressed in a Sean John sweat suit and Timberland boots. He was so black, his pink lips shined underneath the moonlight.

"The man's waiting on you." The monster spoke in an eerily deep undertaker's pitch. "Walk this way."

He waited until I walked in before shutting the door. Standing right next to the Monster, I could now see how gigantic this fool was. I stood six-feet-five, but the monster dwarfed my long frame, which probably put him at seven-feet even. The Negro had hands that could make a basketball look like a baseball. I looked down at the floor in amazement. Didn't know they made Timberland boots that big.

"This way," he repeated. He walked like he was military trained. His gung-ho demeanor was present for all to see. You know the type: straight posture, shoulders held high, chest poked out, stomach tucked in and booty cheeks bunched tight. The only thing missing was a drill sergeant barking cadence.

Highnoon's crib was spectacular. Marble floors, high ceilings, expensive furniture and huge portraits of African Chiefs stared down from the huge walls. After an unbelievable walk that seemed to be five minutes, tops, we finally reached a closed door. Butterflies bounced around inside my stomach at the thought of what could be behind it. I wasn't worried about death. The way my life was going now, death would be a welcomed sight. I would be freed from all problems. No more Malisa, no more worries about the big bad garnishment, family problems, my knee injury, and no more Mail Van!!!

The monster knocked on the door.

"Enter," came a deep baritone from the other side. Before his earlier phone call, I hadn't heard that voice in years. It complemented the morbid atmosphere inside the house.

The door opened. It looked to be some kind of a study, because when I walked in, there were huge bookcases on every wall. The floors in this room were marble as well. The study housed all the latest in office equipment. A few big-lipped African statues sat in every corner. The mahogany desk was beautiful, but the leather high-back chair was facing in the direction of a huge picture window. Cigar smoke floated up over the top. I made the distinction by the way the smoke smelled. I wasn't a cigar man but I could tell the difference between cheap and expensive. Knowing Highnoon's extravagant taste, my dollars pegged the stogie he was puffing as Cuban.

"Rex," Highnoon said, "you may go." Rex obeyed as if he were a well-trained Retriever, closing the door behind him.

The smoke was making me nauseous. I thought I was about to pass out.

"Wisdom, Wisdom, Wisdom." He blew more smoke over the chair. "I guess you're wondering why I called you to my home." He swung his chair around in a dramatic fashion, facing me. I was distraught to see that Highnoon hadn't aged a bit. Because of his lifestyle, I expected my old friend to be riddled by Father Time. But there he sat—looking like the actor Faizon Love—but a picture of good health. If anything, he looked at me like Father Time had been my enemy. I couldn't say his stare was wrong. Putting up with Malisa's crap had earned me a few gray strands on my head and goatee.

"Let's get down to it," I said with a stone-faced look. The bastard was not going to receive any emotion from me.

"Wisdom, still got that down-to-business mentality."

Highnoon smiled at me; teeth and gums. I didn't trust the smile. It was just teeth playing with my mind. It was a smile that had served as the last thing some of his victim's saw before he sent them to that next rest stop.

He gestured to the chair in front of his desk. "Have a seat."

"I'm fine standing."

"Okay, suit yourself. It's gonna be like that, hunh? No pleasantries, no how's the family, no nothing?"

I let the hateful snarl on my grill serve as my mouthpiece.

"Can you remember when we used to play as kids?" He paused for the effect. "We were two punks without a pot to piss in. The pact that we made was one I took to heart. To always be my brother's keeper. We did our little dirt. Robbed a few people, drunk a little wine, lost our virginity to Trenchcoat, the prostitute. We were a regular Batman and Robin. Then, your cousin, Smoke, got into it with my brother, Pat. We didn't think nothing of their little beef because we were all family.

"But Smoke wouldn't let it go. He beat my brother to death with a pipe. That started the family feud. Batman and Robin were no more. No matter how bad I would miss your mother's chicken I had to go my own way." Highnoon was the type that showed no emotions. He was always smiling. That was the first time I had remembered his gold teeth. Highnoon's parents had migrated from Mississippi to Detroit when he was thirteen. The kids in school used to tease him about his golden smile. But what they failed to realize was that the boy with the hip-hop grill was a cold-blooded killer. And that's why his parents had come to Detroit. Highnoon had killed a white boy in self-defense. That was considered taboo down in the Dirty South.

"Look, Highnoon, is there a point to all of this? This walk down Memory Lane—I know all this stuff. I was there." The exasperation in my voice was clearly highlighted by my nasty tone.

He held up his hand as if to hush me. He took a few more puffs on his smelly cigar and smiled at me. "The point is, your cousin might be in jail, but he's still alive. On the other hand, my brother is dead. You can visit Smoke whenever you get ready. I can visit Pat, too…"— he took a few more puffs—"…but the conversation I have with him is mostly one-sided."

"The hell you talkin'?" I said. "Smoke hung himself in jail."

He puffed on his cigar, scratching his chin. "Didn't know that."

I didn't know where the hell he was going with all this, so I stayed quiet. Didn't want to be here no longer than I had to. My constant interruption would only prolong the agony I was feeling.

"Am I my brother's keeper?" he asked, flicking ashes in an ashtray on his desk.

"What are you talking about?"

"Now, I don't have to remind you of how hard it is to lose a loved one. You're going through the same thing now, only your momma ain't dead... yet. But she will be if she don't get a donor." It looked like he was getting off on the look of confusion on my face. "Don't look confused; you know I have connections everywhere. I keep tabs on all my favorite people. I even have connections to obtain medical records." He mashed out his cigar in the ashtray. Highnoon reached under his desk. He set a black briefcase on top, opening it. Then he pulled out some papers. "I know about your mother's illness. It would be a shame to lose such a great woman, to what is it?" He shuffled through the papers. "Chronic Renal Failure? Shame, shame. I have a way you can save your mother."

The Negro was referring to my mother like she was some stranger in the street. He'd eaten many meals at our dinner table. My mother deserved his respect in at least calling her by a formal title. That's how he used to refer to her at dinnertime.

"Get to the point," I said.

"The donor that I spoke about over the phone is me. The conditions that I have for you are simple. Well, before you informed me that Smoke was dead, I was gonna ask you to set him up for my revenge. No need to do that now."

"Highnoon, you're not making any sense."

"Aw hell, Wisdom, my friend, looks like you just took your cousin's place as a sacrificial lamb. That's my deal to you; a life for a life is the price I am asking. I will serve as donor if you give me your life in exchange."

I watched the jerk arrogantly sit back in his chair. Like he'd been fighting a battle for years, and now, he was putting the appropriate pieces into play to win the war.

Indeed, he had dropped a major bombshell on me, and now he looked to be receiving pleasure at my dilemma.

"You can't be serious," I said in my best DMX voice. "She's on the donor list. Don't need your maniacal help."

He sat further back in his chair, showing off all thirty-two.

"Serious as a fat man sitting down to a buffet." He handed me the papers. "You'll see that I'm the perfect match. All the eligible requirements have been satisfied. Right down to blood test and X-rays. I think you underestimate the severity of the situation. I dabble in the black markets, and it's hard to come with one. I'm the only living donor you know."

A brief scan of the letter explained to me that he wasn't lying. "How long have you been thinking about this?"

He grabbed another cigar from the humidor. "It doesn't matter." He lit the smoke. "Time's ticking, Wisdom."

"You mean to tell me that you're sitting on my mother's life and you want her son to die by your hand?"

He arrogantly played with the cigar in his mouth as if tasting victory. "Retribution."

"Revenge, hunh?" My throbbing knee let me know that I'd been standing too long. It was fire down below and I wasn't talking about the movie. Sharp pains stabbed at my knee like somebody was making razor-blade incisions in my skin. But I wasn't about to sit in the chair that he'd offered earlier. "This is insane. This won't bring back Pat."

He removed the cigar from his mouth, leaning forward and resting his elbows on the desktop. "But it's sure gonna help me sleep at night knowing that I've avenged my brother's death. I have a reputation to protect. I respect you, old friend; that's why I wasn't gonna kill you without proper consent. Killing someone like you would send a powerful message that I am not to be trifled with."

I shifted my weight from the bad leg, and perspiration let me know that I had to try a new brand of deodorant. "You coming at me like I was wielding the pipe."

"Of course you didn't. Smoke killed 'em. Blood for blood. This is the only way. Besides, Smoke's dead."

"Vengeance is mine, says the Lord," I quoted from the Bible, hoping that it would change his mind. But I forgot that Satan knows scripture also.

"King Solomon was the wisest and richest king in history. Solomon had first begun to reign when his wisdom received the first test. Two women had come before his throne arguing over a baby. In his infinite wisdom, Solomon summoned for a sword. His aim was to split the baby in half, then give one half of the baby to each woman. This action caused the real mother to speak up. She pleaded to Solomon not to kill her child, but to give the infant to the other woman. The other woman wanted the baby dead. So in all his glory, Solomon restored the baby to its rightful mother. The real mother loved her child so much that she was ready to sacrifice her motherly rights so that the baby could live."

"I'm familiar with the story, but what does any of that have to do with me?"

He flashed me his best golden Colgate smile. "Everything. Sacrifice your life. Your mother didn't name you Wisdom for nothing. That name has a lot of responsibility behind it. Yo' old girl gave you life. Now she's dying. Here's your time to repay her by giving your life for hers. This is a no-brainer." He sat back in his chair, playing with that dumb cigar.

"So this is the only way?"

"Yep." He puffed his cigar. "I'm a businessman. I see that your mother's life needs to be thought about. So here's what I'm prepared to do. I'll give you a week to ponder my proposition." He shoved one finger in the air. "Only one week."

"I didn't kill your brother. I shouldn't have to pay for his death with my life." I pinched the bridge of my nose out of frustration. "I love my mother. I'mma take one week to get my house in order. I'll give you my answer then. I thought you were my brother, but I see now that you're a greasy head cockroach with an expensive smile."

He slowly rolled his chair back around, facing the picture window. "I might be...but your mother is the one who needs *my* kidney." The bank of smoke streaming over the top of the chair told me that I had been dismissed.

The monster was back. He opened the door so that I could leave. "Think long, think wrong," Highnoon said, laughing. "If you only would've stayed home the night of the draft you would've had that NBA money behind you to deal with situations like this."

Damn, did everybody have to keep reminding me of my unfortunate accident? Without another word, I followed the big seven-footer back the way we'd come.

I walked out into the wintery night with a heavier burden than I'd come with. The offer that had been selfishly laid on the table was flashing in my mind like the neon signs of an adult magazine and novelty store. My life for the life of my mother. Somehow along Highnoon's quest for total land domination, the man had lost his damn mind. This bastard was sick to come up with an offer that was so heinous it could've been a money machine for the plot of an A-list movie. I couldn't fathom how somebody that had eaten at my mother's dinner table could hatch out something so evil.

I drove in absolute silence. There was no rush to get home. Instead of the expressway, I traveled the major streets, stunned. This guy had been my best friend. We did everything together. Now he was asking for my life to satisfy his blood thirst. Dracula; Satan; the Ghoul. I tried to find a name that would suit this bastard, but those I came up with were too soft for him. The contract was on the table and he was asking for my signature in blood.

It was almost eleven at night but I needed a drink. I was an occasional sipper, but tonight, I needed something hard and plentiful.

As I drove the dark city streets, I could hear and see small white pellets pinging off my windshield. The first snowfall of the winter was here. It seemed as if I was slowly sinking in the quicksand of life. The proposition kept replaying in my mind. The more I ran it, the more ridiculous it seemed. My mother was already on the donor list. I kept asking myself: what if I surrendered to this madness, then a minute after my death, a kidney came up for Momma? My death would be in vain. All for naught. There had to be another way. I couldn't go through with this. It seemed the more I tried to step out of the quicksand, the more I waded in deeper.

I went to pick up my cell several times to call Rico, but each time I ended the call before the entire number could be dialed. I was in this thing all alone. There was no one in my list of contacts who was qualified to help me ponder this preposterous proposition. My old man was a preacher, and because of his recent shortcomings, the idiot would be no help.

I drove to Brady's Bar. It was an Irish pub that sat in

the crime-riddled streets of Southwest Detroit. It was strange that I thought better in this rough part of town. I had found this bar while frantically searching for a new stop on my route. I'd gotten to know the locals. They'd given me the rundown of all the Mexican gangs that prowled these parts. The color code was red and black, or green and black. All that crap didn't matter right now. I needed to lose myself in a bottle of something hard.

Brady's was a hole-in-the-wall joint. I took a seat at my favorite booth, totally ignoring the hard stares from a few shady-looking young punks sitting at a smoke-filled bar. Their green and black colors warned me that these clowns were the Black Mambas. They were one of the most powerful crews in Southwest Detroit.

Their muscle and hustle kept them head-and-shoulders above all other gangs. The Mambas were known for their public execution-style hits. A crew without fear of death presented problems for adversaries. They didn't care about the value of human life and they definitely didn't give a damn about the punk police. They had a strangling grip on this part of the city with an underlying hatred for non-Latinos. That's why these three taco-eating, butt-wipes were eyeing me like I was scouting out a piece of their property as though I were about to set up a crack business.

A Latina barmaid came over to take my drink order. She was a real hot number with kissy lips and a well-padded bottom. Her silky, long hair sat on top of a face that was made for the silver screen. I ordered a Jack Daniel's on the rocks.

She winked and offered a beautiful smile. I returned her lovely gesture, rendering a Colgate smile of my own. Now flirting in the bar went on all the time and no one paid attention—until now. The three greaseballs who were pimping their gang colors in the form of bandanas at the bar were now staring at me like I was a tasty taco supreme. The green-eyed monster was in the house. I heard that Latino cats were terribly jealous and protective of their women. That bit of knowledge only added to my desire to flirt harder.

She went to the bar and came back in a flash, setting my drink on a napkin in front of me. Skip J-Lo, this woman had that Aztec beauty, and she had dimples to boot.

"I haven't seen you around here before," the pretty lady said with a slight Spanish accent.

I looked in the direction of the Chicos at the bar. It looked as though they were trying to gauge the situation. Trying to filter out what was business and pleasure. I took a sip of my drink. My body tensed, welcoming the sweet-bitter taste.

"Sometimes I stop in for drinks on my afternoon lunch break," I told her while taking another sip. The cigarette smoke was head-locking my sinuses into submission. "I don't usually stop in here at this time. This bar has a whole different vibe at night."

"We can get pretty rowdy," she explained, tilting her

head in the direction of my three buddies at the bar, who now were beginning to get a little hot under the collar. "Watch your back in this place."

"I didn't get your name," I pushed, taking another sip of the drink.

She surprised me when she took a seat across from me.

"Maria," she said, extending her small hand. "My name is Maria."

Her hand was baby-booty soft with fingernails that were polished to perfection. "Pleased to meet you. Maria, you're one beautiful lady. Too beautiful to be working here."

The smoke was starting to sting my eyes and I was trying to blink away the irritation.

Maria must have thought I was trying to be funny because she started giggling. "Can I know your name? You are too handsome not to have one."

"Wisdom; my name is Wisdom."

"That's a unique name, but it's a nice name. It fits your honest face." The fat, stubby bartender yelled over to her, letting her know that she had a job to do. "Well, Wisdom, I have to get back to work. Enjoy your drink."

"I got a few problems, so I'm gonna be drinking here for a little while." I looked at the punks at the bar. They were beginning to look real unstable. I wanted to push them over the edge. I took her hands. "I'll be seeing you around," I said, staring hypnotically into her eyes, inviting her to see the mysteries of the man.

It was as if she drank too much of my mysterious potion. She swayed a little bit. I had her, but the only thing that stopped me from going all the way was the thought of my unborn child.

I let her hands go and she walked back to the bar, occasionally staring backward. I was once again left alone with the proposition. I fell into think mode, and when I came out, my drink had been drained. The sad part was I couldn't remember drinking it. The melting ice cubes were testament to my brief memory lapse. I had been staring at the table the whole time. There was no way in hell somebody could've snuck my drink. The unsettling, paranormal event caused my eyes to rapidly blink as if to replay the scene. My eyes opened once more and saw Maria's beautiful face. She was standing there, smiling, fresh Jack in hand. Maria sat the drink in front of me and stepped back into the smoke bank. It went on like that for a couple of hours. I had managed to drink my problems under the table. Highnoon's ugly, black face had been snuffed out and suppressed by Jack. His gold-tooth smile was a distant memory, surrounded by the fog of alcohol.

All my problems were funny to me now. I'd changed suits, stepping out of my suit of worries and into an inebriated, carefree outfit.

"Wisdom," Maria said with a worried expression on her angelic face, "I think you've had enough."

"How do you figure?"

She put her hands on her hips. "Because you look pretty foolish about the eyes. No more drinks for you. And if cabs came to this area this time of night, I would pour your tall frame into one."

Okay, I'll admit, I was a little drunk, but I wasn't sloppy with it. Couldn't afford to lose my wits in a room full of snakes.

"What's up, *homes*?" the largest of the three gang-bangers asked with pepper in his voice, standing to his feet. I guess my interracial flirting had pushed him over the edge. It seemed his first words hushed the bar. "I see you got a taste for Mexican food, hunh, Homie?" His first step toward me triggered his friends into standing as well.

I offered the greasy head punk Satan's grin.

Everybody in the bar knew that violence always preceded Mamba confrontation. I guess that's what prompted Maria to jump between Grease Head and myself.

"Paco," Maria said, holding up her hands, "this man has done nothing to you. Why don't y'all just leave?"

"Maria?" the smallest of the three piped, "I see you like soul food. Now sit your traitorous ass down somewhere. Paco asked the *vato* here a question."

Maria knew that tone of voice. There were lines you didn't cross. This was her cue to mind her business. But that was cool; it wasn't like I needed a woman to be my spokesperson.

"To answer your question, Paco, I have an international appetite." I stood to my feet, exposing my size. Paco was a big boy, but compared to me, he looked like an obese kid. I could see their eyes widen as if to take in my full frame. To be truthful, I had already punked them.

Paco looked up at me, hesitating. I could actually see the gears in his head working vigorously to come up with a reply. I even heard someone describe the whole scene with one word "Damn."

"Aww, *ese*," the smallest one said, pointing up at me, "you ain't that damn big."

Paco was still speechless, so I decided to hit him with a few choice words. "Listen, Paco, I don't know what your beef is; I'm just drinking off some problems. But if you want a problem, you pissing on the right tree." I couldn't believe my ears. Here I was in the heart of Taco town, trying to punk out the baddest gang in their 'hood. Was it subconscious suicide? Was I purposely trying to bump myself off? I didn't have the science on my own questions. All I knew was that my mouth was working without the aid of my brain. Simply put, Jack Daniel's was trying to get me killed.

Paco stuck his chest out, pulling up his flannel, showing off a black pistol-grip handle of what looked to be a heinous-looking old school revolver.

"You got a big mouth, *homie*," Paco said.

"Big man," I said, my eyes quickly went to the pistol. "So what? You got a heater. What am I supposed to be, scared?" The 23rd Psalm ran through my mind as freely as flowing water. I didn't know which was spookier, the sinister-looking pistol grip peacemaker, or the third gang-banger that hadn't voiced a word yet. Something in his evil eyes told me that I was trespassing in his territory. His eyes flashed dangerously, warning me that he thought of his women as sacred temples and I was in violation of desecration. His silence was enough to frighten anybody. He was about average height and wore a flannel shirt that was two sizes too big. His hair and beard were of good texture; that Latino stuff. His menacing eyes betrayed his average frame. That's when I made, and met the killer of the three. The other two were loudmouths, but this guy came across as psychotic. I had learned to distinguish the difference between the loudmouth and the threat in the schoolyard. The loudmouth was the one that popped off at the lip and couldn't beat up an egg. But the threat was a whole different entity. The threat was the silent assassin. Words were meaningless. Violence was his nature. I tried not to show fear. I swallowed hard, trying desperately to close the lid on my sarcasm. But each time, Jack took control.

"Aye, *ese*, shoot his black ass!" the shortest one yelled out.

Paco grabbed for the gun handle. I could get the drop on him before he pulled it. His huge beer gut would've given me the edge I needed.

It was as if God had heard my silent alarm. A white guy with a bushy mustache walked in our direction, holding up a police badge. He emerged from the smoke bank as if stepping from the Heavens.

"Police!" he shouted loud and clear.

He wasn't quite up on us, and that's why he missed the great pistol disappearance. The trick happened so fast that I thought Paco was Criss Angel dressed in Latino drag. The pistol went from Paco's hand, vanishing somewhere inside the crowd. What can I say? His people stuck together.

"What's the problem here, boys?" the officer asked, stepping between us.

"No problem here, Officer McBrien," Paco said, never taking his eyes off me. "Just having a friendly conversation with my *homie* here."

"Can I break into the conversation?" Officer McBrien asked, smiling.

I couldn't believe that this cop's mustache looked like a red Afro above his lip, which happened to be completely covered. The cop had red hair, glasses, and a banana for a nose.

"We're just discussing the usual: health care reform, the ongoing war in Iraq, high gas prices, and the problems on Wall Street," I said, trying to be funny, knowing damn well that these boys looked dumber than dog crap.

The cop broke into laughter. "Whatever. Look, Paco, you know the rules of this bar. No gangster stuff. Al put you guys out of here a week ago without the slightest thought of you coming back. Now, you and the two stooges here have a choice. You can stay and go to jail, or you can leave with your freedom." He glanced at me. "Your choice," he said, looking back at Paco.

Paco looked at me as if saying with his eyes that this was far from over. They walked out of the bar single file. The cop looked at me like he had saved my black behind. Without a word, he walked back to his table. Everybody resumed what they were doing.

I didn't give a damn how tense the situation, I just couldn't get serious. The Jack had me loose. How bad I wanted to crush Paco's skull, but I couldn't will myself to hit him.

"You must have a death wish," Maria said, copping a seat.

"That cop saved Paco, and his punks," I said, smiling.

"I'm serious. They're gonna be waiting on you out front." Her face was stained by a look of concern for my safety. I had to admit: it felt kind of good for someone to express genuine concern for my well-being. "You might think this is a joke, but Paco is a maniac." She looked in the direction of the back. "Quick, I can let you out the back door. My car is out there." She slid her keys across the table.

My first impulse was to pick up the keys from the table and throw 'em. Was she implying that I couldn't handle a few slimy snakes? Jack told me that she was questioning my manhood. I could hear Jack's voice in my head: *Wisdom, she must think you a punk. Soft. No balls*

*in yo' drawers. What are you? A man or a six-foot-five sissy
in a skirt? You better stand up and get some respect. What's
that little liver-lip broad's name that be pushing you around?
Oh, Malisa. That's the name of that five-foot terror in high-
heels. My name is Jack, and only real men are my friends.
Grow some balls and stand up for yourself.*

While Jack was running off at the lip, my temper was
becoming highly volatile. The voice inside my head was
a rude wake-up call. Jack was right about one thing: I
was becoming soft. I could remember a time when I
would have ripped Paco's head off his shoulders and
beat the other two to death with it.

"What the hell do you take me for?" I said, slightly
raising my voice. "I ain't no punk. I'm a grown man." I
beat on my chest. I pushed the keys back to her. "I don't
need yo' help. Look how big I am. If anything, you need
to get Paco some help." I stood up, stumbling a little
bit.

To my surprise, Maria stood up and hugged me. I was
a little bit confused. Was this some kind of a sign? Was
it her way of kissing me goodbye? I pushed her aside,
walking toward the front door—all eyes on me. I wasn't
sure, but it felt like she put something in my pocket.

Before I left, I took a mental snapshot of the Aztec
beauty, then I stepped out the door.

Snow was falling pretty heavy out. Besides a few rusty
parking lot lights, it was pitch-black. Jack had pumped
me up. I was seriously overdosing off liquid courage.

Didn't get two steps before spotting Paco. He was sitting on my van, nonchalantly smoking a cigarette.

The wind was howling loudly. This was it! Sad to say that I asked for it. I braced myself, getting ready for my final destination. I took a couple steps toward the van when I spotted the two other jackals. They stepped from the shadows and stood right next to the boss.

Paco mockingly put his cigarette out on my hood, starting toward me, sandwiched by his goons.

"Too bad, *Homes*," Paco said, pulling the revolver from his pants. He stopped a foot in front of me, blowing his cigarette smoke in the wind. "McBrien can't help you now, nigga. I hate when you spooks come to our 'hood to hump our women."

"Paco!" the little loudmouth shouted. "Stop talking and shoot that bastard, *ese!*"

The silent one said nothing. He looked at me like he had killed me in his mind ten times over.

A part of me started to panic but Jack was quick with the courage. Looking at the pistol, I came to the conclusion that I didn't want to die. I wanted to live. I wanted to see my baby. My mother. I was seriously outnumbered, ass-out in their territory, but I had desperation on my side, and Paco's stupidity to walk in my face not pointing the weapon. The jerk was still talking when I hit his jaw so hard I thought I broke my right hand.

Shock registered in his face, surprise in mine. He looked foolish because he thought I wouldn't jaw him.

On the other hand, I was surprised because Paco didn't go down. My ego and I didn't stop to ask him how he withstood my power. My second shot was right on the button. This one was a vicious uppercut. The shot left him spitting up teeth and talking in tongues. I was amazed that the other two watched while their boss was being dismantled. I guess they were shocked as well. Paco had fallen to his knees, but he still held the gun. One well-placed knee-lift took care of that. The gun clattered across the frozen ground and under a truck. Paco was out cold. After the short loudmouth one took off running in the other direction, the strategy of taking out the leader first, rendering the rest of the troops confused was confirmed. Had learned that from the Sun Tzu's *Art of War*.

I was amused for the moment—that was until I looked into the deadly eyes of a killer. His face was unreadable. His movement methodical. The butterfly knife seemed to appear from nowhere. He flicked it around in dramatic fashion, the blade gleaming under the parking lot lights.

I didn't have time to think. The animal came at me swinging his knife like a rabid dog, each swipe accompanied by a breezy whistle. I evaded most of his attempts, but the last one cut through my pants, slicing my right thigh. The knife stuck, twisting in my pants, exposing his jaw. I took full advantage of the opportunity with a hellish right-cross. He didn't utter a sound falling to the ground. Was out for the count. I wasted no time getting to my van and pulling off.

My high was leaving me, dropping me back into the lap of reality. Actually, my high had been blown in the scuffle. Jack had left the building, leaving me feeling utterly stupid. Even though my name was Wisdom, there had been nothing wise about me trying to drink my problems away.

As I drove through the dark streets, the mental pain I was feeling was burning in my gut, not surpassing or ignoring the hot pain in my right thigh. The punk had gotten off a lucky stab. I could feel warm blood coursing down my leg. I had no desire to stop and check. Just wanted to get home. Mentally, I bashed myself over and over again for trying to drink my problems away. Trying to make the proposition go away. Wanting to commit suicide by somebody else's hands.

I was confused and all alone. My mother was dying and I was the only one who could save her. I wanted to pray, but so far, it seemed that my prayers were falling on deaf ears. I kept saying to myself that there had to be another way. My mother would be dead and gone before she came up available on the donor list.

I called myself trying to turn my life around. Trying to live somewhat of a decent existence. I wasn't the most spiritual man on earth, but I believed that something good had come out of all this misery: my baby. My baby was the only bright spot in all of this. I couldn't dream of my infant child existing in a cruel world without a father. There was so much I wanted to give my child. To teach it like my dad didn't teach me.

My life for the life of my mother? The unconditional love she'd given me as a child merited my returning the favor. At least I could trust her with raising my baby. She could teach my baby, and keep my memory alive. But I wasn't dead yet. I had a week to ponder the proposition. The man in me wouldn't let me drive myself to the hospital and get professional care for my wound. The wound was the least of my problems. My life was an open wound and no man could help. I had one week, and, in that week, a lot of things had to be put in order.

REVEREND POPPA JONES

My plans were successfully succeeding to perfection. And, boy, was I enjoying every minute of it. The perverseness going on before me was enough to call for an exorcism. An orgy. A straight up orgy that invited Satan, dubbing him as Master of Ceremony.

Deacon Slydale hadn't known who the hell he was messing with. Hadn't known that I could get downright dirty in the ugly eye of revenge. Revenge was mine, said the Lord, but I couldn't wait that long. I had taken off my minister's robe, replacing it with gangster gear.

I laughed at the kinkiness going on in full display on the security monitor. I was laughing on the outside but inwardly dying. The bruise on my right jaw served as a sad reminder of my unfaithfulness coming to bear. It had been a week since the family brawl. I was in denial mode. Still couldn't believe that Yazoo was capable of that much violence. Couldn't believe that he had the nerve to put his hands on his sister. Knew that damn meeting was a bad idea. But once Wisdom got an idea in his head, he couldn't be talked out of it. And since the altercation took place Saturday, Yazoo had been locked up for the weekend. He should've been. Tempest had suffered a concussion and a traumatized neck. He'd hit her, and she'd hit the floor—hard!

My hand went up to the bruise on my cheek, making me burn with anger. Before I could react, the Negro had put me on the seat of my trousers, too. I hated to say it, but if Wisdom wouldn't have interfered, I was gonna put God aside, get my shotgun, and blow that bastard away. Nobody—not even my offspring—put their hands on me.

My eyes widened in amusement at the mischievous activities broadcasting from the monitors.

Somebody was gonna be in trouble.

It tickled me pink to see that in the church some folk could act holier-than-thou, but behind closed doors could be freakier than a drunken hooker with a vibrator.

Somebody was gonna be in trouble!

It seemed that trouble was my middle name these days. My action had picked up. Trying to burn the candle at both ends had me plum-tuckered out. My menu of flesh kept me without pants on. Sister Walker was my morning breakfast with Sister Lawson satisfying my lunchtime craving, and for dinner, my new piece, Sister Williams. I should've been ashamed of myself. Sister Williams had been Robin's auntie; the young girl whose house I'd been over when her husband shot her dead, leaving me to do a four-story swan dive out her window. I couldn't resist myself, because Sister Williams was the spitting image of her late niece. Therefore, I'd been elated when Sister Williams approached me to ask if she could have her niece's funeral at the church. Over a few glasses of wine, Sister Williams had cried on my shoulder, informing me that Robin's husband had blown his own brains out, sitting at a casino blackjack table. He had robbed her of justice.

Sister Williams had been in pain, asking me like Halle Berry was asking Billy Bob Thornton to make her feel good. Who was I not to grant a grieving aunt a wish like that?

The cameras rolled, catching every pornographic deed in the hotel's boardroom. I could only imagine the smell of sex permeating the air inside. Hot sex and naughty deeds. It was gonna make for juicy discussion at the next deacons' meeting. We were in for one wang-dang-doodle of a time.

Indeed, everything was going down as planned. I loved it when a plan came together. Nothing got my blood pumping like a cleverly crafted plan.

I tore myself away from the monitor and glanced around at the small security guard booth, smiling. It had cost me a pretty penny to talk the guard into what I had in mind. The young punk, college student offered a little resistance. That was until I shoved Benjamins into his greedy outstretched hands. Given his greedy looks, I could've bought his momma for a couple more hundred. Some ministers would've looked down on doing some dirty work. Some would've hired dirty-workers, but not me. I was a *hands*-on type of dude. Didn't want no middle-man witnesses. Why send a boy to do a pastor's job?

One of the women on the monitors reminded me of that worrisome broad, Sister Walker. Sister Walker was beginning to get on my damn nerves. My cell was vibrating now, but I wasn't gonna answer it because I knew who it was. It didn't matter how much sexual pleasure I gave her, it still wasn't enough. I had no business thinking this, but I wished she would've been eaten right along with her husband, Wellington.

I looked up at my watch. In a couple of hours, Sister Lawson was going to meet me at the Cadillac dealership. It was predicted that the upcoming winter was supposed to be a rough one. The sister had finally gotten her lawsuit money and was treating me to a delicious upgrade. Had my eyes nestled on a sweet black Cadillac ESV. Her dead husband had cost the city $5 million. I amusedly admit that I had gone through two prescriptions of Viagra to secure the promise of my lavish set of wheels. Had put it on her so mean, she was gonna buy me a truck, and, she was still willing to give the church 10 percent for a tithe. My church would receive a cool half-million dollars. Sister Lawson's generous contribution would go toward construction of a new east wing for the church. My dreams of having an academy starting from grades one through five was finally coming to fruition. My church was growing by leaps and bounds.

I would go through the fire to protect it. And that's why I was sitting in front of monitors showing a triple X-rated reality show.

If I must say so myself, I had set this thing up pretty sweet. Had Deacon Slydale's whole gang in action. This was exactly the type of sickness that the church could do without; a cancerous growth that I planned on freezing, extracting, and casting out.

I glanced at the monitor, looking right into Deacon Kelley's gorilla-like grill. The man was standing there as naked as the day he was born. A quick glance below the belt revealed why this man was so hostile. I chuckled like I was holding a Full House. My poker face was serious, and driven solely for the purposes of winning the game. At that moment, the lady that reminded me of Sister Walker walked up to Deacon Kelley, pointing and outwardly cracking up at the goods he was now shyly covering up.

I didn't know how long these punks planned on partying, but I was there for the show.

"Smile..." I said to the monitor that held Slydale's naughty game show of sex, lies, and deacons. "You're on candid camera, Negro."

❂ ❂ ❂

The snow falling on the ground was one more reason to hurry along in my quest to secure my new SUV. The stuff was coming down in blankets and the rear end of my STS was fishtailing. The traffic on Eight Mile Road was moving at a frustrating snail's pace. Sister Lawson had cell-phoned me twice already. She was either in a rush to spend her money, pleasing me, or, she couldn't wait to see me. The woman couldn't get enough of what I was rocking in my britches.

Against my will, I'd left the greedy security guard to finish up my detail. Had to give that punk a couple more dollars to produce an incriminating DVD. When I got through with Slydale and his gang, they were going to come off in front of the rest of the deacons at the meeting like hard-nosed, porno superstars.

The traffic was stop-and-go for about a mile, then it opened up into a free-for-all of fast, slip-and-slide driving. This was supposed to be the first major snowstorm of the season and these idiots were acting like they had forgotten how to conduct business in a Michigan winter.

I was ten minutes away from the dealership and feeling the joy of a flock of preachers in the presence of a soul-stirring, Holy Ghost convention. Couldn't wait to get under the wheel of my extravagant truck. The truck couldn't have come at a better time. I had a speaking engagement on Sunday evening at Holy Baptist Church.

The pastor of that church drove a four-year-old GMC Yukon Denali. Every chance he got, the man would rub my face in it. Going on about the smooth ride, and all the bells and whistles that came along with the truck.

Well, Pastor Cooper would be in for a surprise. I laughed at the thought of him trying to get his church to up his salary when he got a gander of my mean street machine. The man was going to burn green with envy. And to further his jealousy, I planned to visit Van Dyke's, my favorite men's clothing boutique, and purchase another suit the same color as the truck.

After an incredible drive, I finally pulled in the lot of the dealership. Life couldn't get any better than this. I was soon to be rid of the evil Slydale, and once again be privileged to the new car smell.

I took some pep out of my step as I walked through the parking lot. Didn't want to appear pressed. So I took my time feigning like I was interested in the brand-new cars on the lot.

Sister Lawson was standing by the second cubicle off the door. Her face wore a slight frown. Like she was pissed at my tardiness. But I wasn't worried. I was a charming son-of-gun with a bewitching smile that could melt the coldest heart.

"Hi, my precious Pam Grier," I said, caressing her right cheek. Her frown quickly turned upside down and she blushed like a schoolgirl receiving her first kiss, melting like hot butter between my fingers.

"Pastor, you know that I have a six o'clock appointment. It wouldn't have hurt you to answer your cell phone," Sister Lawson said with a pouty expression on her face. You always can tell when folks come into money—especially black folks. They start buying high-priced possessions that hold no value after the purchase. Sister Lawson was a true testament. Her body was wrapped tightly in a full-length sable coat.

I playfully ran my hand up the right sleeve of the coat, making the whistling sound that people make in admiration of a pricey possession. "I see you found a little piece of justice after all. Sister Lawson, that's a gorgeous coat you have on." My compliment turned a few heads. A very tall black salesman nodded his approval. A white woman he was trying to charm into buying a Cadillac STS couldn't take her eyes off the coat.

"Well, Pastor, the lawsuit won't bring my husband back, but it sure does feel good knowing the justice system finally came through. I can sleep at night knowing that the police involved will be charged with Ross' murder." Her smile was one of relief. The kind of relief that comes with a $5 million relief fund. The lustful look in her eyes didn't go unnoticed. They devoured me as if I were a Krispy Kreme donut, wearing sugary underwear. She came close enough to kiss, but stopped short and whispered in my ear.

"I'm not wearing any panties, Pastor."

"Business first," I whispered with a smile. That's when I noticed the short, white salesman with the shaggy hair standing behind me. Sister Lawson introduced me, then we got down to the paperwork. Of course, they were willing to pay off the remaining balance of my STS.

As we sat inside his claustrophobic cubicle, staring at pictures of his ugly kids, and even uglier wife, Sister Lawson couldn't keep her hands to herself. While Kevin, the salesman, had his head down crunching numbers and working his paperwork magic, Sister Lawson indulged herself in adolescent behavior: stealing kisses whenever Kevin dropped his head to write, playing footies under the table, and mouthing dirty demands.

She was turning me on in the worst way, a way that could jeopardize my position as pastor, and lose my soul to eternal damnation in the process. I was quickly becoming one of the men that I most despised since being called to preach. Men that took bits and pieces of God's Word and flexed and formed and shaped it to justify their habitual, worldly appetite. I was a hypocrite, solely driven by materialism. Satan was leading me around in the world of corruption, dangling the almighty dollar in front of me like a mouse in the presence of a hungry python. I had fallen from my throne of grace with no desire or will power to climb out of my pit of iniquity. I wouldn't stop 'til God put me flat on my back, begging for my life. Frankly, I wasn't gonna stop 'til I hit rock bottom.

We sat there for about two more hours, filling out paperwork. Him asking me if I wanted this or that extra. Extended warranties and extra insurances. I decided to get crazy and asked him since we were paying cash to throw in a set of those stylish rims. The greedy honkie happily agreed. It took another forty minutes to detail the truck. By that time, Sister Lawson was hot, horny, and nibbling on my neck—no longer caring about the salesman sitting in front of us. I could tell that Kevin wanted to get personal, asking if she was my wife, but what did he care? The man had sold a sixty-six thousand-dollar vehicle.

My truck was ready. After peeling Sister Lawson away from my body, I jumped in and immediately fell in love. The inside of the truck was posh. The new car smell was to me as heroin was to a junkie: the ultimate high. I gazed over the steering wheel and felt the power right away. The power I'd heard so much about from other SUV owners. I vowed never to purchase another car again. Once you go truck, you're stuck. I had it like that so high gasoline prices weren't gonna be a problem for me.

The snow was still coming down in buckets and the approaching darkness activated my headlights. Sister Lawson pulled up on the side of me, rolling down her window. She was begging me to sexually reward her for being such a "good girl," in her own words.

I really didn't have the time. Had promised my wife dinner at her favorite restaurant. I couldn't remember the last time that I'd taken Wilma out. Didn't want to, but I had to do what I had to do to shut her up.

The more I said *no*, the louder Sister Lawson professed her love for me. After a couple of convincing, crotch-hardening minutes, I finally gave in. I could use a good stress reliever right now, so I told her to follow me.

Looking at the snow accumulation brought out my inner child. I was in the mood to play, so I activated the four-wheel drive system. I settled into the supple leather, my adolescent mentality screaming a "snow beware" war cry. I pulled out into traffic; Sister Lawson hugged tightly on my bumper. I couldn't believe how easily I plowed through the white stuff. This had to be a *man thing*. My adrenaline was overdosing from total road domination.

Time was of the essence and I was determined not to be blown off course by booty. So I settled on Clark Park. It was a park that sat on the borderline of Detroit and Southfield. There, I could break in the backseat of my new truck without any interference from the law. The park was abandoned and trees and bushes provided excellent cover for our freaky rendezvous.

As I drove through the entrance of the park I passed a liquor store. Wineheads and crackheads stood in front like permanent, tragic corner fixtures. One of the Negroes looked like my son, Jordan, causing me to jam down hard on my brake pedal. It was a good thing I wasn't going too fast, because the SUV skid a few feet before coming to a complete stop. My abrupt action not only scared the hell out of the zombies on the corner, but almost caused Sister Lawson to rear end me. Luckily, the sister had played it safe, allowing ample safety distance just in case she had to break quickly. All the young men on the corner turned toward the street probably looking to see if I was the police. I thanked God that Jordan wasn't one of them. Ain't no telling what I might've done to him. You see, the day he'd disappeared from my house, a Rolex watch disappeared as well. I had four in my possession. I usually kept them in a secured place in my closet. I have nobody to blame but laziness. I had come in the house the night before the family meeting, exhausted. Three ladies in one day will do that to you. I remember grabbing a shower and finishing up Sunday's sermon. That was all I remembered. The next morning the sun gave me a bright wake-up call at the desk in my office. The mistake came when I'd left my watch sitting on my desk. Jordan, using the chaos as cover, had stumbled into my office and couldn't resist my beautiful Submariner. I could only imagine what some pawnshop had given him for my possession. The boy was a crackhead; he wasn't gonna argue about any offer made.

My anger was enough to cause me to pitch my cell in the backseat.

Without explanation to anybody, I continued on my way in search of my perfect spot to ease my tension.

Inside the park, most of the snow set on the ground undisturbed, untouched by the tire treads of humanity. The park's lights made the snow glisten in picturesque fashion. Beautiful landscapes of wintery Hallmark cards.

I wanted to really put my truck through the test, but the muscle of love reminded me to put a lid on my adolescent play. I had business to take care of and Sister Lawson's brand-new Mercedes SL500 was way too powerful for her to be mucking around in the snow.

I drove to the west side of the park—not a soul in sight. It had been that way since we entered. Nobody was out in this weather except fools with four-wheel drives, crackhead fools, and horny fools.

My new truck seemed possessed. It slid into a spot that was picture perfect, trees all around. My manhood was throbbing to a point of being so hard that it hurt. I pulled to the side, parked the truck, but kept it running. I didn't even see Sister Lawson park her car. Before I could look up, her Sable coat was leaping into the passenger seat, closing the door behind her.

Words were useless. We tore at each other with pure, unadulterated animal magnetism. She leaned over my console, meeting my lips, licking them hard. My mouth automatically opened, inviting her tasty tongue foreplay. Our breathing rapidly increased to freakiness only known to adultery. I pushed her back for a second to stare deeply into her eyes. Nothing but lust stared back. We did everything we could possibly do in the confinement of the front seat. Urges to take our passion to the next climactic level forced our party to the back. The heat inside the truck was rising to steamy levels of pure pleasure. The backseat was quickly transformed into a brief moment of paradise, a paradise for prisoners in a world where sin and skin often made beautiful music together.

From some unknown chamber in my mind, Sister Lawson's disclosure of the absence of panties was unlocked and replayed. She straddled me. I unhooked and opened her coat. A rush of body heat escaped, mixing in with mine. She was right. She didn't have on any panties. My finger moving freely inside that hot area was confirmation. Sister Lawson had lifted her skirt before taking a seat on my lap. She grinded her hips, her hot, moist tavern of love closing in around my flip-the-bird finger, letting me know that the littlest things about me drove her crazy. Her eyes had taken on a sensual lazy appearance. Her every moan professed her appreciation for my attentiveness.

With my free hand, I unbuttoned the top four buttons for her blouse. She had a bra full of Victoria's Secrets. The woman had cleavage that I could never get tired of looking at. Breasts that hung like small melons, beckoning for me to taste their sweetness. Gently, but softly, I freed them from their C-cup restraints. Her skin was on fire. My breathing picked up as I gently took one of those melons in my mouth by the nipple. Her right hand unbuckled my belt, zipped me down, went in and grabbed my stiff rod.

Sister Lawson's hair flowed around her shoulders, turning me on as if I were a light switch. We were treading in tabooed-alleys, forbidden valleys of unbridled passion. We were wrong. Dead wrong.

I looked out the windows at all the trees, their branches drooping under the weight of snow. I called myself slick, trying to convince myself that I had picked this secluded spot, hiding from man's law. But eyes were still watching our late-evening acts of adultery. Those were the eyes I should've been worried about. The law that should've scared me as though I were an injured doe locked inside the carnivorous gaze of stalking, hungry, salivating predators.

Be not afraid of those who could kill the body, but him who could kill the spirit.

In all the excitement of my new truck, I'd forgotten to stop and pick up condoms. But that minute detail was lost in a blur of passion, pleasure, and a hefty appetite for pleasurable pain. I was doing what I said I wouldn't do. My pants down around my ankles, I buried myself deep into Sister Lawson without anything between us except skin and sin. The steamy penetration caused my toes to curl. And for the next few moments, I watched her rhythmically slide up and down on Viagra's creation.

All at once, the wind picked up, howling and blowing the truck as if we were about to be carted off into the air and discarded as trash amongst the rubbish. The more Sister Lawson moaned, the more the wind howled. Howling to the point of me distinguishing the disapproving voice of the Maker. The snow was coming down even heavier now as if God was crying snowflakes of tears.

Sister Lawson powerfully climaxed, dropping her head to my shoulder, but not before I reached my pleasure as well.

"Did you like that, Pastor?" the sister said with an anxious look for my approval on her face, her labored breath slowing.

"You know I did. I always appreciate the good times

we share." I could hear my phone vibrating in the back-seat. Not the long vibrations from new messages, but short and angry ones from the same caller. I knew it was my wife. I was living my life in the basement, a floor underneath from where God had given me to dwell.

"You know I have to go," I said, feeling all her weight on top of me, listening to the rise and fall of her chest, hoping God would forgive me one more time.

"I hate being your secret lover, but I understand. I understand that I have to share you with the rest of your congregation, including your wife." She moved from my lap as if her mentioning my wife gave her instant attitude. Sister Lawson, too, recognized the short vibrations of my cell phone. "I had a good time. Call me whenever you feel the urge." With those words, she opened the door and disappeared.

I stayed there for a little while, thinking about my broken covenant. I was feeling the heat from my past catching up to my present. Like bloodhounds sniffing, tracking down a dangerous fugitive. Spooky. It was if I could almost hear the dogs barking. Chomping at my heels. Could see the burning torches of the pursuing officers as they searched far and wide. The fire was so close; I could feel the heat on my backside. And that's when I had enough presence of mind to glance down, noticing that our wild bump and grind had activated the button for the climate control seats.

I pulled up my pants and retrieved my cell. I jumped

in the driver seat and pulled off. Tempest was heavy on my mind. Had to call her to see how she was doing.

She picked up on the third ring. She sounded heavily medicated, complaining about pain and stiffness in her neck. Asked me why was her brother so angry? Answers stuck in my throat. Probably because I was partially to blame. But before I could answer, she started to cry. She let me know that her childhood was an unhappy one. I hadn't called for this, but she felt compelled to unload on me. I asked did she need anything.

"No, Father," she told me. Before I could hang up, she said something that rocked me to the very fiber of my being. "I wish I was never born into this family," she cried, before bursting into more tears. The phone went dead shortly after.

I tried to tell myself that I wasn't a bad father. It wasn't my fault that my children couldn't adjust and lead normal adult lives. I wasn't to blame for the sickness that my wife was now enduring. I'd tried like hell to keep my family together. It wasn't my fault. It wasn't my fault.

For the first time in a long time, tears found their way to my eyes. I had to pull over a few times to wipe them away. The snow was letting up. God's snowflake tears were subsiding. After His tears stopped, mine were merely beginning.

With the four-wheel drive kicking Old Man Winter in the tailbone, it took me half the time getting home than it would've taken if I'd been in the STS.

I pulled up to my condo, wondering what twisted problems awaited on the opposite side of the door. From the snowstorm we had today, I was more than happy to be living inside of a condo community. Landscaping and snow removal were services that came with paying association fees. I was too old to be busting my balls or breaking my back shoveling snow. That was a young man's job. My snow had been neatly shoveled. Rock salt crunched beneath my shoes.

I opened the front door, hoping, praying that Wilma would cancel. I was bone-tired, and badly in need of sleep.

No dice!

Wilma was dressed, with what appeared to be an irritated look on her bloated face. I recognized the look all too well. She was pissed about something and I was way too tired for her nagging. I hadn't got five feet behind the door when she started in on me.

"Why did you not answer your phone, and why are you so damn late?" Wilma asked, her arms folded across her chest.

I set my briefcase down by the fireplace. "Well, hello to you, too." I was extremely exhausted. Short of patience. My fuse was way too short for this type of carrying on. I didn't want to say anything that would hurt her feelings.

"We missed our reservations. But it's a good thing the manager of the restaurant happens to be Dr. Peter's wife. I called her and had her hold them." Wilma's face seemed to swell in size every other day. So much swelling that she didn't look like the lady I'd married at all.

I looked at her with complete disdain. A part of my heart belonged to her, but I despised the other part that wanted her to hurry up and die. She was beginning to be too much of a burden. I was fed up with her verbal attacks. Taking out all her frustrations on me because I was the closet person around. I begged God for forgiveness, but Satan was having his way with my imagination. I could remember a program on Lifetime involving a woman who'd killed her terminally ill husband by poisoning. I questioned myself if I could be that ruthless. Wilma stood at death's doorstep. Seemed that the Reaper was taking too long in opening the door.

"We have to leave right now. Ruthie can't hold the reservations long. You know how crowded that restaurant can get." She was putting on her mink when I strolled into the bedroom. "Poppa, where are you going? Didn't you hear me say that she can't hold them too long?"

I had removed my topcoat and placed it on a chair in our bedroom. I was at the point of erupting. She was gonna have to wait. Her...and Ruthie! I wasn't going anywhere smelling like hot sex on a tropical beach. I heard her footsteps coming so I retreated to the bathroom and locked the door. I finished undressing there. Experience had taught me a valuable lesson. Years ago, I'd gotten undressed in front of her after having sex with another woman. Didn't expect her to smell my clothes, and inspect my underwear. My clothes carried the scent of a woman and my underwear yielded secrets of naughtiness. The woman tried to kill me.

She knocked on the door. "You are a deceitful bastard."

I said nothing as I slid out of my slacks.

"I've been faithful to you all through this marriage. Never once desired another man. But sooner or later, Reverend, you will have to answer to God!!"

Wilma got the point when the roar of the shower drowned out her unwanted conversation.

✪ ✪ ✪

We hadn't said much on our way to the restaurant. Other than the standard questions, we both concentrated on Yolanda Adams' spiritual voice. Wilma liked the new truck, but thought it to be way too much flash for a pastor.

The restaurant sat in the beautiful downtown area of Birmingham. A ritzy upscale community only privileged by the affluent. An area in which a half-million dollars was only enough to purchase a two-room, bungalow-style home.

I maneuvered the truck into the parking lot. A vehicle of this magnitude commanded the respect only valet parking could bring. The young black man in the red jacket helped Wilma from the truck, and through the fancy glass doors of the restaurant. He looked like he was more than happy to slide behind the wheel of the fabulous ESV. The restaurant was a classy ticket. The packed parking lot was proof.

As I strolled through the door, walking on plush red carpets, Sister Lawson was heavy on my mind. The lady had so much money and no husband to share it with. Now, I knew the love of money was the root of evil, but that was the kind of evil I would take my chances with. That woman would marry me in a heartbeat. All I had to do was divorce my wife. I prayed that the Lord would forgive me for mentally drawing up the divorce papers.

I stepped through the double doors, hating the stench of rich folks. All that money and no clue how to use it.

Ruthie seated us in a dining room where folks practiced outstanding table etiquette. I found it hard to believe that some of these folks could actually chew and swallow their food with their noses stuck so far up in the air.

Wilma's jaws were still tight as she scanned the very expensive menu.

"Are you getting the usual?" I asked, trying to break the ice. Right away, I realized that this was going to be a long night. She looked at me and frowned. I was left to my thoughts as I felt somebody tap me from behind.

"Hey, Pastor."

I turned to see Sister Walker's heavy made-up face. Sometimes the woman could wear so much makeup to a point of looking like a walking corpse. She surprised the hell out of me. After the death of her bread winner, I figured this to be the last spot she would frequent.

"Hi, First Lady." Sister Walker reached across the table to shake Wilma's hand. The hesitation Wilma showed before shaking hands was apparent to all. "How have you been feeling? On behalf of the congregation, I'd like to say we miss you dearly. We pray for your healthy return."

"Sister Walker," Wilma spoke up for the first time, "I'm sorry to hear about your husband. How have you been doing?"

Sister Walker was dressed as if going to church: big hat, a pretty dress and matching pumps. I was trying to be nosy; to see who she was with. We were the only black folks in the dining room.

"I've been trying to hold on to God's unchanging hand. My Wellington would want that."

"Amen, Sister Walker. God bless us all that worship Him." I saw a chance at getting into the somewhat stressed out conversation between the two.

The atmosphere had become real tense. Before Wilma had taken sick, she'd suspected Sister Walker and me. All the church gossip didn't make it any better. After a long, uncomfortable silence, Sister Walker wished us a delightful dinner. But not before putting her hand up to her ear as if it were a telephone receiver, silently mouthing for me to call her later. She thought she was slick with it. Thought that Wilma was too occupied by the menu. Nothing was further from the truth. My wife didn't miss a beat. She cut her eyes at the both of us.

As Sister Walker stepped away from our table, I was mesmerized by her bewitching backside. Her booty jiggled upon every impact of her sexy sashay. Her pumps pimped out her calves and her dress highlighted all of her seductive features. I thought my tongue was about to drop out of my mouth when she stepped to the table and sat down with a fat white man. Jealousy rose through my body unchecked. I had been trying to shake that broad, but I almost blew my top when the chubby-faced honky leaned over and kissed her jaw.

"Fuck is wrong with your eyes?" Wilma cussed.

"Say what?" I was startled. There hadn't been many times in my life that happened. I looked down on the floor, trying to maintain my composure. I glanced at her again, hoping whatever demon had jumped into her body was gone.

"I am sooo tired of you disrespecting me—yes, I cussed. What about it? Your back-sliding ass is enough to make somebody want to cut your black ass up and stick your trifling black ass in a garbage bag."

"What is your issue?" I asked, glancing around at some of the faces that were staring back at me. "Keep your voice down. You're drawing unwanted attention."

"Don't give me that shit now. Don't even play that holier-than-thou role. As far as I'm concerned, you love attention. You crave the attention of all those whores in your congregation."

This was the wrong place to get into it. Wilma had

people staring and chuckling at our drama-filled moment. I credited her momentary lapse in sanity to the different medications. She was never this mean. I'd never been so glad in my life to see the waiter approach the table.

"Can I take your drink order?" a rather tall black man asked in a deep, Barry White voice.

I examined the part of the menu that described the different drinks. "I'll have a glass of white wine, please."

"And for you, madam?"

"Nothing," she said rather nastily. Wilma mean-mugged the waiter as if all men were evil. Her coldness toward him frightened me to no end. Didn't she know that this man was in charge of our orders? Boogers weren't a part of my diet.

The waiter stepped away from the table, totally ignoring the bitterness in my wife's voice.

Wilma harshly stared at me, letting the look on her face serve as her voice. She popped her lips; the crows feet at the corners of her eyes strained by anger.

"Sometimes I lay awake at night wondering what it would be like to be dead." She cut her eyes over at Sister Walker. The fat man was whispering in her ear and she was giggling like a silly little schoolgirl. "It's a damn shame that I won't miss you. Instead, I welcome death. It would be better than the misery of a failing marriage. All because my own husband can't keep it in his pants."

"Wilma, this is the wrong place for this conversation and if—"

"Shut the hell up. It's my time to talk." The tone of her voice was blistering. It was as if the room stopped to hear what she had to say. The waiter set my drink and our dinner rolls down on the table. He hustled away, leaving me live on stage in front of all these rich mummies.

"Wilma, I think it's time to leave. You've embarrassed me, and yourself."

I stood up to grab my coat. That's when pain exploded across my forehead. My legs wobbled a bit until I gained my balance. I didn't know a dinner roll could be that damn hard. The bread bounced off my skull and landed on a table of a party of five.

"You will stand there and listen to me, Reverend Do-Wrong. Think about the embarrassment I put up with you over the years. Church members laughing behind my back. You don't even know how to be a father for our kids." She pointed in the direction of Sister Walker's table. "Sleeping with every tramp in your church that would hike her skirt. Jordan stole your Rolex. Big fuckin' deal. You deserved it. One of your tramps probably gave it to you anyway." She stood up to address the rest of the dining room. "People, I'm dying of kidney failure. But my husband, the Reverend here, ain't did a damn thing to make my last days easy. He can't keep his dick out of his congregation to assist his wife."

Our ruckus produced Ruthie. She was a short white woman, but you couldn't tell by talking to her. She had black mannerisms.

"Wilma…" Ruthie put her hands on my wife's shoulder. "Everything all right?"

Why did she have to ask my wife that? It seemed as if the question was a gesture to continue her tirade.

"H-E-L-L to the naw. I'm just getting started."

Drop dead, drop dead, I silently wished. I wanted to push her right out the door. But you didn't put your hands on a lady in Birmingham, Michigan. Didn't know how much more of this I could take.

"This pathetic excuse for a man can't even take me to my doctor's appointments. And you call yourself a Reverend. When it's all said and done, will your soul be going to heaven? Many are called but chosen are few. God called you to shepherd His sheep; not fuck His flock."

I was wondering when the Birmingham Police were gonna show up. They walked into the dining area; arrogant and cocky. Two white men with angry words of white supremacy in the form of police badges pinned to their chest. Wilma was barbecuing my character. It was the beginning of winter but her spring-cleaning was early. The officers looked like they were coming to establish law and order, but one wave from Ruthie stopped them dead in their tracks. I guess what they said about women sticking together was true. It came in a form of all these snobbish white women looking at me like they wanted to put my penis in a blender. I didn't know Ruthie had so much influence.

"Wilma, you're not so perfect. All of us have our

faults. Lashing out at me because God hasn't answered your prayers for a donor. This isn't the right way to do things. I thought you were better than this."

Another hard dinner roll flew through the air. This time I slapped it down with my hand. The thing splattered on the floor into hard breadcrumbs.

"How dare you? My daughter is a whore because of you. My youngest son is a crackhead because of you. And my oldest son is running around the streets with Satan because you weren't there for him. You're becoming the very thing the church could do without: a preacher who preaches for pussy."

Wilma had tears in her eyes. I stood in a room surrounded by misty-eyed women. Wilma had played on the sympathy of every woman there. From the way the two police officers looked, I thought I would be hauled away to jail.

I didn't miss the sneaky smirk on Sister Walker's beautiful face. She was enjoying the parade of skeletons marching out of my family's closet. I was frustrated, angry and embarrassed. I didn't know what to do. If I said anymore words, they would soon be followed up with punches. The little voice inside my head was screaming for vengeance. The man in me wouldn't let me go out like that.

"God will forgive you for your vicious, thoughtless, and cruel attacks on His servant," I said. While I had half an ounce of pride left, I walked through all the evil looks, right out of the double doors and to the valet. I paid the young man, got in my truck and left. Since Ruthie was her new best friend/counselor, she could also serve as her chauffeur and drive Wilma's black ass home.

As I drove through the dark and wet, wintery streets, I had three thoughts on my mind: hoping that this latest embarrassing chapter in my life didn't get back to my congregation, my inevitable divorce and the emergency deacon board meeting that would serve as the evil Deacon Slydale's last stand.

A DIRTY COP SCORNED

Jordan was heavy on Monique's mind. That was until she hit the crack pipe and inhaled. At that point, all her problems seemed to go up in smoke. Monique was in a crackhouse in the heart of the Cemetery. This was the only way she could get Jordan off her mind. Her boyfriend had gone into hiding after he'd lifted his father's Rolex. She could remember as clear as yesterday. Jordan had come knocking on the door of her apartment in the dead of morning. He showed her the watch and it was on from there. The all night pawnshop didn't want to give them jack for the watch at first, but after Jordan threatened to take his business to a rival competitor, the fat Arabic man caved in. They were in smoke heaven after that.

After they'd smoked up the watch, Jordan went into immediate seclusion. A part of Monique wanted to believe that her boyfriend was hiding from the guilt of all the crimes he'd committed for a taste of his little white god. Nothing was further from the truth. The real reason for his magical disappearance: Popeye had picked up his trail. Nothing was worse than a killer with a badge closing the distance.

As Monique took a deep, deep pull on the glass pipe, the last words she could remember her boyfriend saying were, "Hell has no fury like a dirty cop scorned."

The house she sat in was two windows and one door away from being condemned. A crackhead had no choice in where she smoked. Sure, she could've copped and smoked her goodies back at her own apartment but walking through the Cemetery with freshly purchased rocks in one's pocket was considered potentially hazardous. The Cemetery was no joke, and it wasn't even safe for crackheads.

She smoked until her senses were numb. The white clouds that appeared before her reminded her of the one plane ride she'd ever experienced. Monique had taken a trip with her auntie to Florida. Her auntie had politely given her niece the window seat. Monique wanted to be close to the clouds. Her auntie told her not to look directly into them. She warned that God's eyes were in the middle of all cloudbanks. Said that the penalty for staring would be total blindness.

Monique took one last hit and boldly stared into the middle of the cloudbank that had settled around her.

"Blind me." She sat her pipe on the floor. "Blind me... you bad." She threw her hands up over her head as if to intimidate the Maker. Monique continued throwing a fit, but what happened next was enough to sober up the most stoned-out smoker. The strong hands that reached through the fog bank pulled her to her feet. She had issued the challenge and now was left to taste the wrath. When the smoke cleared, what Monique thought were God's hands, in fact, belonged to Satan's stepchild. Popeye's hands were closing in around her throat. Screaming was useless because of the intense pressure he applied. Monique was forced to stare into the eyes of what could be the last person she would ever see in this world.

Her defensive action left claw marks and torn skin on both of Popeye's massive hands. Her eyes were evading their sockets as she desperately fought for air. She kicked and scratched until she was near death. Monique was a heartbeat away from hanging with the Reaper, but Popeye released her. She dropped to the floor, grabbing at her throat, gasping for air.

"Nobody takes me for a joke." He viciously stomped her ribs. "I told y'all that somebody was gonna pay."

Monique painfully got to her knees and got a dirty boot across the mouth for her efforts. What was left of her teeth from years of drug abuse lay in a pool of blood on the floor next to her body.

She looked up into the cop's bloodshot eyes, mumbling something that sounded like, "Why?"

"Now let's try this again," Popeye snarled, snatching her up again. "I'm looking for Jordan. I'm gonna beat on you all night until you get this shit right."

Monique foolishly spat blood on Popeye's boots. She

cracked a bloody smile. "Then I guess you're gonna have to kill me. Because I don't know where Jordan's at."

"Wrong answer." The punch that Monique received to her right temple made her oblivious to the rest of the cop's pulverizing brutality.

TEMPEST

"Oh my God!" I cried into the phone, tears blurring my vision. "I'll be right there." I had been in a painkiller-induced coma before I'd gotten the phone call around ten at night. The phone rang and I'd popped up from my bed in a paranoid, buck-eyed state, readying myself to blaze out whoever had the nerve to interrupt the best sleep that I'd had since my neck injury.

At first, I thought Wisdom had been playing when he informed me that Momma had been rushed to West General Hospital. But once I shook myself to complete consciousness, I noticed that there was no hint of laughter in my brother's voice. In fact, his voice was laced with terrifying urgency.

My husband was visiting family in Chicago and wasn't due back for another couple of days. I felt no need to call him. Instead, I got dressed, put on my neck brace and jetted out of the house, feeling helpless. My mother was all that I had. At that moment, a huge cloud of guilt shadowed the top of my truck as I made my way through the slush and snow. I wasn't the daughter that I was supposed to be. Probably wasn't the daughter that my mother dreamed of having. I silently prayed for her recovery. Sure, Dad and me didn't see eye to eye, but that was no reason to stay away from my mother's house.

I sloshed through the bad weather conditions like police didn't exist. I drove as if I had tunnel vision and my mother was at the end of it.

I was in deep thought when my cell broke the silence.

"Hey, Ma." Geechie's irritating voice vibrated through the receiver. I was so engulfed by the idea of loving my mother that I'd forgotten to check the caller ID before picking up. Not that I was hiding from Geechie's demanding, ruthless ass. I didn't have the strength, nor the patience to put up with his gangster shit. The truth of the matter was that I was beginning to succumb to my senses.

"Yes, Geechie?" I said his name as if it irritated my stomach lining.

"You a hard person to catch up with. I call you, but you don't answer my phone calls. Leaving messages. What's a brotha gotta do to get some conversation?" Geechie let his words sink in. He knew I was afraid of him and he often used that to dominate our conversations. "Do I gotta tell your husband that you don't call me no more?" He laughed harshly into the phone.

I was on the freeway now, halfway to the hospital. "Geechie, I don't have time for this. My mother's in the hospital."

He blew in the phone like the latter was of no concern to him. "Nigga, you better make time. And as far as yo' ol' girl is concerned, you gonna be lying next to her if you don't check your damn tone." Whenever Geechie thought I was being rebellious, threats would be his way of putting me back in place. "Listen, I got something that I want you to do."

"Geechie, I'm trying to make it to the hospital—"

"How would you like to spend some time in critical care?"

I said nothing. I tell you one thing; my arm was getting tired from holding the phone and trying to drive with the other. In my crazy rush to leave, I'd forgotten my Bluetooth that I usually used so that I wouldn't receive a big, fat ticket.

"Why is it that you can't do what I ask?"

I was now riding the off ramp.

"Is it about co-signing—"

"Naw, naw it ain't about that. I got one of my babies' mommas to do that fo' me. Besides, for what I got in mind, I can't use no tramps with police records. I need a nice, clean girl." He paused for a minute, and then said, "Listen to me, and listen good: I was trying to be nice about that co-signing shit. But I'm telling you now, if you don't do what I tell you, not only am I gonna tell yo' old man about us, but I'ma go up to yo' fancy shop and beat the living shit out of that chump you call a husband."

I tried to swallow but my throat seemed to close up,

not allowing saliva the access to the land down under. What had I gotten myself into? Sooner or later, if you slept with the devil too long, you'd eventually get burned— a burning no mortal medicine could cure. Not only was this young punk threatening my marriage, but he'd also threatened to do bodily harm to my sweet and innocent husband.

"The cat got your tongue, Ma? I need you to make a prison run."

Tears welled up in my eyes. "What is a…prison run?"

He was either coldly laughing at my stupidity or getting a major kick out of the fear in my voice. "Fuck, Ma, you ain't stupid. Don't pull that innocent crap with me. My regular girl, Rosie, got popped last week for trafficking over state lines. So I need you to stand in until I find a new broad."

I pulled over to the side of the road. Selfishness was the mindset that had possessed me. I feared for my safety more so than trying to make it to the hospital. I sat there balling at the curve to the entrance of West General Hospital. I should've been rushing into emergency, but the thought of me going to jail was enough to freeze up my actions.

"Ma, say something." I could hear Geechie smiling through the phone. "I need you to come see me. Tomorrow we can kick it about your new gig, Ms. Big Time hair shop owner. And by the way…buy yo' old girl some flowers and a card from me." He hung the phone up in my face, leaving my tears and fears to get better acquainted.

I finally gathered up enough courage to shelve my selfishness and put my mother's health before all. I couldn't believe that Geechie had the balls to even consider me for his petty prison drug run. I had seen plenty of girls locked away behind that mess.

I drove into the parking lot, parking in the spot designated for visitors. My vanity mirror cast a brutal reflection. The woman in the mirror looked lifeless, drained of any energy that could be used to pull her life out of the dark dungeon of negativity and back into the positive light of prosperity. My promiscuous appetite for fleshly thug was jeopardizing the lavish life that I had worked so hard to obtain. The tired, red eyes could be fixed with drops of Visine. The sad tired bags underneath could only be fixed by a complete life makeover.

Somehow, I was determined to rid myself of Satan's son. Geechie didn't know it, but his control over me was weakening. After a few Visine drops, I was out the truck and making my way through the frigid temperatures, headed toward the emergency room entrance.

Momma was in room seven. My knowledge of the Bible was about as short as my appetite for feces. I didn't know much. And being the preacher's daughter, one would think that I should've had it memorized from cover to cover. I did know that there was something sacred about the number seven. Staring at the number of Momma's room had to be a sign that she would be all right.

When I stepped into her room, my faith wasn't as strong as I thought. Different tubes ran out of her body. IV drips hung overhead. Machinery was everywhere. Some beeped, others monitored, and the rest I had absolutely no idea of their function.

Tunnel vision was back once again. Momma lay at the end of the tunnel with her eyes closed, surrounded by what appeared to be robots and looking like a pincushion. My weak achievement at strength dissolved into a landslide of tears, snot and chest heaving.

How could it come to this? My mother had followed almost all God's rules. She'd been a good Christian woman. Was this her reward? Why must the good suffer? It seemed that I should be lying there in her place. I had broken all the rules. Badly crapping all over His covenant.

My legs decided to rebel against me, breaking me down on one knee, blubbering as if they were closing the lid of Momma's casket.

Momma didn't deserve my weakness. It didn't matter how loud I cried. She never opened her eyes to acknowledge my presence. I flinched a little as a strong pair of hands pulled me back vertical.

"Sis," Wisdom tenderly said, embracing me as if I were a little girl, "Momma needs you to be strong. That means you can't break down in here."

Through tear-filled eyes, I watched a nurse come in

to check IV levels. She tinkered with a few of the machines and fluffed Momma's pillows. The middle-aged black woman offered the two of us an encouraging smile filled with loads of compassion.

"You her children?" the heavy-set, fudge-chocolate complexion woman asked.

We both answered, "yes," in unison.

"Is my mother gonna be all right?" I mustered up enough courage to ask, but didn't know if I had enough strength to deal with the answer.

The lady pulled out a tiny cross that was affixed to a thin chain inside her scrubs, glowing with a divine shine. I'd seen this shine many times before. Could remember those days when I was a little girl growing up in the back hills of Yazoo County, Mississippi. Had grown up amongst tons of old spiritual women. Women who listed God as their first priority—opposed to the convenience of some of these modern-day women. You know the type: 'The break glass in case of emergency' generation. She held the little-tiny crucifix between her thumb and index finger.

"Do you folks believe in Jesus?" Her smile seemed to brighten at her mentioning of the Savior.

My brother and I looked at each other, studying eyes for answers. Not just answers to patronize, but heart-felt, soulful answers. We had been through a lot. Our old man had been the culprit to somewhat remove our faith in Jesus Christ.

The nurse seemed to take our hesitation as a chance

to continue. "Children, whatever the doctors deemed impossible—" she held the crucifix in full view, palming it—"God makes the impossible... possible." She smiled brightly. "I'm Nurse Halyberry if you people need anything." The nurse fussed over a few more machines before she walked out the room.

"Wis, what happened?"

My brother pinched the bridge of his nose. I had seen him do this many times before. The action meant that he was extremely angry. He bit his lip to suppress angry, hostile words.

"Your funky-ass father." He punched his right hand into his left fist. "Momma's friend, Ruthie, called me and told me that Daddy..." He bit down on his lip as if it hurt to call his father *Daddy*. "The Negro disrespected Momma and then walked out on her at the restaurant. Ruthie said she was taking Moms home when she had a heart attack. She rushed her here and called me." He paced around the room, only stopping briefly to look at Momma. Wisdom had murder in his eyes.

A sharp movement resulted in an even sharper pain in my neck. I grabbed for the uncomfortable neck brace. "Where's the good Reverend at now?"

My brother stopped sharply, looking like hell was coming with him. "If I knew, I'd be in jail for manslaughter."

The pain inside the neck brace was becoming too much for me to deal with. So I had Wisdom drag a chair to Momma's bedside. I sat down and swallowed a couple of painkillers without water.

"Yeah, getting yourself locked up will do Momma a world of good."

"Momma's kidney is failing. The doctor told me that without a transplant she might not make it. Said that the toxins were ravaging her body."

I stifled an emotional outburst. At that moment, I promised to be there for my mother if she lived. Promised to spend time with her and do those things that mothers and daughters do.

"Have you gotten in touch"—I touched my neck brace gingerly— "with Yazoo?" Touching the neck brace ignited painful memories of me hitting the floor after being manhandled by Yazoo. Even though I despised what my older brother stood for, he still had the right to know about his mother's condition.

Wisdom whispered as if Momma could hear. "We don't need his shit down here. Especially after how that idiot performed at the family meeting."

"But—"

"The boy is hateful, disrespectful and just don't give a damn about anybody but Yazoo. So until we find out what's going on here, *that* nut is not to be contacted."

"Yazoo is still blaming you and Jordan for the death of his father. I have a psychiatrist friend that comes into the shop to get her hair done. After Yazoo nutted up at the meeting, I asked Dr. Morgan about Yazoo's state of mind. I told her about what happened to y'all on the lake that day."

Momma's right arm twitched. Didn't know if that was bad or good. I watched her eyes, praying that they would open. No such luck. Guess God was still busy. He never answered me anyway.

"Can't believe that he still holds me personally responsible for his father—my stepfather. Yazoo ripped me for not making an effort to lend him a hand at saving Jordan. The Negro even had the nerve to go so far as to call me a murderer. He'd flipped out on me when the sheriff divers recovered the body."

The pain in Wisdom's eyes was intense. It was as if he was reliving the whole ordeal again. He blinked back the water that was trying to betray his manhood. I wanted to run to my brother and hug all of his demons away, but my own demons were locked around my ankles as if they were balls and chains. I couldn't move out of the chair.

"How did all of this happen?" I asked as I watched Momma's life bleep across the monitor. Wisdom turned from Momma's bed, his eyebrows questioning my intent. "How did our family become so far apart?"

"Our bastard of a father. You know, I used to blame God for choosing Pop to preach. But the more I grew into my name, I started to understand that it wasn't God's fault. It was Pop's choices. He chose whores over his family."

There was so much hurt in Wisdom's face. So much pain his words. But my big brother was thoroughly skilled at handling his emotions. In a world where the father was supposed to be the backbone of his family, Wisdom filled those shoes for our family. It was his job to stage a good front. He wasn't allowed to show weakness. And that's why he was so damned angry at my father because he didn't have much of a childhood.

"I look at other families and I see how much fun they have together. Staging different family functions. Picnics, trips to theme parks. Not forgetting holidays."

I almost broke down.

"Life is short. God forbid, but if Momma dies, she'll go to her grave knowing that her family was far apart and hating each other." Wisdom looked toward the door as if someone had just come in. "We need to fix this. Sis, we need to get our family back together. Somehow, some way, we need to rediscover the love in this family." With that said, my brother knelt on one knee and surprised me with the most loving embrace a little sister could ask for. I couldn't remember the last time that we held each other. "Sis, I'm sorry for not being there for you in the past. And I wanted to say what little differences we have, I would like to put them behind us." He looked deep into my eyes. "Please?"

I was totally speechless. It was like a heavy boulder gently lifting from my shoulders. For years, our direct lines to each other's hearts had been temporarily disconnected. The power of one word had put us back on line. Restored services.

With the tears in my eyes, and neck full of pain, I hugged my brother so hard that I could feel his heart beating through our winter jackets. "I'm sorry, too. Wisdom, I love you and I need you in my life."

Wisdom sniffled a little. "For Momma. We have to do this for Momma."

This was the start; one down and three more lines to reestablish. Three more hearts that needed to be put back online.

"Have you talked to Jordan?" he asked, standing back vertical, briskly favoring his right knee.

"I haven't heard from him since that night. Wisdom, there are a lot of hearts that need mending, a lot of closets that need cleaning, and a whole lot of ghosts that need to be laid to rest." I scratched my nose. "Jordan needs to get himself together before it's too late."

"You know the night of the family meeting the boy stole the reverend's Rolex."

"Right; wonder what he got for it?"

"Probably not nearly what it was worth. But he didn't care. Just as long as he could smoke. The pawnshop man probably busted a rib laughing after he left." Laughter was just what the doctor ordered. My brother always had an incredible sense of humor. Always knew how to make me laugh. And right now, I could use some humor in my life.

Wisdom sat a chair next to mine. The ice had been

broken and I could feel our sibling bond trying to repair itself. This was the first time in a long time that I felt safe. This was how a woman was supposed to feel. Wisdom was big and strong and if any dangerous dragon presented itself, Wisdom would serve as my brave knight, chopping off the beast's head. We sat and talked awhile, totally unfamiliar with each other's adult life. Our tragic past played as the only common denominator, delivering us as orphans to the doorstep of the present. Childhood wasn't all bad. We did reflect on some funnybone-tickling moments.

"Remember the time when old man Wally's big German Shepherd chased you down the street and you ran out of your shoes trying to get away?" I joked, almost falling out of the chair laughing. Even the pain shooting through my neck had stopped to get in on the hilarious memory. "You jumped on that car and broke the windshield with your bare feet."

"Yeah, they were Yazoo's shoes and the good reverend's car," Wisdom replied, almost choking from laughter.

"You see, we did have *some* good times."

He removed his cell phone from the clip of his belt. Wisdom screwed up his face. Like he was irritated by the number that displayed on the caller ID. "I don't call me almost getting my ass chewed off and bare feet full of broken glass a good memory."

It wasn't until he cursed under his breath that I asked, "How's Malisa doing?"

His eyes pierced my soul. I could tell that it was the

same old shit but a different year. I didn't know his girlfriend too well, but what I did know was that she was a trifling, money-hungry, "looking for the next sucker" tramp. And to be quite honest, I really didn't think her polluted womb held my brother's baby. My brother could do better. I'd heard about Mrs. Thang from a few of the little stripper girls who came to the shop. They'd filled me in on her pole-swinging behind.

"She's doing all right." Wisdom had that look on his face that I usually got whenever Darrius was being worrisome, blowing up my cell phone.

"I can't wait until these last two months are up. Her pregnant ass is getting on my nerves."

"What are y'all having?"

"We didn't go get an ultrasound. Said she wanted to be surprised." He stared in utter frustration at the cell phone. "Hold on, Sis, let me take this." He stood up from the chair and walked out into the hallway. He didn't stray too far from the door.

I wasn't trying to eavesdrop but his fiery conversation could be heard in the parking lot. "Show me some damn respect. My Momma laying in emergency and your ass asking me when I'm coming home. Have some damn respect. I'll get there when I get there." He paused. I guess he was allowing the bitch to get her two cents in. Well, whatever homegirl said, ruffled his feathers. He cut loose with, "Call the damn child support people then." Wisdom was usually a cool customer. Almost nothing could push his buttons. Nothing but that little skank of a button-pusher named Malisa.

"You all right?" I asked, adjusting my neck brace to a comfortable position.

"Yeah, I'm cool. Some days I feel like making that girl come up missing."

My mother's right leg moved. Her heart rate quickened. The monitor sped up—my heart right along with it. But before I could get up and call the nurse, everything went back to normal.

"That's the main reason I won't marry her. The baby was a mistake anyway." He walked up to Momma's bed and tenderly stroked her cheek. "Enough about me. How's your marriage?"

I didn't tell him about Geechie. No matter how much I wanted to drop down and tell Wisdom about the trouble I'd gotten myself into with that punk of a thug, I couldn't cross that bridge. Didn't feel comfortable enough yet. No disrespect to my husband, but I needed the muscles of a maniac to get the monkey up off my back. I loved my husband, truly. Truly, I did. But Geechie would've had him for breakfast. He couldn't protect me. Try as I might, I couldn't bring myself to spill my soul to my brother. A part of me knew how he would react if I told him about the job Geechie had lined up for me. I thought about the fallout. The consequences. I didn't need a detective to figure out that Wisdom plus Geechie would equal out to blood, death and destruction.

Their tempers were identical. Wisdom would either kill Geechie and go to jail, or vice versa. The latter thought frightened me. In either case, I would be compromising my brother's future. And I couldn't have that on my heart. So I was left to do battle with the devil by myself.

We talked for a little while longer when the doctor came in and told us that he was going to admit Momma. Said that they were getting her room ready now. Wisdom and I looked on as the little Asian doctor checked Momma's vitals and scribbled something on her chart. He excused himself, and then left.

Wisdom grabbed his cell phone like he was getting ready to pull whoever the idiot was ringing his bell through the phone and kick some ass. And judging from the sour expression boyfriend sported, I could tell that ass belonged to his soon-to-be, demonic baby momma.

The heifer.

I was looking forward to meeting the tramp. What was my brother thinking? A defective condom, my ass. I was in no position to judge, but Wisdom deserved way more than that stank broad. It wasn't like he had a gold-mine of a nine-to-five. On one of our brief conversations, Momma told me that Wisdom was one paycheck away from begging for spare change and digging around inside garbage cans for a feed.

Wisdom's cell phone rang again. He pinched the bridge of his nose and let out an exasperated sigh. Wisdom had that 'I'm gonna smash this cell phone into itty-bitty pieces' look in his eyes.

"Sis, can you hold down the fort while I take this damn girl some food?"

"That's no problem," I said, trying to offer him an encouraging smile. I looked into his eyes and didn't like what I saw. Pain and frustration were both present. "Big Brother, I hope you're taking care of yourself. You seem to be under a lot of stress. You know high blood pressure runs in our family. Have you had yours tested?"

"I'm straight." He glanced at Momma again. Then he stared my way. I could tell he was deep in thought. Troubled. "Sis, if you had a chance to save Momma's life would you do it?"

He was beginning to frighten me. His perplexed look. The question. "What are you talking about? Yes, if I was the perfect match. I wouldn't waste a second."

He looked down at the ground and smiled foolishly. I knew my brother all too well. He was about to do something stupid.

"That's not what I'm talking about." He leaned in and kissed Momma on the cheek. It seemed as if Momma could sense his touch. Her heart monitor sped up. After telling her how much he loved her, he said, "Sis, walk me out."

We walked and talked. There were stretchers lined against both walls with sick folks. It seemed like every one of these people had picked the same night to get sick. But sick folks weren't the only people in ER. Of course, you had the people who were served up by random urban violence: your gunshot victims, bludgeoning victims and, of course, your stab victims. Everybody was there.

Wisdom was carrying on about how much he wanted a son, and in mid-sentence, he stopped. His eyes grew bigger than dinner plates. His mouth hung open and his breathing was erratic. I thought that he was having an asthma attack. That was until he pointed to the gurney that had supported what resembled a human body. I took a look at the battered figure in front of me, almost tossing my dinner.

WISDOM

"**D**amn," was all I could say without bringing attention to myself and losing precious cool points in front of a group of young women wearing next to nothing, talking amongst each other, standing in front of Ward 3. They were so engulfed in their conversation, I guess they didn't happen to see the badly mangled carcass that had been rolled through the double doors and parked next to the wall.

My eyes were transfixed on the slightly conscious body, trying to determine gender. The chipped-up nail polish on the crusty, rusty fingernails confirmed to me that the body was indeed a woman.

The more I took in the sight of bruises, cuts, bumps and lumps, I wondered had they gotten the license number of the damn truck that did some number on her. Her left eye was swollen shut and her lips were the size of Polish sausages. But what really turned my stomach and made my toes curl in my shoes was her forehead. It didn't look real. Swollen beyond belief. Someone had done a number on girlfriend and had probably left her for dead.

With all this going on, I forgot that my little sister was standing next to me.

"Who could've been so pissed at that lady?" Sis asked, grabbing my arm as if she expected the perpetrators to bust through the doors and pick up where they'd left off.

I'll admit, the last time I had seen carnage like that was when Highnoon went upside poor Bobby Henry's head with a pool cue for cheating in a high-stakes game of Eight Ball.

"It's some real bad people out in the world," I said, noticing that my legs were frozen in a motionless stand-still. I couldn't move. It was as if my memory had imposed its will on my body, not allowing another step until I could remember where I had seen this pile of bludgeoned human hamburger that had been served up on an ER stretcher platter. My mind turned feverishly with notifying clicks of familiarity, but kept firing frus-trating memory blanks. It would've helped if I could make out what her face used to look like. But the agent of destruction had sinisterly contorted her mug so that her own mother wouldn't recognize her. She looked like a lost Picasso. On many visits to the museum, I could remember coming across a Picasso painting that illustrated an abstract view of a lady whose face looked like a jigsaw puzzle. Nothing on her face was in its natural state.

I took another strong look at the lady and figured whoever had done this had probably drawn inspiration from Picasso to create such a violent work of art.

"Wiz, you all right?" Tempest nudged me.

I was so spooked that nothing my sister said was registering. The battered body commanded full attention.

"Do you know her?" Tempest nudged me again.

In the city, a trip to the ER could be almost as hazardous as the circumstances that prompted the visit. Every bed was filled. I guess that's why the staff had left this poor lady lying against the wall as if she were an ancient artifact from an Egyptian exhibit on public display in a ritzy museum.

Whatever the reasons, I was compelled to have a closer look. I allowed my mind to go blank, searching the deepest, darkest chambers of my memory in a vain attempt at recognition. Tunnel vision took over as I neared my creepy destination. There was something in my mind that led me to believe that we had crossed paths. I couldn't put a finger on it.

As I probed harder, the haze of confusion brewing behind my eyes intensified. I was locked into a struggle with temporary Alzheimer's when I felt something cold and clammy grab my right hand. And for one bowel-loosening moment, I looked at my sister for help. Her face was stained by a terrifying confusion.

Tempest looked on as the battered woman tightened her grip around my hand, trying desperately to speak. I couldn't understand the words that were coming from her mouth. So with the only working finger on her right hand, she beckoned me closer. I wanted no part of this. For all I knew, this could be a deathbed confession.

I didn't want to be entrusted with the valuable information that could lead to her would-be killer. For all I knew, the madman could be watching us as I stood. I wanted no parts of what he put on her, but I couldn't let her pass from this world without telling her secrets to another human. With much hesitation, I leaned in to hear.

"JO...JOR..." She violently coughed up blood. "Jordan," she said in a whisper.

That's when her identity hit me like a ton of bricks. Monique!! Jordan's girlfriend. She didn't look like the same woman I'd seen when we were desperately shaking down the projects looking for Jordan.

It was as if time stood still, allowing this tragic play to spin to the end.

"JORDAN," she said a little stronger, tears flowing from her swollen eyes.

I looked at Tempest. She had her hands up to her mouth as if to suppress a frightening scream. I could tell that we shared the same thought.

As much as I wanted to believe that Jordan wasn't capable of this gruesome behavior, the story of him sticking up Popeye's mother and stealing her purse showed his savage nature. Especially when crack was a factor. Maybe Jordan and Monique had come to blows in a violent crack brawl and I was now looking at the loser.

I swallowed my fear, asking, "Who did this?"

"Jordan? He couldn't have done—" I quickly waved

Tempest's words off because Monique had summoned up enough strength to speak again.

Her chest rapidly heaved, then fell. Her one good eye widened with the fear of one seeing a ghost. I thought she was about to flat line. Knew it sounded selfish, but I was praying like mad that she gave a name other than Jordan's before checking out.

"Pop—" She took three quick breaths. "POPEYE!!!!!" she yelled with all the breath left in her cracked-out lungs. Her dramatic confession was so loud that doctors came running from everywhere.

The action was fast and swift. Monique was coughing a wet, hacking cough. Almost like she was going to cough up a lung. The trauma team rushed her off down the hall. Even after she was out of my sight, I could still hear the Grim Reaper resonating from every cough.

Tempest and I stood dumbfounded. I was totally caught off guard. With all the drama going on in my life, I had totally forgotten about the Cro-Magnon-looking cop named Popeye. But I could see that he hadn't forgotten about what my brother had done to his mother.

"Wis, what the hell is a Popeye?" Tempest asked, a look of fear touching her pretty face.

I watched the hallway go back to business as usual. Like nothing had ever happened.

"I guess Momma didn't tell you that your sweet baby brother robbed an old lady, who just so happens to be the mother of a heartless narcotics cop named Popeye."

"And?"

"Sis, I don't think you understand the severity of this situation," I said, my body language reflecting the seriousness of my statement.

"Wiz, you're scaring me."

I pointed toward the direction that Monique had been rushed off in.

"What's left of that lady is Jordan's girlfriend. Somehow, Popeye found out that Jordan was responsible for his mother's robbery and now he's shaking down the city looking for Jordan for payback.

"He caught me coming out my house one day. The cop told me in so many words that Pops was gonna preach Jordan's eulogy."

"Where's Jordan at now?" Tempest was adjusting her neck brace. I could tell she was in pain. The eyes never lie.

"I don't know, but I've had enough of chasing his black ass around the city. I rescued him one time. I have my own problems. I'm not a babysitter. Especially to a Negro that don't want help." My knee was screaming bloody murder and I was bone-tired.

"What are you saying?" Tempest asked, slightly raising her voice while holding her neck brace as if it hurt to talk. "Jordan is in grave danger. It's obvious that Popeye was sending a violent message of promise by mangling that poor girl."

"I don't think that was a message. It was more like a

violent, prophetic singing telegram." I tried to down-play the seriousness of the situation with a sneaky smile.

"I don't think that shit is funny. We already have Momma down here. We don't need her baby son lying beside her."

I threw up my hands, pinching the bridge of my nose. "What the hell do you want me to do? I got my own problems, Sis."

Tempest gave me a look that just about summed up her state of mind.

"Wisdom Jones, you are a selfish bastard."

"I just might be, but right now, I have to go and satisfy the hunger of a woman that threatens me with child support every time I scratch my nuts the wrong way."

I guess Tempest had heard enough; she wheeled around on her heels, headed back to Momma's room without another word. My sister had coldly dismissed me with the turn of her back.

I limped out into the snowstorm, the weight of the world on my shoulders, increasing by the ton, the proposition taking priority over the rest. Momma was growing sicker, and I was running out of time.

YAZOO

To some, revenge is the sweetest dish best served cold. But for me, I didn't give a flying frog's ass about the temperature of the dish. I was hungry enough to wolf down a huge, heaping helping from the four basic food groups of redemption.

I was trudging through knee-deep snow in the roughest alleys of Detroit's Eastside. Old Man Winter was putting his signature stamp on one of the coldest nights we'd had in a long while.

I loved the night. Secrets flowed from every crack and crevice. Mysteries ran amuck, and haunting memories played out in dreams like old black and white Hitchcock films. With every stride, memory fueled my dark and twisted ambitions. If I remembered correctly, it was Geechie who drew first blood—him and his soon-to-be-living-a-short-ass-life cocky Pit Bull.

The cold winds blew as my mind re-created the chilling scenes of the vicious dog attack. Geechie's sneaky smirk as the lights went on in the basement that night.

Geechie and his goon thought it was real funny to set

me up and watch me get mauled. Then he had the damned stones to tell me to forget about it as if he were some Italian mobster.

Forget, hell!

I vowed right then and there, I would never do such thing. An elephant never forgot, and neither did a hungry nigga starved for a slice of revenge.

The first phase of my plan had been—and was still going to be—putting a sizeable dent in Geechie's Gucci wallet, but the second phase of my brilliant planning would introduce some real heartache into his treacherous life. I was about to take the rattle right out the baby's mouth.

A few backyards ahead, I could hear the furious barking of a canine. The harsh weather was not fit for man or beast. Either the mutt was barking angry, disapproving curse words at his owner for animal cruelty, or he could sense my presence and was letting me know that I wasn't welcome in his domain. Whatever the reasons, I braved on. I had a mission to complete. I was determined to let nothing stand in my way.

As I finally reached my destination, the funniest thought in the world crossed my mind. I was doing everything in my power to not let the dog's savage bark drown out thoughts of my sister's unconscious body, lying silently on the floor after I'd put her lights out. And for dessert, I did a little tap dance on my stepfather's skull for his interfering in my business. Hell, it was almost worth going to jail; posting a thousand dollars for bail. Thanks to Geechie's lack of security, I had money hanging out the anus. I paid the "G" and harshly laughed in the faces of all wearing blue uniforms.

I stopped at the gate and could no longer hear myself think. The damn mutt was showing his ass. What fool in his right mind would tie a dog to a fence using a heavy industrial chain in this God-forsaken weather? I hadn't asked that question more than two seconds when a light went on in the basement window, facing the alley. I knew this room, the weight room. I'd studied the habits of the occupants. Knew them like clockwork.

The dog was barking so loud, I thought it would soon raise the suspicions of the creep probably pumping iron or some nosy neighbor. But the neighbors knew that nighttime belonged to the underworld of crime and murder. So, they basically stayed to themselves. Anything else constituted a homicide.

I was directly in front of the dog now. The only things separating us were the chain and fence. For his size, the little sucka was Hercules-strong. Every time he lunged at me, the fence looked ready to give away, but the short length of the chain would act as a bungee cord, snatching the demon dog back before he could get to the fence. The snow was surprisingly shallow where the dog was tied up. He jumped at me again, barking ridiculously loud, cold smoke escaping each bark. The chain stopped, jolting the mutt, almost strangling him dead. I could see that this dog had murder tattooed in his cold, black heart. To have his canines embedded deeply into my throat like a nice, juicy steak for being a good boy had to be the fantasy playing over and over inside his twisted mind.

The snow was falling in huge flakes as if the angels in heaven were engaging in play pillow fights. Visibility was zero, but I could see the dog struggling against the chain, standing on his hind legs, barking like he could actually do me harm.

Regardless of how much the dog barked, Flash, Geechie's bodyguard, was not gonna break away from his workout to attend to a damn dog. Truthfully, he hated that dog and resented every time Geechie would leave the mutt over in his backyard. Geechie was out of town, and his dog was at my mercy. The evil little bastard snarled, showing his canines as he tried like hell to break the restraints.

One last survey of the surrounding houses yielded nobody. Nothing but snow-topped roofs and dark windows eyed back. So, without further adieu and shit, I removed a brown paper bag from the inside of my jacket. Figured I'd had enough foreplay.

"Yeah, you remember me, boy." I fumbled with the bag. "Don't you?"

My toes were going numb, due largely to the mound of snow in which I stood. The succulent T-bone steak I removed from the bag was a full high-grade, prime-cut Angus quality. I had bought one for myself and let a little hood-rat named Brenda prepare it, while I got this one ready for my friend here. And as Brenda served food butt naked, I'd made a few phone calls until I finally tracked down Geechie's prized possession. Needless to say, I'd dished out a lot of loot for my friend to enjoy this. Hoped he like it.

Lately, it seemed like nothing I did could satisfy my soul and release it from the hatred I had for the Man in the clouds, the Being that was responsible for not saving my father. I'd gotten to the point of not even mentioning His name. But that was a horse of another color.

A chilled gust of wind floated the steak's aroma, somewhat knocking the fight out of the little demon dog. Guess he was ready to be my friend now. Could tell by the friendly wagging of his tail. In some strange, twisted way, dogs sometimes resembled people. They didn't want to deal with you—unless you come bearing gifts. And I had the perfect peace offering.

"Here, boy," I said, tossing the meat over the fence. "Chew on that, you bastard." The little punk didn't waste any time sinking his choppers into my offering. I was shivering cold, and I was losing feeling in my left foot. But nothing was worth more than seeing the dog that had attacked me finish off a steak that had been marinated in sulfuric acid.

The last bite of steak brought forth shaking, trembling, and oceans of bloody foam from the corners of its mouth. His insides were on fire. I amusedly stood watching the pure white snow turn an ugly crimson red. The dog violently shook and convulsed as he spewed blood from his mouth and ass.

I thought to myself, a night at the movies couldn't be

much better than this. The aroma of the dog's baked insides smelled like pigs roasting over an open fire. Popcorn was the only thing missing in this box office thriller.

The grand finale came as the mutt lay on his back—his legs still kicking—and his eyes rolled into the back of his head. His last sound in this world was a gruesome, throaty growl. It sounded like a car struggling to start in sub-zero temperatures. It was only fitting. That was the same growl I heard before the mutt had attacked me in the basement that night. Now that the appetizer had been served, the main dish would indeed be far more fulfilling.

Feeling somewhat satisfied, I pulled my cell from my jacket pocket, whispering, "Bring it on." In no time flat, the steak-cooking hood rat appeared at the end of the alley, driving my brand-new, wine-colored Yukon.

While the acid finished devouring the mutt's insides, I stepped away, the chorus from one of DMX's rap songs blaring loudly in my head. *One more bridge to cross, one more risk to take.* X was right. I had one more road to cross and one more nigga to break. My bloodlust had been appeased—for now.

Just before I stepped behind the wheel, I definitely looked toward the Heavens and gave it the finger of disrespect. He was looking. He always looked. The only time when He wasn't paying any attention was when my father was drowning. Heaven's blinds had been closed that day, a big-fat "gone to lunch" sign stuck inside the window.

"You're not the only one who can take life," I said, still looking up as the snow descended.

"Zoo," my little hood-rat spoke up, "you say something?"

"Mind yo' damn business!" I screamed.

I slipped behind the wheel and pulled off, my mind working on a way at properly disposing of my big bad bully boy brother. I couldn't and wouldn't lie to myself. I'd gotten it handed to me at the family meeting. One on one, hand to hand, I couldn't do nothing with Wisdom. But money talked. Where I couldn't do nothing with that big fool, I knew a guy that was larger than Wisdom and just as mean. The nigga would take out a whole ZIP code of folks for the type of cheese I was offering.

I looked over at the rat, letting my eyes roam all over her female goodies. My nickname for her was *Neck Down*. From the neck down, she was a dime-piece, but from the neck up, her grill looked like a sea donkey on crack.

I thrashed around in the snow, showing off for the rat in my new set of wheels. Life was good. And about to get better. Geechie was calling my cell phone. Somewhere in the Bahamas, he was calling me to check on things.

"What's the score, Zoo?" Geechie asked in his usual cocky tone.

This was my next bridge to cross, next risk to take. Geechie didn't know, but he soon would be reunited with his dog on an unbelievable walk through the public parks of eternity.

"Everything's everything," I answered. "Smooth as silk on this end. How's the sun tanning comin' along?"

"Never mind the small talk. I can't get in touch with Flash. Need you to go by there and check on my dog."

The anger in me wanted to relay to the punk that his dog had been checked and ready for a dirt-nap. In my mind, I was taking Geechie's measurements for his final resting place, too.

"Get by there as soon as I can." I was getting a little hot under the collar. Figured I'd better get off the phone before I blew my cool. Didn't want to let the dog guts out of the bag just yet. Setting up his houses to be robbed was a pretty lucrative business for me. He didn't have a clue. The brotha had gotten so paranoid that I'd seen him beat down a few of his workers because they looked like they were going to do something shady.

"Have you seen that Tempest chick around?" Geechie asked. His voice seemed to be a little rattled.

"Talkin' 'bout that broad with the ass that looks like a floatation device?" I said, playing along.

"You look at her ass one more time and I'll chop yo' ass up and feed you to my damn dog!" Geechie yelled.

"You done, boss?"

He let the disrespect he held for me play out as he hung the phone up in my face. If only he knew that the lady he was trying to check me over was my sister. I didn't give a damn about Tempest one way or another, but the sizzling disrespect the nigga had for me was starting to get under my skin.

As I made my way through the dark, snowy streets, visions of my empire played with fantasies of my life after I'd robbed Geechie blind, sending the creep on a one-way trip to where he'd sent all his victims.

"Zoo," my little hood-rat spoke again, "if I don't go to school tomorrow, I'll be kicked out."

"Oh, well," I answered rather harshly.

"I can't be held back in the ninth grade again," she whined.

I hated when she whined. Gave me the feeling that I was babysitting. This was one of my vices. I had a hard thing for teenage girls. Unlike their grown-up sisters, they didn't ask for much. A pair of gym shoes and an outfit was enough to keep me in triple X sex until they developed a brain. I wasn't stupid though. I understood the price for playing with underage freaks. But like they always say: no photos, no proof.

"Chill out, girl." I turned on to her street, pulling up to a somewhat condemned shack that served as the house that she shared with her cracked-out mother. "Go get your stuff."

She looked at me like I was a scolding parent. Before she jumped out, I grabbed her shoulder.

"Don't be long."

The little trick popped her lips and stepped out, leaving me to my thoughts. She was one of many but she was the only one who could stay at my crib overnight. I had

Brenda's mother in check. I wasn't a crack peddler, but I kept enough product on-hand to keep her mother high while I fed my fantasies.

Brenda came out with her overnight bag. We pulled off, headed for my new condo. I was living like a mega rap-star. The only thing stopping me from going triple platinum was the snake in the Bahamas. Numbered were his days. His own money would soon lead to his demise.

"Can we stop and get some Patrón?" she asked, her voice filled with pure adolescent mischief.

"Thought you had to go to school tomorrow?" I replied, stopping at a red light.

"Listen, I play better when I'm tipsy," she playfully teased.

I couldn't press down on the accelerator hard enough to get to the nearest liquor store. Who was I fooling? Everything I possessed, and all the sex I received on a daily basis, still wasn't enough to dull the pain of a life plagued by so much misery. The hole inside my soul was bottomless. No matter how hard I tried to fill it, it stretched deeper and wider. My life was spiraling out of control. A fast life always led to an even faster death. I didn't give a damn, though. Nobody lived forever. If death was the only way to deal with the pain of living, then I was determined to live my life in hyper-speed.

WISDOM

"Oh, yeah!" Malisa boasted from downstairs. "I'm 'bout to run a train of spades on you fools." At eight months' pregnant, Malisa's brainiac plans to turn our dining room into the MGM Grand Casino drew heat from me and our block club consisting of throwback mummies of a time so far gone you'd need a time machine to prove that their era actually existed. Most of the members couldn't get out to meetings due to physical limitations. So, once a week, the able-bodied members would bring the meeting to the homes of the not so fortunate.

Janet Cross was the president mummy of our block club. At seventy years of age, she was ornery, cranky and downright abhorred anybody under the age of fifty. She'd been quoted as saying, "Youth was wasted on the young." Her need to have a cause in her life was her only reason for living. Janet's new cause was to stop Malisa's weekly casino parties.

"If this was a real casino, you'd be dead by now," said a Barry White-sounding man.

"Damn that," somebody with a high-pitched voice responded, "cheatin' is cheatin'!" Keep your damn hands above the table or I'll blow you to kingdom come."

The room filled with drunken laughter. Sounded like it was gettin' real sporty downstairs and Malisa wasn't doing nothin' but laughing her pregnant ass off. Normally, I would be throwing schmucks out left and right. But Malisa's merry band of juiced-up misfits was the least of my worries.

"I told you," I spoke into the phone receiver, "I don't have the money. Without a payment plan, I can't pay you. That's just that."

"Well, sir, this is an attempt to collect a debt. That means we have full cooperation of the state to come after any taxable wage, income tax refund, etcetera." She paused. "Trust me, sir, it won't be pretty."

Karma. It was finally pulling into my station. My ghosts from the past had come back to wreak havoc on my present. Posey and Posey Law Firm was handling the account for Western Motors. My ex, Caliba, was long gone but her debt served as a sad reminder of a life I'd destroyed because of my own selfishness.

"We know where you work, sir," the lady said, her voice was low and threatening.

Glass shattered downstairs, followed by, "Watch yo'self, drunk fool! It's gonna be me and you if you knock over my beer." Another round of sick laughter rang out.

"Everything is so tight for me now. Five thousand

dollars is a lot of money. My girl's pregnant; she's not working. My baby's due any moment. I don't see how I can possibly squeak out a large amount to you monthly," I whispered into the receiver.

I guess you could say that I was getting my affairs in order. With my decision for Highnoon's proposal a few ticks away, I was trying to tie up loose ends. Who was I kidding? Who was going to give a damn one way or the other about a garnishment after I was dead?

From my bedroom, I could hear the front door open. Kirk's voice was very distinguishable. The Negro had a deep, James Earl Jones thing going. I didn't know who was the most irritating, the old hag on the phone who was trying to give me a one-way ride to the po' house, or Malisa's so-called cousin, Kirk.

Suddenly, I started thinking about things I shouldn't have. My imagination ran wild. The vision was something like a heartbreaking comedy. I could visualize a healthy baby being delivered. The doctor proudly hands my little bundle of joy. And to my horror, Kirk's grown-up face is on the baby's body...

"Sir, are you there?" the raspy voice snapped me back to reality. "What can you afford to pay?" I shook off the chilling thought of betrayal.

"Twenty bucks?" I said. The answer came out more like a question.

She coughed harshly. Almost like telling me to go file that answer under "G" for garbage. "Sir, at that rate, you'll be paying this account way into your Geritol years."

"Jokes, hunh?" My attitude was getting testy. Tolerance for nonsense was below zero. "Here's a joke for yo' ass; the twenty dollars I mentioned earlier?"

She bellowed out a funky sounding smoker's cough. Like she was trying to hack up a lung. "What about it?"

"When you kick from lung cancer, I'll take that twenty spot and buy you some funeral flowers, schmuck!"

She hacked again. "You better buy a headstone for your credit as well," she fired back before pulling the plug on our conversation.

I sat on the bed looking at the receiver in my hand like I could actually see my credit report stuffed in a casket in front of hundreds of other bad credit mourners. After my decision, my credit wasn't gonna be buried by itself. Once again, my tongue and temper had conspired to self-inflict nasty, suicidal lacerations of hopelessness on the wrist of my daily struggles.

I managed to pull it together, getting off the bed, hanging the phone up. Had been staring at the receiver so long until it started making the sound it makes when left off the hook. Didn't want to wallow around in self-pity.

The clock on the night stand told me it was time to go check on my mother. She'd been in the hospital for almost a week. The deadline for my decision was upon me, too. Highnoon would be expecting an answer any day now. The snake was probably reveling in the moment, drinking in all the arrogance that went with the title of King Snake. To put it truthfully, the schmuck thought he was God. My ol' girl wouldn't last too much longer without a donor. What would she think about her son trading his life for hers? No doubt, she would try to talk me out of it. Probably tell me that she'd lived a good part of her life. That I deserved a full life and all the pleasures that went along with it. But it wasn't up to her. Solely my choice.

"The crew is in the house." Juanita's unpleasant voice shook the foundation of the house. "Let's get this thing started."

Just what I needed. Gasoline on the fire. Juanita was Malisa's over-the-hill stripper friend. She ran with a band of stretch-marked baby makers from a strip club named Golden Oldies, a place that employed women who were way past their prime. Broads in denial who couldn't shed the limelight, glitter, money and pole for the traditional "paper or plastic," or "would you like fries to go with that" jobs.

I couldn't stand Juanita and she hated me with equal, unbridled passion. Her coming around made Malisa that much harder to deal with. The raggedy body broad with a polluted thong provided a power cloud of bad influences over my baby momma. Juanita was a thug in G-string. What the weave queen lacked in size, the broad made up for in manipulation. Besides all that, the girl was a full-fledged thief. Boosted everything from socks to furs. On a good day, her balls hung lower than mine.

My mind was lost in my problems when I walked over to my closet and pulled out a fresh pair of pants to throw on. That's when I realized that they weren't so fresh after all, but the same pair I'd had on the night I gave Paco and his boys a run for their money. The knife slash through the left leg—stained by dark splashes of blood—looked to be still fresh, like it were the latest fashion in a new line of urban apparel. I disgustedly shook my head thinking back to Malisa's lie. "I'm gonna sew up the leg and wash them so you could have another pair of work pants," she'd lied. Then had nerves like a lion to call me "Boo."

The trifling broad!

I quickly went through my pockets, thinking about how women like Malisa shorten the lifespan of guys like me. Didn't find any money, but what I did find was enough to baffle me until the well-awaited return of Jesus Christ. Maria, my little Mexican dessert, had managed to slip me her phone number. As strange as it sounded, the little flimsy napkin she'd written it on was my calm in the middle of a violent storm.

"I don't know how you expect to take care of a family if your check is garnished because of some freak from the past," my pregnant tornado blew into my thoughts, crapping all over my newfound peace. Better yet, Malisa was more like a money-hungry hurricane that destroyed every healthy pocket in her path.

"Ain't you supposed to be downstairs hosting your illegal gambling party?" I retorted, pocketing the napkin. Didn't want to provide her with any ammo that would entice her to show her tail. Her eyes were glazed over. I could tell she'd been drinking. Something that could harm the baby, causing certain types of physical and mental deformities.

"Lisa, you been drinking?"

"Nigga, you can't even handle your business like a man. You ain't even a real man. How the hell you gonna be somebody's daddy?" she asked, almost raising her voice.

"Don't let that baby come here screwed up—"

"Or what?" Malisa asked defiantly.

"Yeah, or what?" Juanita echoed, her arms folded across her implants standing right alongside of Malisa. Thank God I'd never seen Juanita's bare man-made boobies; they just looked and hung nasty through her shirt. I could distastefully imagine what they looked like in the raw. Like a partially blind Dr. Frankenstein had given her a boob job.

"Juanita, if you don't take your ugly titties back downstairs, I'ma put my foot so far up yo' ass, you'll have athlete's foot on your tonsils," I threatened.

I was trying to be subtle. Didn't want to raise the attention of the rest of the drunken idiots downstairs. I gave it to Juanita because she got on my last nerve. Rattled my usual calm demeanor. She didn't have a man of her own, but always felt an orgasmic need to dispense relationship advice to Malisa's dumb behind.

"No, you didn't threaten me, Boo?" Juanita replied, taking out her cell, attempting to make a call.

"Girl, don't pay that fool no mind. Because of him, I gotta throw these stupid card parties," Malisa said, putting her hand over Juanita's cell. "Somebody's gotta bring some real money into this house."

"One phone call is all it takes," Juanita boasted, holding her cell in plain view.

"You must have me confused," I said, grabbing my coat from a chair in the corner. "Make ya phone call. I hope it's to somebody other than those crackheads you always threatening people with."

By this time, Malisa was standing by the bed. Juanita was blocking the doorway as if daring me to move her.

"What's the problem up here?" Kirk asked. He had appeared behind Juanita, smoking a cigar. The nigga was fresh from head-to-toe—as usual.

"Better get her little dusty behind before I toss her out that window." I pointed to the bedroom window.

Kirk was a little tipsy. With one paw-swipe, he pie-faced Juanita's dusty butt from the door. Besides my own personal paranoia's of Kirk and Malisa, I always thought Juanita was his own private sex slave. As soon as I thought it, I wanted to slap myself—what a horrible visual.

"Get yo' tail from in front of the doorway, starting trouble," Kirk playfully said.

His blatant flirting with the over-the-hill pole swinger in denial was sour-stomach-sickening. Juanita's German

Shepherd obedience was a light bulb confirmation of their septic system taste for each other. Juanita went for bad, always. She never took hot-mouth crap from nobody. But here she was, obeying Kirk without a single smart comment.

"Wisdom," Kirk said, his hand out in front as a peaceful gesture, "don't mind her. You know how she gets when alcohol is involved."

It was now time for walking. With all the pressure and stress I had on my shoulders, I felt that I would snap and catch murder cases from here to eternity.

I shook Kirk's hand. "Don't worry. I don't."

Malisa looked to be receiving the most pleasure from this scene of madness. Seemed like when Kirk showed up, her taste for smart comments went south right along with Juanita's. Either Kirk was well-respected, or a P-I-M-P with game tighter than the Monopoly man's.

As I brushed past Juanita, her look presented dangerous daggers of death. She rolled her neck harder than any black woman I'd seen, and then had the nerve to turn her back.

"I hope they close that geriatric strip club down." I felt compelled to get the last word.

"Get yo' broke ass down those steps." Malisa played one more hand of disrespect.

"That's enough, Lisa," Kirk said. "Let Wisdom go in peace."

Lisa? When did this punk start calling her Lisa? Furthermore, who had licensed this schmuck to direct traffic in my house?

This was an issue opened for serious thought on my way down to see Momma. As I descended the stairs, I left Tweedle Dee, Tweedle Dum and Tweedle Pregnant Dummy standing in the hallway like they were about to pose for a group photo.

The disgusting scene in the living room was no better than upstairs. The place was a total mess. Bums were everywhere. This broad had card tables set up in the kitchen, dining and living room. Beer bottles cluttered the floors, cigarette butts laid alongside them, and somebody was smoking weed. Red flags flew through my head. Total disrespect lay in all four corners of the house. I did a quick walk through, trying to search out the schmuck who was giving me a contact high. The marijuana smoke was so strong, the cigarette smoke was probably getting high as well.

In the kitchen, I didn't find the marijuana-smoking maniac, but I did manage to stumble up on a smoke-black brother who was so drunk the nigga had mistaken my sink for the public toilet.

The moron even looked at me and had the nerve to snarl, "Wait your turn."

I politely waited until he was through before I opened my own little personal can of whup ass. As soon as he zipped, I flipped…his behind to the floor. The poor guy wasn't that big. I drug his intoxicated behind kicking and screaming through Malisa's mini-casino of fools. The people didn't know whether to help or run. My prominent size and Clint Eastwood-type stare were enough to thwart any type of heroic actions.

"You can have what's left in my wallet!" the poor guy yelled as I drug him through the house. The fool actually believed this was a robbery. "Please...just leave me alone!"

After his unbelievable journey of splinters and carpet burns, I opened the door and physically threw his drunken butt out. Upon Mister Piss-Freely's drunken behind striking the frosty ground, I inhaled a gander at the blatant disregard for private property. Now I fully understood what soiled old lady Cross's Depends and the rest of our Golden Years block club. Cars were parked everywhere. Every illegal way possible. In driveways that didn't belong to us. Some numbskulls were even parked on other people's lawns. Everyone was out looking at me like I was the parking lot attendant from hell.

I'd had enough. Removing the keys for the mail van, I deftly backed out of the crowded driveway and took off down the street, but not before receiving nasty glares from some of the irritated neighbors. They were looking at me as if my days were numbered.

How'd they know?

REVEREND POPPA JONES

I was in my study going over some church business when Sister Green stuck her pretty face in.

"Pastor, I have a package for you," she announced.

I popped a mint into my mouth. "You must've smelled my brains cooking in here and came to rescue me from meltdown." I smiled. "I sure can use a break."

Sister Green's perfume was simply intoxicating. The seductive fragrance spelled out adultery, fornication and any other carnal thoughts. I tried to focus intensely on the large envelope in her hand, but her black skirt was so tight, my eyes were seriously misbehaving.

"The package is pretty light," she said, shaking it. "Don't understand why the sender would use this size envelope."

"God only knows why people do some of the things they do."

"I know that's right, Pastor. I was talking to my girl-friend the other day about people and their motives for doing things." She handed the package over to me.

"Satan'll be Satan," was all I could say as I paid attention for the first time that I'd forgotten to straighten Wilma's picture back up. She had upset me so much that I couldn't stomach to look at her healthy face, smiling at me as if everything was peaches and cream. I'd turned the picture face down when I walked into my study after that restaurant foolishness. That was almost a week ago. I hadn't been home since. Hadn't talked to Wilma either. I was making all the worst choices for a man of my magnitude, but humanity allowed imperfections. Sometimes it's hard for pastors to keep their anger in check as well.

"How's the first lady feeling?" Sister Green asked. She was rightfully the most beautiful sister at the church, and a close runner-up to being the nosiest. That title was currently being held by Sister Long.

"One day at a time," I countered. I knew her nosy behind had seen the picture face down. My paranoia took over. Didn't know who knew about the verbal fireworks at the restaurant between Wilma and me. My imagination ran wild with different scenarios.

"A few of the ladies around here, along with myself, are gonna collect money to send our first lady a nice floral arrangement."

I was busy opening the envelope.

"That's good," I said, not really paying her any attention. "Sister Green, can I have some privacy, please?"

"Of course, Pastor," she obeyed, although she was moving in the slowest manner possible. She wasn't slick.

The sister was trying to stall for time. Her nosy nature wouldn't let her exit at normal speed. She wanted badly to see what was in the envelope.

After the door closed, I pulled out a small square case, packaged in bubble wrapping. I twirled the thing around for a moment, silently singing sweet hymns of victory. One thing was for sure, the deacon board was going to be a lot lighter after today's meeting.

My private phone rang. I picked up. "Pastor Jones speaking."

"Boo, are you coming home after the Deacon meeting?" Paula cooed in her best baby voice.

I removed the phone from my ear and walked to the door, cracked it as I peered out. The coast was clear.

"Paula," I spoke softly, "how many times have I told you not to call me here?"

"I know, Boo. But I just wanted to know. Was thinking about cooking your favorite dish."

"Smothered steak, mashed potatoes and mac and cheese?"

"Yes, Boo...and me wearing something so secret, even Victoria wouldn't have a clue." She laughed seductively.

"That all sounds good, but I don't know when."

"Aww, Boo," she pleaded.

"Cut that 'Boo' stuff out."

"Just my affection for you, Daddy."

I didn't know what was exciting me more, all her sexual gestures or the tell-all DVD sitting on my desk.

Let's just say I had wood stiffer than lead for both. But only one was worthy of my full and undivided attention right now.

"Keep my goodies warm for me until I get home, all right?"

"Okay, Daddy," she purred like a sex kitten, down for all my fantasies.

"Paula?"

"Daddy?"

"All my goodies, okay?"

She hung up, lustfully giggling.

After the public tongue-lashing I'd received from Wilma, the same night I'd gone back to the condo and packed up everything my new truck could carry. Without as much as one question, my new piece, Paula, took me in. I wasn't worried about anyone else snooping around. Paula lived inside of a gated community in the ritzy district of Orchard Lake. A place where winter and summer property taxes on a home could run as much as what some people gross in a year. I was wrong. Dead wrong! My life was so twisted, I couldn't do anything else. Figured God would straighten this mess out when He got tired.

I wondered how my wife was getting along in the hospital by herself. Wondered if she missed me yet. How long would it take her to come crawling back on her hands and knees? It was her fault anyway. If she never had gotten cute with me at the restaurant, none of this crap would've happened. I wouldn't have had to shack up with Paula.

The more I pondered, the angrier I became. Took a couple of deep breaths to slow my heart rate.

The private phone rang again. I picked it up, all set to go the hell off on Paula. "Didn't I tell you—"

"Tell me what?" my past spoke in a husky female voice.

This game had gone on long enough. Time to crap or get off the pot. "So I guess this phone call means you didn't have that little bastard yet?"

"My, my, my, preacher. Finally grown some balls?"

"Watch your mouth when you're calling the house of the Lord," I softly yelled.

"You didn't watch your dick, did you?" She snickered childishly. "Fucking hypocrite. You 'member, don't you, Pastor? I can 'member like yesterday. Yo' ass feeding dollars into my G-string in that hotel room. Me dancing—just like it was yesterday. You wouldn't stop tracking me down. Sending your deacon around to my job. The laying on of the hands. Who you thought you was foolin', hunh? Runnin' that preacher man hype. Talkin' 'bout you had to exercise the whorish demon out of me before I could become your wife. Can't believe I fell for that one—hook, line and sinker."

"God forgave me. Why can't you?" The clock informed me that it was time to extract a few evil weeds from my garden. "This game is over. Time to confront demons. Make things right," I confessed.

I wasn't prepared for the unsettling moment after my closet cleaning confession.

"No!" she shrieked in a tone that sounded monstrous. "You think I'ma let you take away my glory like that? You have to suffer just like me and my trifling-ass man. Be prepared to be cast into a lake of fire!"

The ensuing silence was louder than her deranged shouting. Sweat beads poured over my forehead. My ministry passed before my eyes. Losing the very thing I'd slaved for. I couldn't, I just couldn't let this evil witch take it all from me. Something had to be done. Didn't know what, but I had to do something quick. This Negro was asking for a ridiculous sum of money. Something like two hundred thousand. One confession to the newshounds would take my church and finish tearing my family apart.

I'd be ruined. Desperation bred drastic measures. This called for something totally out of my realm of reasoning. Chilled me to the bone just thinking about it. There was a light knock at the door.

"Pastor, the deacons are ready to start the meeting," Sister Green reminded me.

I didn't answer. Just sat there with the receiver still in my hand, staring stone-faced. She lightly tapped the door again.

"Pastor, you in there? You all right?"

"Yeah. Tell the gentlemen I'll be one or two minutes longer."

"Okay."

My hand had been forced. The queen had made her move, somewhat placing me in check. I absolutely abhorred what my next move would be. But whatever it was—however it turned out—my life would never be the same.

❂ ❂ ❂

Deacon Slydale's face wore a confident smile wider than the Detroit River. From the way he looked, you would think that the ugly Negro held my life between his chubby palms. But it was the other way around. His fate was sealed tighter than the envelope I was carrying. The sick smile continued as I made my way to the head of the conference table.

"Gentlemen," I greeted. Really, I was acknowledging everybody other than Slydale. He was a thing. Not even a real human, and in a moment—jobless.

All eyes came to rest on the huge envelope I set on the maple finish.

"Pastor," the men greeted in unison.

"If I may," I said, neglecting to take a seat, "I would like to address a serious issue that crossed my desk earlier this morning. The wicked behavior displayed by a few of us here today is in question." Brows arched curiously, while Deacon Slydale's cocky smile incinerated into a guilty expression of concern.

Nobody moved a muscle as I opened the package. Each man was stewing in his own world, trying to replay the last couple of weeks, praying like mad that he hadn't done anything that would land him in front of a hot spotlight and a barrage of embarrassing questions.

I took my sweet time opening the envelope. Toying with emotions. Savoring the power of knowing who the guilty parties were and watching them squirm under the tremendous pressure that exposure could bring.

"We have a few brethren in our mist who are in serious need of prayer, followed by reprimand," I began. Earlier that morning I'd had Deacon Clay to set up a TV/DVD. He'd wanted to ask why, but had thought better of it. The Deacon knew if I didn't say anything, I was probably saving it for the meeting.

As I walked over to the DVD player, still fumbling with the package, a slight murmur penetrated the silence. The thirty-six-inch color television sat on a brownish steel mobile stand. It was positioned where every eye had a good view. Nothing would be missed.

I finally pulled the case out and held the thing up in full view.

"This was addressed to me. Came by way of UPS. Gentlemen, what I'm about to show you is shocking, disgusting and downright wicked."

Without further procrastination, I slipped the DVD in and pushed "play." The strangling tension in the air was thick enough to give a chainsaw trouble.

The picture was snowy at first, but quickly cleared up, revealing an undisputable picture of Deacon Slydale humping the hell out of a lady who looked like Sister Walker.

"This is an outrage!" Slydale yelled, jumping to his feet. "I never did anything like—"

"You're doing it right there." I pointed to his hairy, fat butt rising, and then falling.

The murmuring was back, louder than before. Slydale started for the television, but was quickly put in check by Deacon Clay.

"Slydale, you have some *'splaining* to do," Clay said in his very best Ricky Ricardo voice, waving the *shame, shame* finger.

"Gracious God," Deacon Shoe blurted, clutching his heart. "Sodom and Gomorrah."

"Jesus Christ," somebody added as Slydale flipped the woman on all fours, then eased in from behind, riding like his name was the Lone Ranger. The woman yelled whenever he smacked her butt, which acted as his green light to thrust faster.

Deacon Kelly jumped his grits-eating, gorilla-looking self up, screaming. "This is preposterous! A slander in the eye of my Lord." If Slydale was Lone Ranger, then Kelly was Tonto.

"Kelly," I said, trying hard to conceal my heightened pleasure. "We have some of your greatest hits as well." I fast-forwarded to Kelly's pudgy-fat, tar-colored body.

He tried to play shy at first. Stood there as the girl dropped to her knees in front of him and started taking his shriveled manhood into her mouth.

A round of disgusting grunts saturated the air. I looked at Kelly. Sweat drenched his brow. The armpits of his dress shirt were plagued by betraying rings of perspiration.

Things didn't look so well for Deacon Roberts and Deacon Long either. Slydale's other two partners in crime. Although they weren't featured, the two could be seen in the background performing like high-profile porn stars.

"Can't you see what he's doing," Deacon Slydale hollered out of desperation. He pointed a chubby finger. "He set us up. We were framed."

"That's not me," Deacon Long yelped.

"He's trying to do us like they did that R-Kelly boy," Deacon Roberts cried.

Cry as they might. The proof was evident for all to see. I made a personal note to drop by the hotel and thank the young security guard for his brilliant job. Didn't know much about his major. Just knew he had a good career in film if he chose that route. Could see his name in the same sentence as Spike, John, Fuqua, and a few others.

"Gentlemen," I said, my hands outstretched in a calming gesture. "In light of the overwhelming evidence against the deacons in question, I move for an immediate dismissal of Deacon Slydale, Deacon Kelly, Deacon Roberts and Deacon Long."

"I second it," Deacon Shoe chimed in. The old man was sitting, sipping a glass of water. For a minute, I thought we were going to have to call an ambulance. Once he'd seen the incriminating footage, he'd started clutching his chest, talking in tongues. "We can't have that type of behavior going on amongst the leaders of our great church. Sinful. Just plain sinful. Wicked. God please forgive them."

"The motion is unanimous," Deacons Clay, White and Braxton sang out, still shocked and appalled by what they'd just witnessed. Deacon Kelly immediately broke down, crying like a two-year-old girl denied of goodies at the grocery store. Deacon Long and Roberts were holding on to their innocence like a couple of guilty men sentenced to twenty years hard time in a federal pound-me-in-the-ass penitentiary.

I would be lying if I said I wasn't enjoying this execution. That was until Slydale lost it and tried to attack me.

"I'll kill you," he growled, his hands out in front, headed for my throat. He was met by a wall of resistance named Deacon Braxton. Braxton was the youngest of the Deacons. At thirty-five, the man was built like a Hummer. Neck like Mike Tyson. Hands large enough to choke out a grizzly bear.

Slydale was no match. It happened so quickly. One minute, Slydale was locked into a lung-burning bear hug, the next, he was lying on his back, looking up at the ceiling of the church. Dazed. Trying desperately to shake off the cobwebs, groaning like he was still receiving pleasure from the Sister Walker wannabe.

"I think it's safe to say that this meeting is adjourned," I concluded.

As soon as Slydale came to, I had him and his partners in crime escorted from the building. At least this chapter of my life was closed.

The evil Deacon Slydale was a disgusting, distant memory. But my problems were far from over. One day I would be held accountable for my deceitful ways. Made to pay for all my bad deeds. I figured since God hadn't slipped the rug from underneath me, yet, I might as well head to my office. I'd picked up a new prescription of Viagra. It was Sister Walker's dinnertime. I would be her dessert.

WISDOM

T his was the day. It was a Friday evening and unfortunately, my deadline. Highnoon was about fifteen minutes away from finding out if he was going to quench his blood lust. And I was fifteen minutes away from making the biggest decision of my life. It did cross my mind that if I didn't go through with the deal, Highnoon would rub me out anyway. There was no honor among thieves. But I'd planned for whatever. Momma was stable, even though she still had tubes everywhere. Wished I could've seen her one more time. But I was afraid if I went back, I probably would've changed my mind.

"Didn't think I would hear from you again," Maria's angelic accent flowed through my cell.

"I must've been some kinda drunk when you slipped your phone number in my pocket," I teased.

"Drunk and foolish." She laughed.

"I had everything handled," I bragged, trying hard to impress.

"By the way, how's the leg?"

"How'd you know?"

"Paco's my brother." She admitted that like she was extremely proud of her genetic connection with a guy that had the IQ of a Diet Pepsi. "He came home pissed about you knocking him out. Said that before you knocked Hector out, he tried to slice your leg off."

"He got lucky," I said, laughing.

"How so; you still were injured?"

"I know. The dude got lucky because if I hadn't been drinking, my reflexes would've been much sharper and the idiot would've received more than an aching jaw. So yeah, I say he was lucky."

She laughed a bit. "So, let me get this right, if you wouldn't have been drinking, then you wouldn't have had a reason to come to the bar? Therefore, I wouldn't have had a chance to meet and slip my number in the pocket of a man that I'd been hoping would walk through the doors of that bar and sweep me off my feet."

There it was. Delivered in black and white. Her little confession made my head swell to the point of heaviness. Pride ran like wild water rapidly through my body. In the past, before Malisa, I'd been known by the ladies for my superb hunting tactics. Thought that there wasn't a woman alive who I couldn't charm out their digits. I was all that.

"Thank you, but I've been known to be a man dripping with mystery, charm and charisma. Even when I'm drunk, I'm still deadly with game. Now, tell me. What did I say that night that left your heart yearning for desire?"

"You really wanna know?"

"Go 'head, baby. Regale me with tales of mad game and good looks."

"Absolutely nothing," she confessed, sweetly snickering at the air now escaping my swollen head and manly ego. Women would never admit it, but they enjoyed taking men down from their own pedestals of arrogance and pride, deflating egos like nail-punctured hot air balloons, splattering male conceit all over the black top of masculinity. Ways that left weak men sitting in the middle of the floor, legs crossed yoga-style, babbling baby choruses of "ga-ga, goo-goo."

"That was kind of cold," I replied, picking my face off the floor of the van heading toward fate.

"Mister, Mack," Maria joked, "it wasn't you. My momma—God rest her soul—had the gift."

I ran smack dab into the heart of rush hour traffic. The freeway was locked up tighter than a head cold. The King Snake was expecting me around seven. The gold teeth schmuck even told me not to be late. Said that a real man had three things in this life he lived by—actually I thought I could remember Tony Montana mentioning two things, his word and balls.

"What gift's that?" I asked while trying to give my undivided attention to her, but watching some impatient punk in one of those Nissan Pathfinders, four cars up. The fool was acting like he was a doctor late for surgery, jumping from one lane to another, horns of peeved motorists sounding off disapprovingly.

"My mother could tell what type of person you were by one touch," she revealed. "And no, she wasn't a witch."

The girl was in my head. I was spooked because that is exactly what I was thinking.

"Wisdom?"

"I'm here."

"What's the matter?" she asked with concern in her voice.

"Is that what happened? When I touched you in the bar, you could tell *that*?"

"Yes," she said with so much passion and conviction.

"You're deep."

The traffic was starting to move at a swift pace. Not to my surprise, the State Troopers had the schmuck who was driving the Pathfinder pulled over and were going through his truck as if they'd expected to find millions of dollars. The opened beer bottles sitting on the hood of the Pathfinder betrayed the driver's reckless behavior.

If this was supposed to be my last ride, I sure wasn't acting like it. I used to wonder what went through the minds of condemned men when that last walk came. Did they have thoughts of other family members when the switch was thrown?

I sure wouldn't. The conversation I was having with someone who actually gave a damn about another person was refreshing. Wondered what she would say if she knew I was exchanging a life for a life? As quickly as the idea came, it vanished. She was nice, probably with a completely different set of problems. Didn't want to get her caught up in my mess. Hadn't even told her about Malisa's scandalous ass. Felt no need to. Because in a few minutes, my life would probably be extinguished.

With five minutes to go, I told Maria that if I lived through the night, I'd call her first thing in the morning.

"I love your charming sense of humor. Every *Chico* around here is so dang-on gangster-serious."

I wished this was all conjured up by an outta control sense of humor. But it wasn't. This was the real deal. The last ride for this broken down B-baller with debt up the wazoo.

My only bright spot was that Malisa wouldn't be able to threaten me with child support anymore. With that in mind, I figured dying wouldn't be half bad.

Right before we ended our phone conversation, Maria cut loose with a little sense of humor of her own. "Don't get killed before I prove to you that my gift is always right."

The big knot of uneasiness in my throat only allowed me to chuckle. She didn't know how close to the truth she was. Strongly against my will, I ended the phone conversation, whipping the van into the parking lot of a dreadful, spooky-looking warehouse. The thing looked like it could've been rented for Halloween to scare the living hell out of the thrill-seeker looking for the ultimate, gruesome rush. Abandoned wasn't the word. From the outside, the building looked completely dark. Every window. Every door.

The snow had started to subside. I couldn't believe that I was probably watching my last snowfall. I sat there, taking it all in. The unexplained beauties of this world. Its subtle creations of life. The ups-and-downs. Why evil men profited, and the righteous got the shaft? Why my mother was battling to stay alive? And why my father was searching for his next piece of ass? Then it hit me like a penetrating kick in the nuts. I was about to make the greatest sacrifice. Not as significant as Jesus', but significant to me. Jesus was the unblemished lamb. But me, I had far too many flaws to even say that I was the chosen one. This was indeed a living sacrifice. Myself for my mother.

The directions Highnoon had given me led me to one of his old abandoned warehouses, somewhere in the shadiest parts of Pontiac, Michigan. Just a little flyspeck on the map, a low-brow, factory district with other buildings that looked just as spooky as the place in which I sat.

The only creatures stirring were me and some emaciated mutt out on a homeless stroll of scavenging garbage cans, praying for a feed. I guess one could say that my life ran parallel to the mutt's. We were out here in hell town looking for life. He was looking for food to continue his and I was laying one down to save. The mutt acknowledged me—with me doing the same as I exited the truck. The van looked like it was already mourning the loss of its driver.

"Goodbye, old friend," I mumbled, stepping off into the cool evening air. Being that the factory was abandoned, I guessed Highnoon didn't see it to have the snow removed. The crap was knee-high deep, making my last mile somewhat unpleasant, even treacherous.

I stared at the darkened skies, praying that my cell would ring. There would be so much screaming on the other end that I couldn't make heads-or-tails of what my sister was saying. Then she would calm down and say that Momma had just received a donor. Highnoon's space-black face would scowl as I gave him the wonderful news with a few choice words and that fabulous middle finger people enjoyed flashing so much.

That miraculous phone call would never come. The silence my cell displayed from the grueling trek from the van to the overhead doors around back had given me the answer I was looking for. There would be no divine intervention. This was meant to be. There was no other way.

Suddenly, the overhead doors began to slowly slide upward. Nothing but the creepy, rusty mechanics of the chain could be heard as the door slowly ascended. I braced myself for the inevitable. Would it be quick? Or would Highnoon want to see the pain in my eyes as he showed me pieces of myself. I figured him being the same old person from our dust-kicking days of running the streets. The S.O.B. was ruthless, cold, calculating. The lunatic took pleasure in torture and maiming. I was sure he would try to start out with feeling-padded tactics, but after a few moments of reliving his brother's murder, seeing my cousin standing over Pat's slain body, pipe in hand, the Negro would flip out. He would totally be on some ol' Freddy Krueger crap. Would I give him the satisfaction of hearing me scream? Or would my dignified silence heighten his barbaric will to punish me until he heard the howling break of a tortured soul? Achieving his avenging goal, setting his brother's tormented soul free, feeling satisfied to go wherever, knowing that vengeance had been served.

No sooner than the noise from the chain stopped, I heard somebody fumbling around in the inky darkness, now staring at me. Goosebumps traveled the length of both arms. Expected to hear gunshots, but instead, I was hit by a high-powered beam of light. My sight was lost.

"The man's been expecting you." A gruesome, gruff voice penetrated the light. I knew that voice from anywhere. The vocals belonged to Highnoon's Frankenstein monster of a bodyguard, the tree trunk wearing Timberlands that had met me at the door of Highnoon's ritzy crib that night.

I shaded my eyes. "Is this really necessary?" I asked coldly.

"Sit tight," he commanded.

Two huge Bigfoot-looking schmucks with real angry mugs walked from behind the light. One creep patted me down, while the other gorilla waved a metal-detecting wand over my bomber jacket on down to my boots. Didn't know if the idiot thought I was a terrorist wearing explosive Timberlands or what.

"What's this about?" I voiced. "This Negro wants my life!"

"We can't be too careful," the monster replied. "Business is business."

They shook me down for another couple of minutes, then smuggled me through the darkness to a room with one lonely chair placed under a bright light, like it was about to be used for interrogation purposes. The rest of the room was creepy dark.

"Sit yo' ass down," one of the Bigfoot brothers rudely ordered. The way these bubblegum gangsters were treating me made me want to knock one of these fools upside the head. They were seriously disrespecting me, like my size didn't amount to a hill of beans.

More lights went on as I sat down in the chair, revealing other enormous predator-types. I understood the rude treatment now. It wasn't that they were disregarding my size; it was strictly a numbers game. I was the smallest cat in the room, surrounded by dudes that made me look shorter than a midget on his knees. They were all staring at me like I was a bucket of Kentucky Fried

Chicken—extra crispy. Now I knew how a turkey felt right before Thanksgiving.

These damn lights were getting on my nerves. And right when I was about to lose my cool, the King Snake made his star-studded appearance.

"Wisdom, Wisdom, Wisdom," Highnoon said. The fool was sporting a high-priced fur jacket. Mink. Leave it up to that jewelry smiling punk to flaunt his riches in my face on my last day.

"What's with all the dramatics?" I pointed around the still room of darkness at all the bodies.

"This kinda deal can't go down nowhere else," he said. He walked in front of me wearing some loud-ass alligator shoes. "Don't think I'm receiving pleasure from this. Because I'm not." The closer he got, I could see that this clown wasn't wearing his coat in the normal fashion. He was all pimped out. His coat draped his shoulders, pimp-style, making it easier for one of his thugs to remove it. And, on cue, the Negro stopped in front of one of his goons, exposing his back to 'em and rolling his shoulders like he was in that movie "The Mack." The goon removed the coat, stepping backward. Highnoon was wearing blue jeans capped off by a very fashionable bulletproof vest. Strictly kingpin attire.

"What's with the basketball team of husky football-playing Negroes?" I asked, becoming a little uncomfortable with this scene.

"Ain't no telling what you might run into out here in

Yak Town," he replied. Yak Town was the slang term given to Pontiac by its hip-hop generation of local thugs, hooligans and gangsters. "Pays to be prepared."

"So," I said, looking at all the super-sized goons that were collected around me. "This is the only way?"

"I have no say-so over the matter in question." He licked his crusty lips. "Pat's death is the only thing I listen to."

It was South Pole-cold in this desolate dungeon. My knee started in on me, letting me know that it disapproved of the climate. I only wished it had eyeballs to see this scene that I was caught up in the middle of. And if it did, my knee would've shut the hell up at the sight of what appeared to be a nice-sized crate being brought in the room by the same Bigfoot brothers who'd felt me up earlier.

Highnoon played off the question in my eyes. "Wisdom, Wisdom, Wisdom." I absolutely abhorred when the clown sang my name like that. It meant doom. In the past, he would sing his victim's names in this exact manner— right before he sent them on that next bus ride to eternity. We'd done plenty of dirt together. And seeing the crate spelled bad news.

"I admire your courage, Wisdom. Truly, I do. Laying down your life for the life of a family member. Is that not unconditional love? I envy you. Unconditional love and all." He was putting on a pair of black leather gloves like the ones made famous by O.J.

"You have that love that comes naturally." He nodded

to his gang. "Not the shit that has to be bought and paid for." The fool walked over to the crate, opening it. The lid was easy to lift. Not that this moose of a man would've had any problems. Highnoon removed a stainless steel briefcase with handcuffs fastened to the handle.

"These are the official papers," he indicated, removing them from the case and handing them over to me.

My hands were so cold I could barely grip them. I tried to blow on them to get a little circulation going.

"How do I know this is legit? Like you're not going to double-cross my black ass, kill me, letting my momma die?"

"Wisdom, Wisdom, Wisdom. I thought you knew me better than that."

I looked around the room at his small army. "I thought I did, too. But"—I held the papers up—"look what you're making me sign. Death papers."

He flashed that gold mine smile again, dripping with arrogance. "Now that was low." He covered his crotch. "That was a real low shot, pal." It was colder than penguin booty in this joint, but Highnoon's gang stood deathly still, undaunted by the biting temperatures.

"Not low enough," I cut back. "This is low." I shoved the papers again. Highnoon clapped his gloved-hands together twice. I thought the fool had installed one of those clapper products, but a wimpy looking white man appeared from the shadows, carrying a black leather briefcase, dressed in crow black. The idiot looked like Alfred from those batman mini-series DVD box sets.

"I guess this is the Avon Lady?" I sarcastically asked.

"No, my brother," Highnoon answered, "this is the man who's gonna make this thing official." He pointed to Alfred.

"This is my lawyer—by the request of my counselor, he shall remain nameless. Told you, brother, this deal has professionalism all over it."

Alfred didn't speak. He immediately took the papers from my hand and started going over them. There were three sheets there, but it didn't take him long to read them.

"Put your signature here." He flipped through the pages. "Here, here and there."

He handed me a black fountain pen.

"Am I supposed to believe this?" I asked, growing a little bored of this game of cat and mouse. Besides, my knee was paining beyond belief. I was ready to get this over with.

"That's up to you," Highnoon said.

Now it was my time to smile.

"I know."

Highnoon's eyes grew blank with confusion and arrogance.

"You didn't think I would completely put my trust in a snake, did you, my brother?"

"What you talking about?" Highnoon's eyes bucked wide.

I opened my coat, pulling up my shirt. It was then I'd reminded myself that this quick action had mistake written all across it. The improvisation brought guns from every direction. The goons that had stood silent were now animated, each pointing their own unique brand Clint Eastwood sized-cannon at my noggin.

"Wait!" I yelled, throwing my hands in the air.

"Put 'em up!" Highnoon barked the command. And as quickly as they'd appeared, the goons holstered the weapons.

"That was stupid, Wisdom," Highnoon said, laughing. "You almost cheated me out of my chance." He smiled sinisterly. "Now let's see what you almost got yourself shredded for."

The lawyer reemerged from the shadows. His face was a cowardly portrait of fear.

"Like I was saying," I continued, just a little shaken, "I don't trust you to go ahead with our deal after my death." I removed a mini-microphone wire that I'd taped to my chest before I left home. "I took precautions just in case yo' big ass tried to back away from the operating table." I held the wire up for all to see.

"What's that?" Highnoon asked. Some of his arrogance had disappeared at the sight of the wire. I was wearing the granddaddy of all smirks. Had the attention of every gorilla in the room. If I was going to die, it would be for a cause. And I would defiantly go out knowing that I'd regained a little power. I would do this my way—on my terms.

"This is a wire," I lectured as if this was show-and-tell. "There's a person on the other end of this thing who's taping this whole deal. In any event that my momma don't receive the kidney, the tape will be handed over to local authorities," I bluffed. Had seen this ploy work a few times for the A-Team. Hannibal was my favorite character. He just loved it when a plan came together. I silently prayed for this one to go the same. Hannibal would've been proud.

"Quit bluffing, Black. We know you ain't got a leg to stand on," Highnoon countered. Sweat was perspiring on his forehead. "You ain't got the plums to pull off something that sophisticated."

"Try me if you think I'm bullin'." My eyes convincingly held the threat of promise. The big fellow composed himself. He pulled a Cuban from somewhere and lit the thing.

"Like I said, Wisdom, this thing is legit. You have my word." He puffed the cigar.

"One other thing," I voiced. "Before I sign this thing, we need to write in two more contract clauses." I waited on Highnoon to acknowledge my comment before I continued. "And in the event that my mother's body rejects your filthy kidney, or it's not her type, you'll have the glamorous job of locating her another. So think about that when your goons are out killing whoever opposes your majesty. Have somebody remove the kidney and see if they're a righteous fit. One last thing. My family must be able to find my body. Closure, asshole. That don't mean dividing my body into compass directions, sending parts east, north, west or south."

"Anything else?" Highnoon asked, rubbing his hands together. Didn't know if he was gloating or cold.

Alfred got right on it. The twit pulled out a laptop from his briefcase and got busy. He made a few phone calls.

"Wisdom, I wish this didn't have to be."

"It is what it is," I replied. "I can't expect a loser like you to understand."

Highnoon called for the two Bigfoots that failed at successfully patting me down. Somehow, I knew he was smoking at the thought of me dotting the I's and crossing the T's. But what the Negro did next surprised the hell out of me.

Highnoon reached into the small of his back, coming out with a pistol the size of a small violin.

"Boss!" The first one threw up his hands, wide-eyed. "I'm sor—" Highnoon raised the pistol and shot him twice in the chest. The goon dropped like a wet loaf of bread. The shot had been muffled by a sound-suppressing silencer neatly fitted on the barrel.

"Damn!" the second loser yelled, trying to run. Two muffled sounds later, the second creep had taken both in the back, the force violently pushing him forward, causing him to trip over some scrap metal lying on the floor. His body came to rest in a twisted wreck.

The cold-hot smoke steaming from the sound suppressor refreshed my memory, confirming the fact that this fool was a cold-blooded killer.

"One thing I can't stand is incompetence." His all-business face melted back to a sinister smile of gold and lies. He looked at me, all thirty-two showing. "You'd think with the money I pay out, I could get some mugs who could handle the job of conducting a proper pat-down."

The lawyer stopped what he was doing. The fear on his lemonhead-shaped face was plentiful. He tried to continue what he was doing, but the gump was shaking worse than a priest in a crap game.

For the rest of the goon squad, it was business as usual. Their nonchalant attitudes informed me that this type of crap happened on a daily basis.

"Was that really necessary?" I asked in a voice that was not impressed or frightened. Even though I'd turned my life around, I was no stranger to random acts of violence. I was no saint. Had my share of violent situations. That's why I didn't care too much for guns. I'd stood on the business end of them in my past, trying to make sure undesirables didn't have a future. Highnoon knew it. Think he was just trying to make a point to himself. That he still had the stuff to mass produce corpses. The two gorillas ready for body bags with holes in their bodies the size of grapefruits were a testimony.

"Ignorance like that," he pointed the pistol at the bloody bodies, "can be dangerous." He placed the pistol back into the small of his back.

"I-I-I think everything is in order," the lawyer stuttered, finally getting the apples to speak. He nervously handed the papers over. The new clauses were implemented. I took the pen.

"Wisdom, you're a disappointment to me," Highnoon

said in his very best Michael Clark Duncan voice. "Why didn't you continue your career as a full-time gangster?"

"That's not to worry." I signed the document. "In a minute, I'll be dead, but you're still looking at trouble."

"What you talkin' about?" His look was drenched by confusion. I decided to play my last card. "Word on the street. This cat named Geechie is looking to take your crown." Rico had called me right after my sister and I had made up. Told me as a favor from one of his informants, that he had learned Geechie was trying to force my sister into being his mule—taking drugs into prisons. My family was in turmoil. We weren't exactly the Huxtables, but I wasn't about to let scum prey on us. My plan was to pit one snake against the other.

I didn't think God would be exactly patting me on the back, giving me the well done servant routine, but Geechie had to be dealt with. My sister's life depended on it. I would have to take my chances with the Big Guy in getting into Heaven. But if it took this to get that leech off her back, then that Negro deserved to be with me on that same bus ride to eternity.

"Is that so?" Highnoon said, hanging on my every word.

"Very much so," I replied, smiling, trying hard to sell this. "You don't know who Geechie is, do you?"

"A Westside nobody."

"Maybe not to you, but he got those fools in his area convinced that he's the next Highnoon."

"You serious?"

"As kidney failure."

"This is going to take some checking into," he said.

"Study long, study wrong." I quoted that exact same line he'd given me before I left his house the night he'd confronted me with his proposal.

He pondered a little while longer before going into the wooden crate; removing a device that looked so wicked that it chased the poor lawyer out of the room.

"So that's my one way ticket, hunh?" I asked with no fear in my voice whatsoever. "You order that thing from Amazon?"

"Funny," he responded, setting his sinister device up. The detail that caught my attention was this crate being far too big for the device. The device was no bigger than a car tire, but the crate looked to be my size. It left me with one question on my mind—could I be looking at my makeshift casket? If it was, I was freaking out. Not too many people had gotten a chance to peep out their box of slumber. Morbid. Extremely morbid. Highnoon's entire proposal was unconventional. If for some reason God blessed me with some divine intervention, I'd take this story and parlay it into a bestselling novel.

For some strange reason, my leg started to tremble.

All sorts of thoughts bounced around inside my skull. I was still sitting in the chair, but without restraints. In college, I had been known for my lightning speed. I could break and run in a zigzag pattern so I wouldn't end up like the poor schmuck that had taken two in the back earlier. But the man in me was about facing any and everything life put on my plate. All spirit-breaking obstacles were welcomed. Besides, my mother was worth it. Worth the pain and suffering inflicted by any madman. So I sat back in the chair, bracing myself for one nightmare of an ending.

It was after Highnoon had finished installing what looked to be jumper cables on his death device that I said, "That thing looks kinda personal."

"Well," he answered, "when you lose the only person in this world you really care about, by some bullshit that could've been avoided…everything is personal."

"So," I said, bending and rubbing my aching knee. "One more time—just so I can tell your Maker what qualified me to take the place of a man that died in jail years ago?"

"Blood, Black," he explained, "blood." I didn't know what to make of the welding glasses he put on. My only guess was that things were about to get bright. "Like I said at the house, I was robbed of my chance at bringing justice to that faggot of a cousin of yours." The fool fired up the machine and Holy Jesus! The hum was enough to kill a person.

I was just about to change my mind when Highnoon made a hand gesture, bringing life to his silent soldiers. They grabbed me before I could get up. One big one held my neck, while two others bound me to the chair with heavy industrial strength chains and padlocks the size of my fists.

This was it. I was on my way to the Great Beyond. Highnoon slowly approached me, his fist clutching the grips of the cables. Just to show me what he was doing was on the real, the ugly schmuck touched both metal endings of the grips together, sparking fire.

I didn't even flinch. Instead I took a deep, calming breath. Highnoon's face held that deadly snarl from when he'd gunned down his two gorillas.

"Any last words, or wishes?" he asked. He was close enough for me to see my reflection in the tinted lens of his glasses. People used to say that I was my mother's masculine twin. I had her eyes, nose, mouth, forehead and high cheek bones. It was then that my mind started replaying events from the past. Like I was watching a silent film inside of my head. I could see my mother at all my basketball games, cheering me on, fueling my spirits to perform at my highest level. Then, without warning, the film quantum-leaped to my high school graduation. Momma was so proud of me walking across the stage. So proud that she almost kicked the crap out of an usher who told her that she couldn't approach the stage to take pictures. It took me leaping off the stage in my cap and gown to pry his hands from her arm and give myself one helluva graduation present in the beating I'd laid on him. Nobody touched my mother!

I could see that Highnoon had a flare for the dramatic. He bumped the metallic tips again, sparking fire. "I asked you if you had anything else to say?"

"Yeah," I said, a remorseful look on my face. "My only

wish would be that I could have one week to put my family back tight with the Lord, and each other."

Highnoon was inches away from my left cheek with the fire of his hot revenge. I closed my eyes, trying to put myself somewhere else. You never know how much you love people until you're faced with your own mortality. Suddenly, I wished that I could've made things right between Yazoo and me. Told him how much I loved him, despite what happened in the past. Wished I could've sat my old man down and told him how bad he had hurt the family with his selfishness. Then we could've embraced, chasing away the ghosts from past deeds. And Jordan? My heart yearned to help someone who didn't want to help himself. My only bright spot was my baby, and making up with my sister. Had visions of my sister babysitting my brat, showing him, or her, the ropes. I smiled, wondering why I hadn't felt the pain. Maybe because Highnoon had pity on me after all, shooting me in the head, saving me from hair-curling pain.

I opened my eyes expecting to see St. Peter, but instead, I stared right into the ugly eyes of Satan. It was funny to me. I couldn't remember any Bible stories describing Satan wearing gold teeth. That's when I noticed Highnoon switching off the machine.

"You got one week, Wisdom," he announced. The Negro clapped his hands and his apes removed the chains and locks.

I let my stare serve as a thank you. I stood up kinda

wobbly. Had been sitting for quite some time. Shaking some blood back into my limbs, I tried to say something but was quickly waved off.

"Wisdom," Highnoon said, removing the glasses. "We have a signed agreement. If you don't come back after one week, then I release the dogs of war upon your entire family."

I felt God over me. My guardian angel had finally come through. All lines to Heaven were now open again. This was the divine intervention I was hoping for.

Somehow, I found my way through the darkness. I was almost to the exit when I heard, "One week. The clock is ticking."

I felt no need to ask him a thing. I'd been delivered and spared with one goal in mind. Didn't know how I was going to accomplish the task, but I would bring my family closer together...even if it meant the ultimate sacrifice—my life!

ABOUT THE AUTHOR

Thomas Slater is a native of Detroit, MI. He is the author of *Show Stoppah* and *No More Time-Outs*, and under the pen name, Tecori Sheldon, he is the author of *When Truth is Gangsta*. He hopes to create a footprint by stepping off into the cement of literary greatness. Visit the author at www.slaterboyfiction.com, facebook.com/thomaseslater and Twitter @EarlWrites.

READER DISCUSSION GUIDE

1. What was the true nature behind Yazoo's rebellion against God?

2. Which two people did Yazoo personally hold accountable for his father's death?

3. Why didn't Yazoo want Geechie to know that he and Tempest were related?

4. What college did Wisdom play for before tragically blowing out his ACL?

5. When did Wisdom begin to suspect that there was something going on between Malisa and Kirk?

6. What was the name of Reverend Poppa Jones' church?

7. Who was the mysterious, but very unstable voice that stalked Reverend Poppa Jones' personal phones?

8. What was the promise that Wisdom made to his mother?

9. Why did Wisdom's mother think that she could trust him in keeping her promise?

10. What was Highnoon's insidious purpose for his proposition?

11. Did Wilma Jones know of her husband's infidelities? If so, did she ever confront him?

12. Who did Tempest blame for her promiscuity?

13. What did Geechie use to try and blackmail Tempest into being his drug-trafficking mule?

14. What ruthless act did Jordan commit that earned him Popeye's deadly attention?

15. Under what stipulations did Wisdom accept Highnoon's offer?

16. What Bible story did Highnoon use in trying to secure his deal with Wisdom?

17. Wisdom exhibited the highest summit of unconditional love. What limits would you travel for a loved one in trouble?

TAKE ONE FOR THE TEAM

BY THOMAS SLATER

CHAPTER 1

I sat outside on the bleachers of a neighborhood park that the locals had nicknamed "The Hole." It wasn't too cold out, but my knee was singing me the blues rendition of the national anthem. Cornflake-sized snowflakes gathered around the shoulders of my gray uniform jacket. The last two months of my life were replaying inside my dome like some ghetto-version of a Shakespearean tragedy. Tyler Perry would've been tossing Bentley Coupes through my bedroom window for an opportunity at the option of transforming my dysfunctional family drama into one of his record-breaking, box-office smashes.

To recap: My mother was dying from kidney complications and needed a donor, like yesterday. When, out of nowhere, this gold tooth-wearing serpent named Highnoon slithered from my past with a sleazy proposition. He'd found out about my mother's condition and wanted to help. It turned out that he was the exact match for a donor. There was a deadly catch to it. His generosity had been spawned by revenge. And I was the closest living relative to the one responsible for his pain. The proposition: He would give my mother a kidney if I surrendered my life to him for his sick, twisted pleasures in quenching his thirst for revenge. There was nothing that was too special for my mother so I agreed by signing Highnoon's contract. We were in his version of *The House of Pain*, about to fulfill my end of the bargain, when he asked me *the* question: Did I have one last thing to say?—or something to that effect. He was at my left eye with something that looked like a blow torch when I answered, "Yeah. I wish that I could have one week to put my family tight with the Lord, and each other." Highnoon turned off his machine of torture and gave me seven days, one whole week to restore my wayward family to its place of purity in God's eyes.

I was amongst fifteen chumps who occupied seats on cold bleachers waiting patiently for a turn to get into a pickup game that was in progress. Over the years The Hole had gotten its fair share of bad press, a virtual media-feeding frenzy. Almost every other month, it was nothing to turn on local news and see coroners dragging bodies from the place. There, the possibility of a pickup game ending in gunfire was more common than hemorrhoid flare-ups. But regardless of its brutal nature, some of the biggest stars in the NBA once did battle on its black top. Young, hood-hopping hopefuls still flocked to the park to mix it up with the old-heads in the glorious pursuit of that next level reputation.

Light snowfall made conditions on the court slick as flakes melted upon surface contact. It did very little to stop the action on the court as play heated up. A punk named Pogo was showing his ass. He went baseline and threw one down on some tall, lanky guy named Alex. The park exploded with "oohs" and "aahs" as Pogo landed, offering a double bicep pose, feeling himself. Me and this Negro had history. Bad blood that dated back to my injury. The jerk had been the one responsible for me shredding my ACL. And knowing it, I couldn't explain what type of madness that had drawn me back here, to the same place where my knee and basketball career had been shattered. For me, The Hole was a place where my dreams had ended and my nightmares had begun.

I could no longer fool myself. My reason for today's visit was pure evil that was solely sponsored by Satan. Inadvertently, Highnoon had turned me into a monster with the proposition. I could do anything to anybody and wouldn't have to worry about the consequences from the laws that governed man. Pogo was about to feel my wrath. The Bible stated that revenge belonged to the Lord, but I couldn't go to my grave knowing that the fool responsible for costing me an NBA career was still serving up Negroes on the basketball court. Of course, Pogo had given me a song-and-dance about it being accidental, a case where his athleticism had taken a backseat to his passion for aggressive play. Of course I never believed the shit, not for one moment. From day one, Pogo had been a jealous-hearted bastard with a nasty reputation for being a dirty player. He hated on my game, ups, handle, and the fact that my career was taking off, while his flew way below NBA radar.

I sat back, knee throbbing, going over a violent list of things I'd planned for my old enemy when Pogo got into the passing lane and intercepted the basketball. The anticipation of a highlight reel dunk captured attention. Pogo exploded down the court, beating defenders, getting his steps together, and launched himself from the free-throw line—like MJ. I wasn't hating on the brother or nothing, but the Negro's sneakers were player-eye level, as he floated by and two-handed monster-dunked.

"Game, nigga!" Pogo shouted, cold smoke escaping his mouth as he hung from the rim. "Get the next set of victims out on this bitch!" The nine other guys walked off the court dressed appropriately for the weather in sweats, hoodies, and sneakers to grab a seat or hydrate.

"Good game, my nigga," a sloppy-looking cat said to Pogo.

"I don't know why yo' ass didn't go pro," said another chump with a big nose, sloping forehead, and rocking a unibrow.

Victim was right, I thought. Because after today, Pogo was going to need the assistance of a pogo stick to ever reach his vertical-leaping maximum again. He saw me and immediately walked his cornrowed R-Kelly-looking ass over like he'd never robbed me of a golden opportunity at gracing a cover of *Sports Illustrated*.

"What up doe, kinfolk?" He fist-bumped me. The schmuck was about six-two and wearing a hoodie that boasted a *Just do It* slogan across the chest, a skullcap and some crusty, water-soaked Olympic Air Jordans, number 6's. I had to hand it to him. Pogo had a huge set of grape-fruits.

My fist met his. "I see that you haven't lost a step. Nice game."

"Thanks, kinfolk! You know these young cats come up in here to make a name. They'll never style on my watch."

I removed my jacket and placed it on the aluminum,

exposing my gray uniform shirt. Under any other circumstance I would've never worn jeans with black work boots to get it in.

"I hear you."

"I ain't seen you around here in a minute, not since the evening of the accident." My temper was on boil. I couldn't believe that this trout-mouth little punk was still tagging his jealous rage as an "accident." But I stayed cool.

"Damn, Wisdom, I don't see how you could come back here anymore. Me personally, I would've put a pistol up to my head years ago and pulled the trigger. It would've been too much for me to lose all the money and fame that came with the NBA." He glanced in the lot where my mail van was parked. "I guess I ain't as strong as you are." I hadn't missed Pogo's cute little diss. It was all good, though.

Normally, I would've conducted a thorough evaluation, skimming the sidelines for talent before I made my selection. But I didn't have winning on my mind. So I randomly selected four nobodies from the side.

The moment that the ball was inbounded, I was all business. My knee was screaming bloody murder the first trip down the court. Being back in the saddle had me feeling like I was invincible. I had to check myself. I wasn't here for the thrill of the game. And Pogo found that out the moment he lost his man and tried to go all Michael Jordan with it. An alley-oop was tossed and Pogo catapulted himself off the ground to grab it. If this had been an NBA game, the flashbulbs would've been blinding in an effort at capturing his effortless flight, and the roar of the fans would've been deafening. But this wasn't the NBA and Pogo wasn't Kobe Bryant.

Much in the same manner, I lowered my shoulder like he'd done years ago and delivered a nasty undercut. I would like to say that time stood still to watch Pogo suffer the same fate he had given me on the evening of the NBA draft. I stood erect and took great pleasure in watching his wiry body do a somersault over my six-five frame like a propeller that had busted away from the hub of a plane while crashing through thick trees. Pogo tumbled to the cold, unforgiving ground, landing flat on his face. I'd been saving that undercut for quite some time now. It was executed perfectly, but I wasn't aware to what degree this idiot had been injured.

Pogo lay there perfectly still. I thought I might've killed his ass until he groggily rolled over onto his back. In the place where his face had lain, there was a pool of crimson-red blood mixing with a small puddle of water. Thought that I hadn't done enough, until he cringed, opening his mouth. I was satisfied because his once healthy smile had been vandalized by a mouth filled with bloody, jagged stumps. And although I was filled with pleasure resulting in the rising pain on his face, I knew somehow, that it would never equal out to the millions I would've earned in the NBA. Seeing him gag on his own blood and spitting out tooth fragments was priceless.

My job here was done.

Nobody said shit to me as I walked off to the side and

slid on my jacket. I didn't have to offer an excuse for my actions. A few of these cats were around when Pogo had taken away my NBA opportunity and a chance at giving my family a better life. They knew the deal. It was the big payback.

The others probably looked at it as though it was a senseless cheap shot. There were a couple of bums from his team trying to help Pogo to his feet. But every time they tried, he sank back to the asphalt. I'd completely fronted on my team in pursuit of my own smash-mouth brand of justice. I was pumped and ready to take on those that had the nuts to step up and play Captain-Save-A-Hoe. Other than a few stares, like I'd lost my damn mind, everybody else was fixated on the carnage left behind on the court. I was cold but I wasn't completely heartless. So I went into my pocket to fetch my Metro PCS. I was about to dial 9-1-1 when I heard somebody yelling from a distance using a familiar tone. I turned slowly but with the uncertainty of somebody caught between running like a coward and mannin' up. Walking across the snow-covered grass, in the distance, maybe fifteen to twenty guys were coming my way.

This was about the time that I figured out coming to this part of town by myself had been baptized in stupidity. The newcomers had walked onto the court and watched as two of Pogo's team members dragged his worthless carcass away. I'd won a small victory. But something told me that this army was here to win the war.

I recognized the leader: Small schmuck, extra-large mole on the chin with his right hand clutching a pistol. The barrel was about the size of one my extra-large feet. Most of the guys that had been there before these fools rolled up had taken flight at the sight of the pistol.

"So, Sasquatch," Molechin said with all the disrespect one could muster. "We meet again. But this time"—he looked around at his crew—"instead of your big mouth boy Rico getting the drop on us, we got you."

It was one of the BeBe kids that me and Rico had rolled up on the night we were searching the ghetto for Jordan.

"You still pissed at Rico for taking your strap that night and telling you to get your ass back in school?"

Moleman brought his weapon into full view as if experiencing an orgasm at the sight of it. "No worries. I got a replacement here. We 'bout to cause you some serious brain damage, nigga."

None of his soldiers said a word. It was as if they were awaiting his command. All were dressed in black Timbs, same color Dickies, and Carhartt jackets. Stone-faced killers. I cursed myself for being so stupid in putting myself in the line of fire. Highnoon's contract would be worthless if I didn't make it back. And Momma would certainly die.

It surprised me that a few morons had stayed behind to see how this would play out. But it didn't come as a total shocker that one of the spectators was Pogo. The Negro was livid. Whatever the color of the towel that he'd been using to absorb the blood leaking from his mouth, it was now completely red.

Moleman raised his piece. "Nigga, this is gonna be nice. I'd been hoping to run back into you. I've been dreaming about putting yo' ass in the dirt for so long that my dick itches."

"The pharmacy has creams for conditions like yours." The first thing that came to my mind was the night that I'd beaten the brakes off Paco and his goons in southwest Detroit. But Jack had my mouth quick with the insults that night. I was completely sober at the moment. This time I didn't quite know where the insult had come from, but it triggered life from his soldiers.

"You niggas chill!" the mole-chinned little gangsta commanded his troops. "I got this one."

He closed the distance between us, but stayed out of my reach. In dramatic fashion he yanked back the slide on the pistol and turned it to the side like the Black modern-day gangstas in the movies. "After I do you, I'm gonna find yo' crackhead brother Jordan and send him to see you. That bitch owes me money."

The little runt was about to squeeze the trigger when five black Hummers appeared out of nowhere. The powerful trucks dominated the snowy terrain as they drove across the grass with urgency, fully maneuvering like they had driven right off of the big screen and out of a Michael Bay action movie. Everybody froze as the trucks seemed to stop, blocking off every possible route of escape. The doors opened on four of the vehicles and out jumped cats who were dressed in army fatigues and combat boots, bald heads and packing some serious heat. Nothing but AR-15's surrounded Moleman and his crew. Where the little chump's troops once stood with the ferocious posture and stone-faced resolve of glorified killers, their faces were now animated by sheer terror.

Once the area was locked down, the driver from the last Hummer stepped to the back door and opened it. Highnoon stepped out dressed like his small militia and smoking a Cuban cigar.

"Wisdom, Wisdom, Wisdom," Highnoon sang my name in his usual flat, irritating cadence. "You didn't think I'd let you out without bodyguards, now did you?"

Over the years I'd built up a tough reputation on the streets as a man who could hold his own when it came to watching his back. And I could've ridden that wave of pride, but it would've been total bullshit. I was inwardly smiling and trying hard to hide the look of relief on my face. For once, I was pleased to see Highnoon's gold-toothed grill.

"Wisdom, go and take care of your business." Highnoon stared at his men. They raised their weapons, all trained on Moleman and his crew. "I'll finish cleaning up here."

Without words, I walked to the mail van. I didn't owe him a damn thing, not even a thank-you card. I saw the save as him protecting his investment, looking after his portfolio.

Before I could close my door all the way, Highnoon said: "Seven days. Don't waste them. The clock's ticking."

Regardless of all the insidious players that were involved inside this high-stakes game of life and death, I had to pull out the win. My mother's life absolutely depended on it. There was no turning back. In front of me the game had begun. This was that last second heroic shot that every little kid around the world dreamed of making. I would go into battle armed with the knowledge that I had no more time-outs left to successfully take one for the team.